THE REGENCY
LORDS & LADIES
COLLECTION

**Glittering Regency Love Affairs
from your favourite historical authors.**

THE REGENCY LORDS & LADIES COLLECTION

Available from the
Regency Lords & Ladies Large Print Collection

The Larkswood Legacy by Nicola Cornick
My Lady's Prisoner by Elizabeth Ann Cree
Lady Clairval's Marriage by Paula Marshall
A Scandalous Lady by Francesca Shaw
A Poor Relation by Joanna Maitland
Mistress or Marriage? by Elizabeth Rolls
Rosalyn and the Scoundrel by Anne Herries
Nell by Elizabeth Bailey
Kitty by Elizabeth Bailey
Miss Verey's Proposal by Nicola Cornick
Prudence by Elizabeth Bailey
An Honourable Thief by Anne Gracie
Jewel of the Night by Helen Dickson
The Wedding Gamble by Julia Justiss
Ten Guineas on Love by Claire Thornton
Honour's Bride by Gayle Wilson
One Night with a Rake by Louise Allen
A Matter of Honour by Anne Herries
Tavern Wench by Anne Ashley
The Sweet Cheat by Meg Alexander
The Rebellious Bride by Francesca Shaw
Carnival of Love by Helen Dickson
The Reluctant Marchioness by Anne Ashley
Miranda's Masquerade by Meg Alexander
Dear Deceiver by Mary Nichols
Lady Sarah's Son by Gayle Wilson
One Night of Scandal by Nicola Cornick
The Rake's Mistress by Nicola Cornick
Lady Knightley's Secret by Anne Ashley
Lady Jane's Physician by Anne Ashley

MISTRESS OR MARRIAGE?

Elizabeth Rolls

First published in Great Britain 2001
Large Print Edition 2009
Harlequin Mills & Boon Limited,
Eton House, 18-24 Paradise Road, Richmond, Surrey TW9 1SR

© Elizabeth Rolls 2001

ISBN: 978 0 263 21034 7

Set in Times Roman 15½ on 16½ pt.
083-0309-85756

Printed and bound in Great Britain
by CPI Antony Rowe, Chippenham, Wiltshire

Chapter One

Lady Maria Kentham viewed her only surviving great-nephew in what appeared to be unmitigated exasperation. Lord knew the boy had always been stubborn, but this was beyond all belief! Not that there was much left of the youth she remembered, apart from the obstinacy, of course. Twelve years had wrought a greater change in him than they had in her.

He'd filled out rather nicely, she thought critically, as he stood glaring back at her, green eyes snapping. His breadth of shoulder and powerful chest were admirably displayed by the close-fitting black coat. His pantaloons were all they should be as well. Lady Maria did not always approve of modern fashions in clothing—indecent, some of them were. But when a pair of pantaloons was moulded to legs like those…well, she had to admit, if only to herself, that there might be a point in them.

His snowy cravat was a monument to discreet

elegance—a single diamond, snuggling into the intricate folds, flashed its chaste fire without detracting from the artistry of the arrangement. All in all, his attire was everything a gentleman's should be, and more.

And he was just as handsome as ever, she thought approvingly, with the Melville green eyes and jet black hair. His mother's delicate bone structure had combined with the heavier features, which had characterised his father and elder brother James, to produce a chiselled strength, aristocratic in the extreme.

David Melville, the present Viscount Helford, eyed his Great Aunt Maria with mingled exasperation and affection. The last thing he'd expected when his butler announced Great Aunt Maria was that she'd stalk into his library and open fire without even a declaration of war. He thought ruefully that he had obviously been away too long, if he had forgotten Great Aunt Maria's tendency to speak her mind with frequently shattering candour. Nevertheless, he was damned if he'd dance to this tune!

'Don't you think, Aunt, that it might be a little early for this discussion? After all, I only arrived back yesterday. Perhaps I might be permitted time to look up my old friends before I exhaust myself in the hunt for an eligible bride. Or rather before they come hunting me. And would you kindly stop looking me over as if I were a prize stallion?'

A dangerous flash in her black eyes, Lady Maria corrected him on two points. 'This ain't a discussion, Helford! I'm telling you! The succession is in some danger and it is your duty to marry *at once*! James died over a year ago and the people are starting to wonder where you are. You have a ten-year-old niece who requires attention as well as a three-hundred-year-old title and estate in need of the same!'

She fixed him with a steely glare. 'As for looking up your friends, you have my full permission to look 'em up. On the dance floors!' A very unlady-like snort escaped her. 'Who knows, if you run across Peter Darleston in town, then he might even help you! From all I can see, he's embraced the married state again with what I can only describe as vulgar enthusiasm! Which should be a lesson to you. Just because you had some stupid boy-and-girl attachment to Felicity doesn't mean you can't form an eligible connection with another female.'

Her voice and eyes softened slightly as Helford stiffened at this blunt reference to his early infatuation for his elder brother's wife. 'Lord, boy, did you think I didn't know? It was obvious enough you was head over heels in love with her! The only person who didn't know was James!' She pursed her lips. 'Mind you, he never saw anything, not even Felicity's *affaires*. And God knows there were enough of them!'

Obviously startled, Helford was betrayed into revealing speech. 'James didn't know? That I—' The firm lips closed abruptly.

Lady Maria Kentham stared at him in disbelief. 'So that's it,' she said slowly. 'You thought James offered for Felicity, knowing how you felt about her. That's why you joined the army and stayed away all these years. Because you thought James had purposely stolen your bride. For heaven's sake, boy! Your mother suggested the match to James. If he'd known how you felt, he'd never have offered for her!'

Her nephew just gaped at her in stunned silence. She didn't really expect an answer. He'd never been one to confide, even as a boy, and she didn't think he'd changed all that much. Lord, so he'd been blaming his brother all these years for supposedly stealing a hussy who'd have broken his heart! Well, he knew the truth now and nothing more she could say on that head would be of the slightest use.

So she returned to the main thrust of her argument. 'You do intend to marry, I assume, Helford?' Using his title, she reasoned, would remind him of his duty. He was not merely the Honourable David Melville, younger son, any more. He had responsibilities…to his name, to his people. He must not be allowed to shirk them on any count, certainly not for the memory of his brother's wife, a woman who had been dead for more than a twelvemonth. A woman who, if the boy were to be totally honest with himself, had not actually cared for him in the least.

His jaw set hard, Helford answered. 'As you say, Aunt Maria, I have no choice in the matter.'

She relaxed. Good. He was going to be sensible.

'Very well, then. There are bound to be any number of personable young ladies out this Season. I will—'

'No!'

A frosty glare greeted this summary interruption of her detailed and all-embracing plans.

It was met by one as chilly. 'I am entirely capable of choosing a bride by myself, thank you very much!' grated the Viscount. 'It may surprise you to know that I can just about remember how to make myself agreeable to the ladies.'

Lady Maria permitted herself an amused smile. 'Can you indeed, Helford? From all I've heard, you're a little out of practice with the ladies…'

'The hell I am!' exploded Helford.

'With the ladies, I said, dear boy,' purred Lady Maria sweetly, not in the least put out by her nephew's choice of language. 'I've not the least doubt of your expertise with the brass-faced hussies of the Viennese Opera.' She rose to her feet before her outraged nephew could think of a suitable riposte and continued, 'And if the way you've received me is any indication, then I should think you can do with all the advice you can get. No offer of tea, Madeira, cakes! It passes all bounds.'

This backfired slightly. The blazing green eyes suddenly crinkled with laughter, adding disastrously to their owner's already nigh-on lethal charm.

'Oh, no, you don't, Aunt Maria! That cock won't fight! I distinctly heard you inform Haversham that you never maudled your insides with tea at this hour and considered it far too early for anything stronger! You also told him to concentrate on making himself useful rather than forcing you to eat food you neither wanted nor required.'

'Humph. You could still have offered!' she snapped, not in the least mollified. 'Still, it's all of a piece with your generation. Not the slightest notion of respect for your elders.'

She rose to her feet with the aid of a walking stick that Helford was morally certain was his grandfather's old sword stick. He supposed he ought to be grateful that she hadn't pressed her point with that.

'I'll take my leave of you, Helford. I'm putting up at Grillon's.'

He flushed. 'Whatever for? You're perfectly welcome to stay here for as long as you like. You know quite well that I have a considerable affection for you, quite apart from any respect you may feel I owe you!'

'Humph, I dare say!' Seeing that he looked quite sincerely upset, she relented. 'I've no taste for racketing about town these days. I'll stay another day or so at Grillon's, then go back to Helford Place.

Shouldn't leave Fanny much longer. That child needs taking in hand.'

He frowned. 'Aunt Maria, did you come all the way down from Warwickshire merely to put me in the way of my duty?' The mildness of his voice belied the frown.

'Certainly not!' she lied unconvincingly. 'I've every intention of going to the opera!'

After seeing his great-aunt to her carriage, Lord Helford returned to his library, but somehow the peace and quiet he had been enjoying was shattered. The shabby old leather chairs seemed to repel him so that he paced up and down, and the leather-bound books lining the walls all nagged at him, reminding him of his forebears who had amassed them. The wisdom of generations was held in those covers, he thought whimsically. And all it could do was urge him to a step he had shunned for years.

Marriage. Something he had set his face against for over twelve years.

His memory lurched back to the day Felicity's father had calmly told him that he had received a better offer for her hand, that he was not to approach her again. An order which he had not the slightest intention of obeying. He had not found out who the lucky suitor was until he had reached home that night after riding all day in a thundering rage, fuming as he laid his plans for rescuing his love from an unwanted marriage.

He'd found out when he got home, muddied and exhausted, and discovered James celebrating with their mother. *She* had known. Had tried to explain to him later that James, with his title, had a better claim to Felicity's hand and fortune. She had smiled gently, cynically, when he'd cried out that he loved Felicity. Had told him that he would find another attractive fortune one day. He'd never spoken to her again.

The next day he'd managed to intercept Felicity on her morning ride with her groom. She'd seemed very embarrassed to see him and when he'd insisted on riding ahead with her, had agreed very reluctantly.

He could remember her light voice now. 'But, David, dear! You cannot expect me to marry you in the face of Papa's displeasure. Why, he has positively ordered me to marry James.' There was a brief, pregnant pause, during which he'd assimilated the variance of her claim that her father demanded the match, with her unruffled tone and demeanour.

She continued. 'We must be sensible about this, David. After all, once I have fulfilled my duty and provided James with an heir, there is nothing to stop us… I mean, if we were discreet.' Innocent-seeming blue eyes had smiled up at him beguilingly. The soft pink lips he'd longed to crush under his curved in the most tempting of smiles and the pale spring sunshine had glinted on golden curls.

He felt nothing but disgust. And fury. Fury with

himself that he could still want her. That even knowing what she was, he could still desire her, long to have her as his wife.

Somehow he'd managed to speak. 'A gratifying offer, Felicity, but I think I'd rather stick to *honest* whores.' The words, and the biting tone in which he'd uttered them, had struck home. A flush had suffused the petal-soft cheeks, an angry glitter had sparked in the blue eyes and the delicate bow of her mouth hardened.

'Really, David!' she expostulated. 'You are being most unreasonable. You know as well as I that marriage in our class is a contract made for the better preservation of property and the provision of heirs. My father demands that I marry James. What more is there to say?'

'Absolutely nothing, my dear,' drawled David, wondering how on earth he had missed seeing her mercenary streak before this and realising that love could indeed be blind. 'It remains for me to congratulate you on your catch and beg your pardon for having distracted you from your duty to your ambition. Good morning.'

He'd spurred his horse into a canter, then a swift gallop, and left her. Not once had he looked back, either then or in the years of wandering that had followed.

The next morning he'd left, only pausing to ask James if he'd purchase him a pair of colours, and from that day to this he hadn't stepped across any threshold belonging to his family. James had looked puzzled at his request, but had agreed immediately with the easy generosity that had always character-ised his dealings with his younger brother.

And he hadn't known. Helford swore bitterly. No wonder James had been so puzzled, particularly by his refusal to come home after that. His refusal to come to the wedding. Even knowing the truth about her motivation, he had still found that the thought of seeing Felicity married to his own brother was unbearable.

By the time he'd come to his senses and realised that he'd made a fool of himself, he had been too proud to come home. And he could not have borne to see Felicity, to be reminded of the callow youth who had loved her only to discover that his idol had feet of clay. All during his years in the Peninsula and then in Vienna at the Embassy odd scraps of gossip had filtered through to him. Scraps which told him he was far better off out of marriage with her. Or with anyone.

Never again had he made the mistake of caring for a woman. They were toys, playthings. He avoided marriageable females like the plague, seeing in them only reminders of his own foolishness. And now he'd have to marry after all. Very well. So be it. But it would be on *his* terms. The terms Felicity had taught him so effectively.

His bride would be a woman of birth, beauty and fortune. And irreproachable conduct. He was damned if he would provide cover for a high-class little whore as James had obviously ended up doing for Felicity. He thought about it carefully. Titled. She needed to be titled and from one of the oldest houses preferably. That way she would have been brought up to know her duty. She would see her rank as an accepted responsibility rather than as a prize to be won at all costs. The bargain between them would be an equal one. And he would make damned sure he picked a bride with little disposition to flirt or encourage the attentions of other men. He'd learned his lesson the hard way and he was going to make quite certain that he profited by it!

And now that he had decided all that, he would go for a stroll along Bond Street and let the world know that he had returned.

He had quite forgotten what Bond Street could be like at this hour. The clop of hooves allied with rumbling wheels was deafening and overlaying it all was a buzz of chatter. It seemed that most of the fashionable world was here at three o'clock on a bright spring afternoon. For a moment time rolled back as though the intervening years had never happened. But for one inescapable fact, David thought, he might never have been away.

Twelve years ago he would have been recognised by any number of the elegantly gowned ladies whose fluttering muslins gave the street the appearance of a flower bed. The strolling gentlemen would have known him as well. He would have been most unlikely to have been walking alone. He would have been part of the milieu rather than this faintly cynical observer.

Just at the moment his anonymity suited him perfectly. There was an odd satisfaction in being able to view his world almost as though he were invisible to prying eyes and immune to gossiping tongues. He felt as though he were free to observe, not yet part and parcel of the glittering London world which all too soon would know of his return. No doubt by the time he had been back a week the news would be out and any number of people would be claiming long acquaintance. In fact, he rather thought he could count on Lady Maria to spread the glad tidings.

He strolled past Stephens' Hotel, wondering idly if any of his friends were inside but not sufficiently interested to find out. This feeling of being invisible was very pleasant. No one had seen him at all!

His feeling of invisibility was pure illusion, of course. Whatever the gentlemen might do, it was not likely that any lady could possibly pass by an unknown gentleman of his quality without observing him very closely, albeit surreptitiously. Naturally one would not like to stare and be thought a vulgar hussy, but one could and did cast a fleeting sideways glance at the tall, powerful figure, moving with such leonine grace and dressed with such unobtrusive elegance.

The illusion of invisibility continued as far as Jackson's Boxing Saloon. It might have continued even further had it not been for Helford's observation of an entirely new phenomenon. Never before in that distant time that had known him as a frequent and welcome visitor at Jackson's had he seen such a large dog sitting patiently outside the door. The creature was more than large, it was the size of a small pony, he thought. And what was even more amazing, no one, not even the ladies, seemed in the least bit concerned about it.

You would have thought, he reflected, that many of the ladies would have given such an animal a wide berth. But no, most of them went by without taking the slightest notice. The only ones to acknowledge the dog's presence were the ones who actually stopped to pat it. These attentions were received with a slight thump of the tail on the pavement, no more. Clearly a dog of discrimination, thought Helford in amusement.

He wondered who owned the shaggy grey beast. It had to be someone very highly regarded. Unless London society had altered out of all recognition, he could think of few men who would dare to plant an animal like that outside Jackson's and expect to get away with it.

Coming closer, he slowed to observe better. Sensing his regard, the dog turned its great head and gazed at him out of tawny brown eyes. The tail remained motionless and one was left in no doubt that only a fool took liberties with this animal if he didn't know you. There was nothing in the least threatening about his behaviour, just a sort of massive dignity.

He was conscious of an odd urge to incline his head to the dog before continuing, but all at once the dog's attention was not on him. He had turned to the shut door of Jackson's and was standing up, wagging his tail furiously.

Now we shall see who owns him, thought Helford. The door opened and a gentleman as tall as himself stepped out on to the pavement. An athletic fellow with curly black hair and dark brown eyes. He greeted the dog with a pat and then caught sight of Helford, who was staring at him as though seeing a ghost.

The brown-eyed gentleman's jaw dropped, just for a moment, then a smile of unshadowed delight lit a face which more than one romantically inclined damsel had in the past held to be positively Byronic in its brooding good looks. He held out his hand and it was taken at once in a strong grip. Blazing green eyes laughed into brown as they had not done for nearly eight years.

'David Melville! Good God! We all thought you were fixed in Vienna, distracting the ladies of the opera there! What the devil brings you to town? Apart from the opera, of course!'

Helford merely grinned at this reference to his generous, if scandalous, patronage of the arts and riposted, 'You can't talk, Darleston! I seem to have heard that you developed a bit of a reputation with the ladies too!'

The brown eyes laughed at him, 'All in the past, Melville, all in the past! Now come, what brings you…oh, of course! Melville, indeed! Helford, I should say! I forgot all about it. It's over a year since your brother died, isn't it?'

Helford nodded. 'Just over. I should have come earlier, I suppose, especially since I am guardian to James's daughter. But quite frankly I've little turn for children and Aunt Maria seems to have the matter well in hand. So… er…Vienna was more appealing!' There was a raffish twinkle in his eye.

The Earl of Darleston chuckled understandingly, 'Was she, indeed? How very pleasant for you! Where are you off to now? Are you busy or can you give me your company?'

Helford laughed and said, 'If you will promise not to break my incognito to anyone, you may have my company for as long as you please.'

'Incognito?' Darleston grinned. 'Do you mean to say a whole, live, single Viscount managed to get this far along Bond Street without being mobbed? I had not thought it possible!'

He began to walk, the dog closely to heel. 'Eight years, isn't it? The last time I saw you was the morning we left Waterloo village.' His voice was studiedly light.

Helford nodded slowly, remembering that roaring, smoking hell. 'It probably was. Although I saw you much later in the day, I would doubt your having been in a condition to remember. Carstares was just heaving you on to your horse to have you led to the rear. Neither of us thought you'd survive.'

Darleston smiled. 'I still have Nero. My wife rides him now.'

His voice took on an oddly gentle cast and Helford looked at him sharply. His wife! Shouldn't have thought he'd let a female near a horse that had stood over his fallen body in the heat of battle, let alone ride it. Although hadn't Aunt Maria said something about Peter remarrying? Not to mention that letter he'd had from Carrington. Suddenly he remembered the letter.

Peter has remarried, you will be interested to hear. Married for convenience and an heir and it turned into the greatest love match of all time. Carstares and I are still laughing about it...

Something like that. 'That's right. I had a letter from Michael. Is it too late for congratulations?'

His friend shook his head. 'Not at all. And even if *you* think nearly three years is too long for congratulations, you can always congratulate me on the arrival of my children.'

Helford did some quick calculations and said, 'Children, plural? In that time? Even for you…' He left the sentence hanging.

Darleston had the grace to look faintly embarrassed, 'Penelope is a twin, you see, and—'

'Twins? You are the father of twins?' Helford put back his head and roared with laughter. 'Well, well, well! And what are you blessed with?'

'Boy and a girl, just turned two,' said Darleston without the slightest attempt to disguise his pride.

'Congratulations!' said Helford in wholehearted delight. 'Now I have just one burning question. Where in God's name did you get this?' He indicated the great dog pacing beside them.

'Gelert? Oh, he belongs to my wife,' answered Darleston. 'Part of the marriage contract, you might say. Where she goes, he goes generally. Even into Sally Jersey's drawing room, would you believe!'

Helford mentally conjured up the image of this huge dog cluttering up the drawing room of London's uncrowned queen, one of the patronesses of Almack's, a woman who could destroy the chances of any aspiring debutante or hostess with a single word. It just wasn't possible! Lady Jersey would never tolerate such a thing, not even for the Countess of Darleston.

Grinning at the patent disbelief, writ large all over Helford's countenance, Darleston said, 'If you aren't otherwise engaged, come and have dinner with us this evening. George Carstares is staying with us and Penelope's youngest sister Sarah. Come and join us. An extra place at the table won't be a problem, I assure you.'

'If you are sure that Lady Darleston won't mind, then I should like that very much,' said Helford.

'Penelope never minds anything,' said Darleston with a sublime confidence that his friend was far from sharing. In his experience, when a man married, his wife tended to regard his old friends as so many intruders.

They continued along the street slowly, filling in the past eight years and laughing over old gossip and the fates of various acquaintances.

'Now, are you settled in town? You say no one knows you are back,' continued Darleston, as they strolled along past Hookham's Library.

'For the Season,' answered Helford. 'I'll probably be organising a house party at Helford Place at some point during the summer.' There was a faintly questioning note in his voice.

'Oh, yes, we'll be home by then,' responded Darleston. 'The children are a great deal happier in the country and Penny and I prefer it. We're really only up for Lady Edenhope's ball in a couple of days. You come too. She'll be so thrilled to be the first to entertain you formally, she won't mind in the least if you turn up uninvited.'

'Seems as good a place to start as any,' was the enigmatic reply.

'Start what? A mill?' asked Darleston with a wicked glint in his eye.

Helford chuckled, 'I only did that once and the bounder deserved it! Besides, I was foxed!'

'Once was enough, in all conscience!' said Darleston indignantly. 'I still have nightmares about trying to persuade Lady Edenhope not to call your father from the card room! Now, enough! What are you up to?'

'Getting married, according to Aunt Maria.'

'Congratulations,' said Darleston and raised his brows in mute surmise.

'You're a little premature,' said Helford. 'I haven't popped the question yet.'

'Oh. I see.'

For a mere three words he managed to get a wealth of unasked questions into them, thought Helford. But, after all, Darleston was almost as well acquainted with the formidable Lady Maria as he was.

With a sigh he said, 'You know how it is. I suppose you remarried for exactly the same reasons. Convenience and an heir.'

'I did, of course,' agreed Darleston. 'And very soon discovered my mistake.' His voice held more than a shade of amusement.

'Mistake?' Helford was surprised. 'Aunt Maria seemed to think your enthusiasm for the married state was positively vulgar.'

'Oh, it is!' smiled Darleston. 'I meant that I was mistaken in marrying for convenience. It didn't work at all! But enough of me. Tell me who you have in your eye.'

Helford shrugged. 'Does it really matter? Frankly, I've just got back. Aunt Maria descended upon me this morning and proceeded to enumerate to me my duties to the name of Melville. So…' He grimaced. 'Hence I'm in the market for a bride with the following qualifications: breeding—she must be titled—and good looks, of course. And a reasonable dowry. She must be well behaved and accomplished…sensible…capable of running a large household. You know the sort of thing.'

Darleston nodded slowly. 'Did Lady Maria stipulate all this? You surprise me.'

'Hardly,' said Helford with a reluctant half-smile, thinking that he must have sounded remarkably cold-blooded. 'That's my own recipe for a bearable marriage.'

'Oh,' said Darleston. Again he managed to invest the monosyllable with a world of meaning.

They strolled along in a silence broken at last by Helford in a tight, bitter sort of voice. 'I know what you are thinking, Peter, but I learnt my lesson early and I've no intention of mixing business with pleasure.'

'More than one lesson to be learned in life, old chap,' said Darleston thoughtfully. 'Mind you, I'm not saying it wasn't a good thing Felicity taught you to be wary, but one can take one's suspicions too far.'

Helford snorted sceptically. 'If you'll pardon my frankness, Peter, I should have thought that you of all men would have been doubly wary.'

Darleston did not seem at all offended. 'Oh, I was, I assure you!' He hesitated and then said, 'That's precisely what I meant. I didn't even recognise love at first! And probably just as well, since I should have run a mile if I'd realised. It just sort of sneaked up on me. I certainly didn't go looking for it. In fact, I caused Penny quite a deal of hurt while I was floundering about wondering why she bothered me so much!'

Helford was unconvinced. 'Well, it won't do for me. I'd prefer to know exactly where I am in my marriage so I'll settle for convenience. Come on, enumerate to me all the impeccably bred, attractive fillies currently parading in the auction ring.'

With a resigned smile, Darleston considered carefully. 'Well, there is the Clovelly chit, quite attractive and well behaved. Not titled, of course, but the Clovellys are looking high, I believe. And besides, she *would* be titled if her great-great-great grandmother hadn't told Charles the Second to keep his hands to himself! Or, if you insist on the title, there's Lady Lucinda Anstey—Stanford's chit, you know. She's held to be a very regal-looking girl. No doubt there are a score of others, but those two come to mind as...er...embodying the qualifications you mentioned.'

'Point 'em out to me,' said Helford. 'I thought to spend the Season looking about and courting here in town and then invite the girl and her mother to that house party I mentioned. You know, see her at closer quarters before making a final decision.'

'I see,' said Darleston, and his voice suggested that he did see. Perfectly. 'Very well. Penelope and I will engage to point out all the most impeccably behaved and bred damsels we can think of.'

Helford grinned. 'Aunt Maria, at least, will be eternally in your debt. I knew I could count on you, Peter. If you are quite sure Lady Darleston won't mind my turning up...'

'At eight, then,' said Darleston. 'We are keeping town hours. I must be off to the park now, David. Do you care to come and be presented to Penny?'

'No, no,' said Helford, hastily. 'I will look forward to that this evening!'

They parted and Helford turned back along Bond Street. Darleston's amused reaction to his matrimonial plans had thrown him slightly. Peter would never criticize, of course, but it was plain what he thought of Helford's marriage campaign. He shrugged. Peter *might* have been supremely lucky in his second marriage, but he'd reserve judgement until he'd met the second Lady Darleston. And he certainly wasn't going to run that sort of risk himself!

Helford presented himself in Grosvenor Square at the fashionable hour of eight and was admitted to Darleston House by the elderly butler.

'Good evening, Meadows. Are you keeping well?' asked the Viscount, handing the startled man his hat and cloak. He remembered the old boy from his school days when he had frequently ridden over to join Peter Frobisher and his other cronies at Darleston Court a bare ten miles from his own seat.

'Master David! That is…my lord! Well! His lordship did say he had a surprise guest for this evening, but he wouldn't tell anyone who.' The kindly old face beamed as wrinkles chased themselves delightedly all over it. 'You are looking well, if I may say so. Come this way, the family are all in the drawing room.'

'Thank you, Meadows.' He followed the old chap up to the first floor and said with a twinkle, 'I do trust you are going to announce me in style, Meadows.'

Suppressing a chuckle wholly at variance with his usual dignified manner, Meadows opened the door of the drawing room and said into a sudden silence, 'Lord Helford!'

The group before the fire stared in amazement, except, of course, for Darleston, who was obviously taking a mischievous pleasure in the shock he had given Carstares and the ladies.

Carstares had changed very little, thought Helford as his friend surged forward with outstretched hands.

'Helford! Good God! Where did you spring from?'

Helford seized the outstretched hand and wrung it. No, Carstares hadn't changed, still the same cheery blue eyes and tousled fair hair. The same merry open countenance.

He clapped George on the shoulder. 'Got off the packet yesterday morning and went on the strut down Bond Street. Just to see if anyone recognised me. Didn't see a soul I knew until I met Peter outside Jackson's.' He shook his head. 'Lord, it's good to see you two again!'

Darleston strolled forward, 'Come and be presented to my wife and sister-in-law.' The odd note of pride in his voice made Helford glance at him sharply. If George had not changed, Darleston most assuredly had. When last he had known this man, he had been in the depths of a bitter depression over the infidelities of his first wife. Now he was again the warm, easygoing man Helford remembered from his youth.

The reason was not far to seek. Penelope, Countess of Darleston, was a very lovely woman; a riot of auburn curls and smoky grey eyes were not the least of her charms. Her expression held a great deal of sweetness and a hint of mischief. And there was something in her eyes when they rested on her husband that made Lord Helford's heart contract sharply. Briefly he wondered what it would be like to have a woman look at you like that. Abruptly he dismissed the thought. He was not looking for love in his marriage. That was far too dangerous.

Lady Darleston came forward to greet him, 'I am so pleased to meet you at last, Lord Helford. Every time we drive past your gates in the country Peter is moved to reminisce about his long-lost youth and all the dreadful things you used to do!'

Helford bowed low over her hand and said, 'The pleasure is mine, Lady Darleston. Peter told me that it was not too late to offer congratulations on his marriage. And I understand that he is now a father. You cannot imagine how ancient I feel!'

The Countess laughed, 'I think it makes him feel old at times too. May I present my sister, Miss Sarah Ffolliot?'

She drew forward a slender girl with more brown than red in her curls but the same smoky eyes and friendly smile. But if Lady Darleston might be said to have a hint of mischief in her eyes, this chit had a great deal more than a hint. She seemed to be bursting with energy and, after being introduced, said to Helford, 'It must have been terribly exciting being abroad and in Vienna of all places. I should so much like to go there one day!'

He chatted to her for a few minutes, responding

to her artless questions about life in the Austrian capital, until George came to lead her in to dinner. He was startled to see the look that passed between them. A look compounded of deep affection and, at least on George's part, of desire. Good God! Carstares thinking of marriage? How were the mighty fallen!

Helford enjoyed his first social engagement enormously. It was good to pick up his friendship with Darleston and George Carstares. Their long separation had not loosened the bonds between them. Even Darleston's marriage did not seem to have affected his friendship with Carstares. It was plain to see that Lady Darleston held George in great affection, treating him with an easy camaraderie, and by the end of dinner Viscount Helford was in a fair way to envying his oldest friend.

That Darleston's marriage was ecstatically happy could not be held in doubt. His lovely auburn-haired countess was utterly delightful. Darleston was a damned lucky fellow, thought Helford, as his hostess had them all in stitches with her description of her first Channel crossing when she had been appallingly seasick.

'Poor Peter tried to be noble and hold the basin for me,' she said giggling. 'Which would have been fine had I not completely missed the basin and sullied his sacred Hessians! I don't know who was more upset with me, Peter, or Fordham, who had to clean them!'

Peter grinned and said, 'Not to mention the rest of my attire. Fordham was vastly put out.'

He changed the subject, 'Shall we escort Helford to Aunt Louisa's little do, Penny? He wishes to make his bow after such a long absence. Shall we lend him our…er…patronage?'

She smiled at Helford, seated on her right. 'Do you care to come with us? I am sure Lady Edenhope will not mind in the slightest. Will she, George?'

This last to George Carstares who said cheerfully, 'Devil a bit! Be glad to be one up on all the other tabbies, shouldn't wonder!'

Darleston eyed him in fascination, 'Are you referring to our esteemed friend, Lady Edenhope, as a *tabby*, George?' He shook his head. 'How very brave, isn't he, Sarah?'

'Or foolish,' suggested Miss Sarah Ffolliot with her usual candour. Helford was amused. Miss Sarah had a disconcerting habit of saying exactly what she thought and positively fizzed with naughtiness. He liked her, and hoped she was not going to hurt George. From a couple of remarks Darleston had made about minding her estate interests, it was plain she was an heiress. In his bitter experience, heiresses did not throw themselves away on younger sons, no matter how charming.

'Do come,' she said to Helford. 'It will be capital sport to see all their faces when you are announced!'

'Like the beasts at the Royal Exchange being fed?' asked Helford, amused.

'Something like that. I love going there with George. But would you consider yourself as a beef-steak?' laughed Sarah.

A groan of mock despair came from Darleston, 'We'll never marry her off, Penny! How can we when she refers to eligible *partis* as "beefsteaks"? Those that she doesn't beat all hollow at chess. There's nothing for it but to put her in a convent!'

Not in the least abashed, Sarah put her tongue out at him and continued to eat her syllabub. 'Oh, pooh,' she said between mouthfuls. 'If Helford is a friend of yours and George's, he must be perfectly accustomed to outrageous behaviour. Besides, George can beat me at chess now!'

'Well, thank God for that!' broke in Penelope. 'I've been tutoring him for months!'

Helford left Darleston House well after midnight to walk home. It occurred to him briefly as he strolled along that perhaps he ought to consider waiting a while before he married, see if he could find a girl to love, but he dismissed the thought immediately with something very like panic. Admittedly Darleston had been lucky and it looked as though George would be just as happy. But he shuddered at the thought of the risk he'd be taking. He'd made a crashing fool of himself once and he didn't fancy doing it again.

And it would take time and time was one thing that he didn't have. His brother's premature death had put the succession in some danger. It hadn't really needed Aunt Maria's intervention for him to realise the importance of his marriage. He was the last of the Melvilles now, except for his niece, and it behoved him to marry as carefully as possible to carry on the name creditably. No, he would marry for the title and family name. His own pleasures would be carried on as they had always been, outside the marriage bed.

Besides, he shuddered as he contemplated the sort of hurt that Darleston was wide open to. He did not for a moment think that Penelope would ever betray her husband. That was out of the question. Even his cynical mind could accept that. But how would Peter survive if anything ever happened to Penelope? It was better to guard against that sort of pain. He remembered the agony of grief after Waterloo as one by one he realised how many of his friends had died. No, it was safer to settle for convenience in marriage and attend to his pleasures elsewhere. Love, whatever it might be, was for others.

Three nights later he trod up the steps of Lady Edenhope's mansion under the gaily striped awning erected for the occasion in company with the Darlestons, Miss Sarah Ffolliot and George Carstares. Numerous glances were cast in their direction and

Helford was tolerably certain that his incognito had been blown by the time Louisa Edenhope's very starchy butler announced their party.

'The Earl and Countess of Darleston, Viscount Helford...' Despite the stentorian tones of Lady Edenhope's butler, an upsurge of exclamations and chatter drowned the announcement of Miss Sarah Ffolliot and Mr Carstares. Neither of whom cared in the least. They were too entertained by the spectacle of such a crowd of fashionables jockeying to be among the first to greet the new beefsteak, as Sarah had christened him, without appearing odiously pushing.

As the hostess, Lady Edenhope was the first to greet him. 'David Melville! How dare you turn up like this without so much as warning me! I nearly fainted when I saw who Peter had in tow. So, you are back to plague us, are you? Well, I shall give up my box at the opera and I warn you, if you start a vulgar brawl this time then I will have Darleston and George cast you out! Not to mention having Sally Jersey and the others bar you from Almack's. Although I don't suppose that would bother you in the slightest.'

'Dear Lady Edenhope,' said Helford, bowing low over her hand and kissing it. 'I have lived for this moment!' He twinkled at her outrageously.

'I dare say,' she said. 'Stop trying to turn me up

sweet and go and find some other female to play off your cajolery on. I'll have you know I'm far too old for your tricks!'

'Never, dear lady,' protested Helford dramatically. 'The day you are too old for me will be the day after I cock up my toes!' His lofty tones and resonant voice made the vulgar expression sound positively romantic.

His hostess snorted. 'You're cutting a wheedle, Helford! You can give me twenty years...more I dare say!'

'For you, I'd give them,' he assured her with a smile which she privately thought was enough to make any unwary female tumble head over ears in love with him. And as for those eyes! Well, they were enough to give any female, wary or otherwise, palpitations.

'Take him away, for heaven's sake, Peter!' urged Lady Edenhope.

'With pleasure, Aunt Louisa!' said Peter with alacrity. He looked at Helford in amusement. 'Are you practising for the benefit of the impeccables? Rest assured, you're in fine fighting trim.'

The evening passed in a blur of music and champagne judiciously mixed with the stream of faces, familiar and new, which whirled past his lordship. True to his word, Darleston had persuaded Penelope to present him to as many of the young ladies as possible. Most of them he dismissed from his mind at once, including the charming Miss Clovelly. He found her giggle rather irritating and not all the legendary virtue of her great-great-great-grandmama was enough to reconcile him to a life spent throttling the urge to throttle his wife.

Lady Lucinda Anstey was quite another matter. Penelope had not at first presented him to her, but the dignified carriage and glossy black ringlets caught his eye.

'Who is that, Lady Darleston?' he asked very softly.

She followed the direction of his gaze.

'With the black hair,' he prompted, seeing her hesitate.

Damn! thought Penelope Darleston. Damn and double damn! She knew nothing against Lady Lucinda, but she just couldn't warm to her. The regal carriage people raved over always struck her as top lofty. The cool air of confidence said more to Penelope about Lady Lucinda's conviction of social superiority than anything else. She *was* lovely, though. Those glossy curls and rose-petal complexion were a lethal combination and, when added to deep blue eyes and a tall elegant figure, the sum total was quite out of the common way.

'That is Lady Lucinda Anstey,' she said reluctantly. If he married her, then any social intercourse with Helford Place would be of the most stuffy and formal variety, she reflected. Lady Stanford's entertainments were renowned for the positively stifling degree of pomp and ceremony which characterised them. Lady Lucinda, however, appeared to revel in it.

'Is it, indeed?' responded Helford. He looked the lady over with the eyes of a connoisseur. Tall, very elegant, a definite air of distinction. He supposed that she was beautiful—truth to tell, his preference was for smaller women of a more rounded aspect. Not plump, just a trifle more curvaceous than Lady Lucinda. The sort referred to as a *cosy little armful*, in fact. He reminded himself irritably that he was selecting a Countess, a consort, a woman to be respected, not tumbled in the heat of passion! He could set up a mistress later.

'Will you present me to her?'

He didn't sound terribly interested, but Penelope accepted the inevitable. Peter had warned her that Helford was not looking for a love match. 'The three Bs, my love: Breeding, Behaviour and Beauty,' he had said with a slight twinkle. Well, she certainly had all that, and if Helford didn't require a warm heart in his bride then it was none of her business.

With this in mind she led Helford up to the lady. 'Good evening, Lady Stanford, Lady Lucinda. May I present Lord Helford, who has recently returned from Vienna? He wishes very much to be made known to you.'

Helford bowed over Lady Stanford's hand and then Lady Lucinda's. Neither lady appeared to be in the least awed or flustered by his evident desire to make their acquaintance. He didn't mind that in the least. It suggested the sort of dignity and breeding he wished for in a wife.

They all exchanged polite pleasantries on the weather, the overcrowded room and the prospect of it becoming more so as the evening progressed. Helford was agreeably impressed by Lady Lucinda. Well bred, a serious turn of mind and definitely a young lady of striking appearance. Superbly gowned in cornflower blue silk which emphasised the sapphire blue of her eyes, she was clearly an eminently suitable candidate for the position he had in mind.

Of Lady Stanford he was not quite so approving. She had, he felt, a grating sense of her own superiority, not to mention a sublime ignorance of anything outside London.

'I am delighted to make your acquaintance, Lord Helford,' said Lady Stanford. 'You must be glad to be back in England after so long abroad. You must have desired the sound of your own language very often. And I understand that the tone in Vienna is not always what one would like.'

He wondered sardonically just what language Lady Stanford thought they spoke at the Embassy. He had been in no danger of forgetting the sound of his native tongue and besides, when a girl whispered German sweet nothings in your ear as temptingly as that little charmer Lottie, then the only desire of which he was conscious had nothing to do with the English language. Certainly he had no complaints about the tone she had used. The thought was instantly dismissed.

'Quite so, ma'am,' he agreed politely. 'And I am the more aware of what I have missed when I see such a gathering as this.' Lord, what a stupid thing to say, he thought. I'd forgotten how polite and stuffy it can be!

He realised that the orchestra had struck up a waltz and smiled at Lady Lucinda, 'Might I have the honour of this dance? If you are not otherwise engaged…' He thought that it would be unusual for a girl of this quality not to be engaged for every dance, but to his surprise Lady Lucinda shook her head and said,

'As a matter of fact, I am not engaged and I should be honoured to dance with you, but—'

Her mama cut in. 'Of course she will be delighted to be your partner, my lord.' He missed the warning look Lady Stanford directed at her daughter and the disapproving look that Lady Lucinda returned. Smiling, he offered his arm and led her out onto the floor.

Completely stunned, Penelope Darleston watched Helford lead out a girl who had never danced the waltz in public on the grounds of her mother's disapproval of innocent damsels spinning around in a male embrace. She was only saved from a social indiscretion by the fact that her husband came up and said firmly, 'Our dance, my lady.'

He swept her on to the floor, saying, 'David has taken up quite enough of your time for one evening. He now knows enough impeccably bred fillies to found a stud should he wish to do so.'

She shook with laughter at this outrageous comment and felt his grip tighten.

'What on earth will we do if he marries that one, though?' she enquired, slightly breathless at the hard strength of his arms as they encircled her.

'Resign ourselves to some excessively tedious dinner parties at Helford Place, my sweet. And if Lady Stanford agreed to this dance, then I should say our fate is sealed as far as she is concerned.' He drew her closer so that her silk-clad thighs brushed against his and whirled her through a turn, effectively dismissing all thought of Helford's matrimonial concerns from her mind. If Helford wanted convenience, it was entirely his own business.

He held Penelope's gaze and whispered something that brought a flush to her face and a soft glow to the expressive eyes.

Watching them, Helford felt his heart lurch at the way Lady Darleston's mouth quivered into an adoring smile, the way she seemed to melt even more appealingly into her husband's embrace as they danced. The beauty in his own arms was quite unyielding. Much safer, he told himself firmly. Dull, perhaps, but safe.

Chapter Two

Lady Lucinda's first waltz took the *ton* completely by surprise and before it was over bets were being quietly laid that the Stanford stronghold was in a way to being stormed. It was well known that Lady Stanford deeply disapproved of the waltz for unmarried girls. At least, so the whispers ran, until a *parti* so eligible as to make a hopeful mama clutch her vinaigrette in excitement had solicited the Ice Maiden to stand up with him for the disgraceful dance!

Perfectly aware of the ripples of conjecture eddying out from them, Helford had continued to guide his rather unyielding partner around the dance floor, conversing with her on the most unexceptionable topics he could think of. While the sobriquet Ice Maiden did not occur to him, he did compare Lady Lucinda somewhat unfavourably with little Lottie, who had danced the waltz not at all as if she were laid out cold for her own burial. Sharply, he reminded himself of what he required in bride. Lottie's skills and charms were not part of it.

Lady Lucinda was also only too aware of the furore that this dance was causing. She was pleased to note, however, that finding herself in such an intimate embrace was not at all likely to make her lose her head. Indeed, she might as well have been dancing with one of her brothers, for all the thrill it gave her to be held in Lord Helford's arms. She had to admit, though, he talked like a sensible man and did not appear to be the amorous type.

Passing them on the dance floor in George Carstare's arms, Sarah Ffolliot said *sotto voce*, 'Do you think she's noticed that it's a waltz yet? Should we tell her?' Her grey eyes brimmed over with mischief.

In extremely un-loverlike tones George said, 'For heaven's sake, Sarah! Shut up, she'll hear you!'

'Well, but if she doesn't know it's a waltz...' Sarah encountered one of her lover's rare frowns and promptly shut up. If George looked like that, then he was serious.

By the time the *ton* left Lady Edenhope's ball the main topic of gossip was the Helford assault on the icy Stanford ramparts. Whatever might be Helford's intentions, Lady Stanford had clearly signalled hers. This was Lady Lucinda's second Season and there were two more daughters in the wings. Although the regal beauty had never lacked for suitors, none had ever come up to scratch. Obviously her ladyship was not going to put any rub in the way of my Lord Helford.

At the end of a fortnight society was still buzzing with gossip about Lord Helford's attentions to Lady Lucinda. He had ridden beside her carriage in Hyde Park during the fashionable promenade. He had called twice at Stanford House and had been admitted on both occasions. He had even danced the waltz with her at several balls. Lady Stanford had explained, most unconvincingly, that in her second Season a girl might be said to have proved herself.

By the middle of April most people regarded the match as a foregone conclusion. Helford had admittedly paid some attention to one or two other damsels, notably Miss Sarah Ffolliot, but no one was in any doubt about his intentions. Lady Lucinda was to be the lucky girl. The only bet you could get odds on in the clubs was whether Helford would pop the question before his friend George Carstares could get up his courage to offer for Darleston's sister-in-law.

Returning home one evening in early May from escorting Lady Stanford and Lady Lucinda to the opera, Viscount Helford found himself in a mood of introspection. He couldn't for the life of him think why. His courtship was going to plan. Quite obviously he only had to pop the question and he would be sending notices to the papers.

His intended choice was everything he had stipulated. She had breeding, conduct and beauty, even a respectable fortune. What more could he want? He entered his recently refurbished town house using his latch key. An argand lamp burnt on a marble-topped console table supported by improbable sphinxes. He took up the lamp and laid his opera glasses down in its place. What more, indeed? He had been startled to realise midway through the performance of *La Cenerentola* that he was paying more attention to the charms of one of the chorus than to Lady Lucinda.

Thoughtfully he mounted the stairs. Well, what of it? He had little doubt that Lady Lucinda would turn a blind eye to his amorous dealings if he were discreet and did not make her a laughing stock. Obviously she expected him to make her an offer, but it was ridiculous to suppose that there was any more sentiment on her side than his. Their marriage would be a business arrangement for the begetting of children, preferably sons, and the orderly devolution of property.

He reached his bedchamber and began to undress. Somehow he was dissatisfied. Now, when he had managed everything according to plan, suddenly the plan seemed flawed. Rubbish, he told himself sternly, as he divested himself of his black coat. You want a marriage of convenience and that's precisely what you are getting. He threw his shirt over a chair, resolutely thrusting away the vision of Peter and his lovely wife, who had also been at the opera. They had visited his box at the interval, the affection between them apparent for anyone to see. His breeches followed the shirt with unwonted violence.

A nightshirt was laid out for him. He donned it thoughtfully. His house party was nearly arranged. The Stanfords were off to Brighton for several weeks, but he had little doubt that if an invitation to Helford Place were extended, Lady Stanford would have no scruples in leaving her own spouse to the joys of Brighton while she secured a husband for her daughter. He had formed the intention of paying a morning call at Stanford House the following day to invite them. He had invited several friends, but Lady Lucinda was the only unattached female. It looked a little particular, but that suited his purpose admirably.

He sat on the edge of his enormous bed with its extravagantly carved headboard and blew out the lamp. It occurred to him as he lay waiting for sleep that perhaps he should have discreetly set up a mistress. That might have eased the odd feeling of dissatisfaction that haunted him. Too late now, he was leaving town in a couple of days to make sure all was in order for his house party. Besides which, it was probably time he introduced himself to his ten-year-old niece and ward, Miss Fanny Melville. He thrust away a feeling of guilt. After all, surely no one expected him to act as nursemaid to the child.

At ten o'clock the following morning Helford left his house in Cavendish Square to stroll around to Stanford House in Grosvenor Street. He met George Carstares in Grosvenor Square and hailed him with pleasure.

'Hullo, old chap. Haven't seen much of you recently. How are you?'

George grinned, 'Never better, thank you.' He appeared to be bubbling over with high spirits, unusual in one of his preferred matutinal habits. 'Offered for Sarah last night and she accepted!'

Helford stared, speechless for a moment, all his cynical, sceptical convictions flung into disarray. An heiress, and one much sought after, had accepted the hand of a second son with no chance of inheriting. Despite having expected this for weeks, the solid fact shook his cynical soul to the core.

'Congratulations, George,' he said, squashing the unwelcome tinge of envy that arose in his breast. He did not envy George *Sarah* specifically, just that look of transparent joy and completion that he and Darleston radiated. 'Please wish Miss Sarah happy for me. I will be leaving town tomorrow. Time I went down to Helford and sorted things out there. And I have a small house party arranged for next month—as a matter of fact, I'm just on my way to invite Lady Stanford and Lady Lucinda to grace it.'

George hid his horror very creditably. 'Oh! Then…?' He almost held his breath awaiting the reply.

'No. Not yet,' answered Helford, correctly interpreting his friend's unvoiced question. 'Only fair to let the girl see where she is going to live beforehand. Besides, it will be as well for us to spend some time together first. Make sure we don't annoy each other too much. I shall speak to Stanford this morning and make sure he has no objection.'

None of this gave George any comfort. There was no way Helford could get out of making the girl an offer if he spoke to Stanford. And he had little doubt that the offer would be accepted, if not with enthusiasm—for George could not imagine Lady Lucinda being so vulgar as to betray such a human emotion—then with dignified good breeding.

With no hint of his true feelings George said, 'I'll wish you luck then, old chap.' No harm in that, he thought. Besides, if Lady Luck *did* happen to glance in the direction of Helford Place, she might just decide to meddle!

An hour later Helford left Stanford House, determinedly aware that he had set things in train for exactly the sort of marriage he had envisaged. Lord

Stanford had given his permission for him to address Lady Lucinda with a complete lack of surprise. Lady Stanford and Lady Lucinda had accepted his invitation to Helford Place with a marked degree of gratification. Everything was as he had planned.

So why the hell did he feel as though a trap were closing about him? He had engineered everything himself. He had certainly not been caught by a scheming mama. On the contrary, he had been totally in control of the whole situation and would remain so.

He reminded himself of this frequently on his journey down to Helford Place, until his unacknowledged excitement at coming home at last finally rose up and drowned all other thoughts in a flood of expectation.

Indeed, he found the last part of his drive down to Helford Place to be a very odd experience. In the past twelve years, on the few occasions he had been in England, he had only visited London. Now, driving the last few miles, he found that everything was much the same as he remembered it. Yet he felt very differently about it.

The road was as rutted as ever, the hedges towering overhead crowded with pale pink dog roses and honeysuckle. Their heady scent drifted on the light breeze, seeming to float suspended in the golden aftermath of a brief shower. Glittering droplets bejewelled each blossom so that it sparkled. Twelve years ago he would not have noticed such things. Then, if he had been on this road heading for home, it could only have meant that he was in dun territory yet again, depending on his brother to give him a tow. Or to pursue his infatuation with Felicity. He'd certainly never had any inclination to notice the beauties of nature.

He thought cynically that, at least after he'd quitted Helford Place for the last time, he had learnt how to live on his pay as a soldier and his patrimony. Even added to it by careful investments, so that he'd been a relatively wealthy man in his own right before he inherited the title. So determined had he been to have nothing more to do with his family that he had learnt the value and handling of money.

He had made good time on the journey. He had sent his horses forward and this final pair of chestnuts he had picked up at Tattersall's had been an undoubted bargain, prime bits of blood and bone. Not quite sixteen-mile-an-hour tits, but nearly so. Their action was admirable, forward stepping and very easy. And their mouths were something to dream about. Better than the bays he had had twelve years ago, he reflected. Or perhaps it was just that he was a better whip now, capable of coaxing the best from his cattle.

His mind still in the past, he swept around the last corner before the village of Little Helford at a pace which he later admitted to himself to have been far too fast. He was within two miles of home and eager to reach it.

The road was not particularly wide and the church stood just outside the village with the parsonage beside it and it was from the lane beside the church that disaster so nearly struck. He could see a female on his left walking towards him alongside the churchyard. She looked up at the rumble of the curricle as it approached and he clearly saw her face turn to horror as she ran forward shouting and waving. Then, so fast that he could never afterwards be sure exactly what happened, a small boy on a makeshift trolley came tearing out of the lane. The trolley hit a rut in the road and flipped over, depositing its shrieking driver directly in the path of the oncoming vehicle.

Helford swore and hauled desperately on the reins with scant regard for his horses' delicate mouths. The pace was too swift. Seeing in a flash that he had not the slightest chance of stopping in time, he attempted to yank them around, but they were thoroughly upset and did not respond fast enough. Horrified, he realised that the child was going to be killed.

Then somehow the girl was on the child and had caught him under the armpits, swinging him out of the way before trying to leap clear herself. She was not quite quick enough to avoid a glancing blow from the shoulder of the off-side horse which sent her spinning into the ditch. There was an appalling cracking, splintering sound as hooves and wheels crashed over the trolley.

Petrified at what he might find, Helford pulled up his pair ten yards further on. White and shaking, he set the brake and flung the ribbons to his equally shocked tiger with a terse, 'Hold 'em!'

He vaulted down into the road and ran back, inexpressibly relieved to see the girl struggling to her feet and the small boy trying valiantly to control his sobs.

'Are you hurt, girl?' he snapped, fear making his voice sharper than it might otherwise have been.

The girl looked up at him, rubbing her left shoulder vigorously, and he was staring into the most appealing little face he had ever seen. She had a warm, creamy complexion, which just now was streaked with mud and becomingly flushed; the nose had the merest suspicion of a tilt and more than a suspicion of freckles scattered over it. Soft brown curls had escaped a knot on top of her head, adding to the disarray of her person. And a small, slender yet daintily rounded person it was too, he noted, despite the dowdy and rather shapeless grey dress she wore. Definitely what he would describe as a cosy armful!

He felt sick in his guts as a nightmare vision of what might have happened rose before him. The slight figure lying broken and battered in the mud. He closed his eyes and shook his head to dispel the thought.

But perhaps her eyes were her most startling feature. He supposed one might describe them as hazel, but they were in reality the strangest mixture of green and brown, fringed with the longest, thickest black lashes. Delicate black brows arched over them in direct contrast to the softness of the rest of her colouring. Never had he seen lovelier eyes.

And never had he seen eyes quite so angry!

'No! I am not hurt! But it's small thanks to you if I am not! How dare you drive at such a *wicked* pace around a corner into a quiet village!' She positively quivered with fury. 'You could have killed Jemmy here!' She turned on the boy. 'Not but what you have been warned often and often not to ride that trolley on to the road! You ought to be ashamed of yourself. Why, you might have hurt the horses badly!'

'My thoughts precisely,' drawled Helford, relieved beyond all measure that the little vixen was at least unharmed enough to rake them both down. He reached into a pocket and drew out a shilling. 'Take this, Jemmy, and don't do it again or I'll warm the seat of your pants for you!'

Stunned at such largesse and barely able to mutter his thanks and apology, the boy accepted the coin and took to his heels before a crowd could gather. By some miracle no one was about and he could entertain reasonable hopes that his escapade would not reach the ears of his mam who would not wait for his next infraction to warm his seat for him. Especially if she ever found out how close Miss Sophie had come to being runned over!

Amused, Helford turned back to the girl and said, 'Are you quite sure you are—?' He stopped mid-sentence and swore. Her nose was bleeding copiously.

'Damn! Here, let me!' He found a large silk hand-kerchief in his coat pocket and applied it firmly to her nose, cupping the other hand behind her head to hold her steady. Startled eyes stared at him in outrage over his handkerchief, but she remained still in his grip. His fingers, threaded through the soft curls, trembled slightly. There was a curious familiarity in the intimacy of silken locks tumbling over his hand in such disorder. It was far from the first time he had tangled his long fingers in such soft tresses. But under the circumstances he was shocked to feel a twinge of desire in his loins. Ruthlessly he shackled the unwelcome thoughts and concentrated on her bleeding nose.

After a few moments he released her carefully. 'That should do it,' he said with misplaced confidence.

For a moment the girl stood stock still and then he noticed that she was trembling and breathing rather oddly. His eyes widened in horror as he realised what was about to happen but there was no time to dodge. In sheer self-defence he grabbed her and clamped the handkerchief to her nose again.

'Aaaachhhoo!' The sneeze and its effects were thoroughly extinguished by the handkerchief, but he realized, while trying unsuccessfully not to laugh, that this time the girl had obviously had enough. Firmly she took the handkerchief and removed herself from his grip.

Her voice came slightly muffled from behind it. 'It's nothing! Please just go away unless you wish to see me reduced to a sneezing ruin!'

'But—'

She cut in coldly, 'I am perfectly all right and I can sneeze without your assistance! Please go away! I am not hurt in the slightest, despite your best efforts, and will be glad to see the last of you!'

'Damn you! The accident was not my fault!' he said, stung by her contempt. 'If you had stayed off the road—'

'Jem would be dead!' she flashed at him. 'I do not say he ought to have been there, but had you not been coming at such a *wicked* pace you would have had time to pull up! Did you not hear me? I called out to you to stop!'

He shook his head, 'No, of course I could not hear what you were saying, you fool of a wench! The horses and wheels were making far too much noise. In fact, I should have thought that hell-born brat would have been able to hear me coming and alter course! Now, if you are really uninjured and require no further assistance, might

I suggest that you go on your way and permit me to go on mine!'

'Why you…you…arrogant, conceited coxcomb!' she exploded, while still trying to staunch her nose. 'How dare you speak to me like that! No doubt in my position you would have let Jem be killed!'

She was shaking with rage and Helford suddenly realised that she was close to tears. Shock, he thought. Reaction. *For God's sake, man, control yourself! She's little more than a child herself and you damned nearly killed her!*

'No, I wouldn't have,' he admitted ruefully. 'But please put yourself in my position. I dare say I was driving too fast, but I was horrified when I saw the child and realised that I couldn't avoid him. Can you imagine how I felt when I saw you go flying into the ditch?' She stared at him in shock and he continued, 'Come, you are undoubtedly upset! Go home and try to believe that I would have been devastated if I had killed or injured either of you. I will even go so far as to thank you for sparing me such an ordeal.'

'I…I beg your pardon,' she said stiffly. 'I should not have lost my temper like that.' This grudging apology was uttered into the blood-boltered handkerchief, but she cautiously lowered it and sniffed carefully. Nothing happened, so she folded the handkerchief up and held it out to him. 'Er, do you want it back?'

He glanced at the gruesome relic and shook his head. 'Not really! You keep it, in case your nose bleeds again.' She nodded and bestowed it in the pocket of her gown.

He asked gently, 'Have you far to go? Might I take you up?'

'Thank you, but no. I have an errand to discharge on my way home and it will take some time. Good day, sir.'

'Good day,' he responded and stood watching as she walked away. She did not look back and he wondered who the devil she was. Her speech suggested that she was gently born, yet she had no maid to attend her, despite her youth. He did not think she could be more than twenty-three or so. Obviously she had no pretensions to wealth and fashion in that gown, but there was a certain dignity in her bearing which even her tumbled curls and muddied face could not destroy.

Puzzled, he went back to the curricle where his tiger was walking the mettlesome pair up and down.

'No harm done?' he asked.

'None, me lord,' responded his henchman. 'Leastways, not to these fellows. I'll warrant that mort'll pull up stiff tomorrow though! Lor', she did take a tumble! Thought she'd be kilt fer sure when I saw what she'd be at!'

His noble employer grunted. It had felt as though his stomach had fallen into his boots when he had seen the girl leap into the road for the boy. He had fully expected the pair of them to be trampled to death. And it would have been his fault. He had been going far too fast!

'Why the hell didn't you tell me to slow down, Jasper?' he asked crossly.

'Acos you mostly in general damns me eyes fer it,' was the very disrespectful answer. Jasper had been in Helford's employ since before he went out to the Peninsula in 1811. He had been in numerous scrapes with his master and had actually dragged him off the battlefield on two occasions. His was a privileged position and he spoke his mind very frequently.

'I dare say! Next time I do something this stupid, hit me on the head!' growled Helford.

There was a chuckle from behind him, 'I dessay the thought of that little bit of a lass tearin' strips off you like what she did will do the trick. Little spitfire she were!' The appreciation in Jasper's voice was marked.

Helford slewed around in his seat, 'You behave yourself, Jasper. She's a respectable lady!'

'You keep yer glims on the road, me lord. Don't have to tell me she's quality! Could see that fer meself! Real flesh-and-blood quality at that.' This last was muttered to himself. Jasper had his own opinion of Lord Helford's choice of helpmeet. For the life of him he couldn't think what the master was playing at. For his money, the little spitfire who'd raked him down in the roadway would be a better choice than that there statue back in London. Still, that was one subject where he'd do better to dub his mummer! The master wouldn't take no interference there! Not by a long shot he wouldn't!

Chapter Three

Miss Sophie Marsden wriggled her left shoulder irritably. It still ached from her tumble in the ditch two days ago. In fact, if she were to be strictly truthful, most of her still ached. She had woken up the following morning as stiff as a board. A careful examination had revealed her upper left arm and shoulder to be badly bruised along with her entire left side. Since this was where the horse had struck her and she had also managed to land on that side, the stiffness and bruising were only to be expected.

What really bothered Miss Marsden was that she could not get the gentleman's face and startling eyes out of her mind. He had been as white as a sheet as he came striding back to them. And his eyes! She had never imagined such blazing green eyes. And it was not just his eyes. The lean, powerful frame had simply radiated arrogant masculine strength. But it was the memory of his hand in her hair that was really occupying her thoughts.

Those long fingers had tangled in her curls in a way that made her tremble when she recalled it.

Crossly she forced her attention back to the household accounts. Just because she had never seen such a handsome man before was no excuse to be making so many mistakes over these accounts. He was undoubtedly some traveller passing through whom she would never lay eyes on again and the quicker she stopped thinking about him the better. Even if she did see him again, the chances were that he would not even recall her face and, if he did, it would probably be in connection with her shocking loss of temper.

For a few moments the accounts reigned triumphant but then her pen slowed and her mind drifted. For some reason his face bothered her. She was nearly sure that it was oddly familiar, but she was quite certain that she had never met its owner before. Her reflections were interrupted by the door opening.

She turned around to see her elderly companion, Miss Andrews, and their maid Anna. The former looked distinctly apologetic. Anna, on the other hand, simply looked annoyed.

'Oh, dear! What has he done this time?' asked Miss Marsden resignedly.

'Can't find him nowhere, Miss Sophie,' asserted Anna. 'We've looked everywhere an' he's gorn.'

'Everywhere?'

"Fraid so, Miss Sophie. He's gorn.'

Miss Andrews said, 'I am truly sorry, my love. But I left him for no more than a moment, just to fetch the Latin primer. And I put him on his honour not to leave his books.'

'And he still left?' Sophie was shocked.

'Well, yes,' said Miss Andrews. 'But he took his books with him.' She seemed to feel that this in some way mitigated the crime.

'Little pest!' said Sophie indignantly. She sighed, 'Very well. I shall have to go and look for him. Again.' This was the third time in a week that her orphaned ten-year-old nephew had taken French leave from his studies. She shut the account book and stood up carefully, suppressing a curse at the soreness. She had not mentioned her escapade to any of her household, having a constitutional dislike of being fussed over. The muddied gown had been explained away as the result of a passing carriage.

Several applications of arnica had gone a long way towards relieving the soreness, but she was by no means her usual lively self and the thought of a long tramp after her truant nephew Kit did not appeal to her in the slightest.

She smiled cheerfully, realising that Anna was watching her closely. 'Never mind. I dare say a walk will blow the cobwebs away. I simply couldn't make my accounts add up.'

'I shall go over them for you, then,' said Miss

Andrews, very pleased to think there was something she could do to atone for her foolishness in letting Kit slip his leash. She was vexed to think that she had not remembered to put him on his honour not to leave the room.

'Don't you dare, Thea!' Sophie was outraged. 'I am to have a pleasant walk over to the river, where Kit is no doubt tickling trout. Why should you not have a morning off? The accounts will wait. In fact, I have a very good notion about them. We will make Kit tot them up as his punishment. He can do it after dinner instead of his usual playtime.'

Miss Andrews was impressed. Like most small boys Kit loathed arithmetic. But he would certainly appreciate the justice in this arrangement!

Old Anna nodded sourly. 'Happen he'll think twice afore he does it again.'

Ruefully Sophie said, 'We can hope so, but I suspect there is something more to this than mere small-boy naughtiness. He doesn't even appear to *enjoy* his escapes. When I came up with him the last time he looked plain miserable, even before he saw me.'

Five minutes later, clad in a light cloak, bonnet and list boots, she was crossing the meadow behind the house, her skirts brushing through the purple clover. Several cows glanced up at her, their jaws moving rhythmically. She thought they must be getting used to the sight of her by now. Kit was making a habit of this.

It was odd, she thought. As she had said to Anna, he didn't seem to be enjoying his excursions. So why was he doing it so often? The only explanation she could come up with was the death of her sister six months ago. At the time Kit had been grief-stricken, of course, but he had appeared to recover, if not his usual spirits, at least some semblance of the merry boy he had been. Now he was playing truant all the time and even seemed to resent his aunt's authority. Oh, he still obeyed her, but she had the distinct impression that he didn't want to.

What exactly was behind it all, she didn't know. He wouldn't talk to her about it, just clammed up when she tried to discuss his behaviour. Give him time, she thought. It's hard for a child to lose his mother. She missed Emma bitterly enough herself. Even when she had been following the drum with her soldier husband, Emma had written regularly to her little sister, telling her all about their adventures, keeping in touch. Now she was gone completely and it would have been her birthday next week…

Sophie froze. Good God! How stupid of me, she thought. We always made such a fuss of Emma's birthday, picking flowers, making her a present. He's thinking about all that, of course. No wonder he's such a picture of misery. Oh, dear! What on earth can I do?

She continued on alongside the hedge until she

came to the corner. There was a gap. Small enough to keep the cows in, but large enough for her to brush through the tangled honeysuckle, which spilled its scent and petals down over her shoulders. Large enough for Kit too, she thought, noting a scrap of wool caught on a twig. He's torn his stockings again! Well, at least I know what's bothering him now. Perhaps we can do something about it.

Insensibly cheered, she went on towards the river with an easy swinging stride. Her mind now largely freed of its concern, she was able to enjoy the walk. It was a favourite that she and her sister had often taken with Kit. Despite this being private land, the previous Viscount Helford, from whom she had rented her house, had always made her free of it.

'You can't do much harm,' he'd said in his bluff way, when he came by to apologise after one of his keepers had warned the three of them off. 'Just don't let the lad fall in the river.' He had waved aside their thanks. A kindly man with his green eyes and black hair. She and Emma had truly mourned his death…they'd hardly ever seen his fashionable Viscountess… Green eyes? Black hair? Good God! Now she knew why that face had been so familiar! He looked just like his brother. Well, not just like—Lord Helford had not had that air of rakishness about him and he had not been so appallingly handsome. But the resemblance had been enough to niggle at her memory.

Merciful heavens! She had actually had the effrontery to abuse her own landlord on a public road in the presence of a small boy and one of his own servants. If he ever found out who she was, she'd be lucky if he didn't evict her. No! The denial came sharply from an odd, secluded corner of her mind. It was inconceivable that he would be so churlish.

Little details of their encounter assured her of that. The look of sick terror on his face as he strode back, the gentle way he had held her while trying to stop her nose bleeding. The memory of his long fingers tangled in her curls brought a most peculiar sensation to the pit of her stomach. Firmly she dismissed it. He had been angry enough, she thought. But not because *I* nearly splattered him with blood! She giggled as she saw again the dawning horror as he realised what was about to happen. No, he hadn't cared at all! Just tried again to help her. He'd even laughed.

She felt a trifle guilty as she recalled how she had ripped up at him. No wonder he'd lost his temper with her. He wasn't to know that cologne sometimes made her sneeze. But he had curbed his anger almost immediately. Had he seen how upset she was? The whole affair had suddenly got home to her, making her quite sick with delayed fear. When she had seen Jem's danger there had been no time for fear. She had acted without even thinking. Only later, when she had been safe, had she begun to shake and feel cold. It was always the same, she thought ruefully. She went tail over top into action and then thought about the consequences later.

Even now…crossly she thrust the memory away. What a ninnyhammer, to be trembling like a leaf over an avoided accident two days old! Depend upon it his lordship—she entertained no doubts that it *had* been the new Viscount—had forgotten it already. If her memory served her correctly, then this Viscount Helford had a reputation as a considerable rake. Vienna! That was it! He had been at the Embassy, his brother had said. A badly dressed country nobody with no pretensions to beauty was hardly going to lodge in his memory.

Riding out that morning on one of his late brother's horses, his lordship was very far from having forgotten the encounter. He was strangely haunted by the business. He had seen death often enough in the army, horrible lingering deaths of mangled bodies and maimed limbs. Deaths which had been a mercy when they came. But none had ever affected him as did the thought of that girl battered by his horses and dragged under the wheels of his curricle. He had woken the previous night in a sweat having dreamed of it. The details were horribly clear and he had shuddered in relief to realise that it was merely a dream.

Now in the bright sunshine as he cantered across his flower-starred fields he had leisure to wonder who the girl was. A lady, unquestionably. But who? He had casually enquired of his Great Aunt Maria about the various gently born families currently in residence, but none of the persons she had enumerated tallied with his little termagant. And why the hell was he bothering anyway? She could be nothing to him. He had applied for permission to court Lady Lucinda and that should suit him admirably.

Of course she can be nothing to you, soothed the odd voice in his mind. But it would only be polite to call on her and assure yourself that she really did take no hurt. And to suggest that her parents or guardians should take better care of her. A chit of her quality should not be wandering the countryside unattended. It was outrageous. The more he thought about it, the more he was convinced that he should find out who she was.

A movement on the far side of the hedge he was riding beside caught his attention. He stood up in his stirrups for a better view and there, on the other side of the meadow, was a familiar form. He could not possibly be mistaken even at this distance. There was something very distinctive about the way she moved. A suggestion of lithe grace about the lissom body. He was surprised that the unknown girl should have so wormed her way into his thoughts.

He watched for a moment and wondered where her companions were. He could see no one else, just one unattended girl heading, if his memory served him, for the river flowing beyond that belt of oaks. Riding further along the hedge, he came to a gap. Turning his mare, he rode back a little and then pushed her into a canter. Her ears pricked daintily as she saw what he would be at. A snort of enthusiasm told David that she was not at all averse to jumping. Gathering her quarters under her, she sailed over effortlessly, picking her feet up daintily.

The figure by the far hedge had obviously heard them. She had stopped and turned to see who was coming. Now, thought David, I can find out who she is. And what the hell she is doing trespassing on my land!

The thud of hooves had alerted Sophie to the fact that she was not alone even before the familiar chestnut mare came over the hedge. She recognised her at once. Lord Helford's favourite mare, Perdita. And ridden by the gentleman in the curricle. His seat on a horse was magnificent, she saw at once, and he handled the lively mare with the ease of a born horseman. He was obviously coming to find out who the trespasser was so she waited, wondering if he would even recognise her.

His first words settled that. 'Do you never take a maid with you, or a companion? I cannot think it right for a girl your age to go about unattended.' He had not meant to be quite so direct but somehow the words were out before he knew it. It must be the eyes which unsettled him. They were even lovelier than he remembered.

Sophie stiffened. He would be quite within his rights to castigate her for trespassing, but how dare he call her to account for her behaviour! Insufferable man! With an effort she recalled that he was her landlord and a Viscount to boot, and that common courtesy required her to suppress her natural inclination to tell him to mind his own business.

'Good morning, Lord Helford,' she said sweetly. And observed with pleasure the jolt she had given him. He had certainly not expected her to know who he was.

'I confess, ma'am, you have the advantage of me.' He acknowledged her hit with a charming smile and dismounted, drawing the bridle over his mare's head. Perdita, recognising a well-wisher who on numerous occasions had bestowed an apple or even sugar upon her, promptly gave him a shove and insinuated herself between them, rubbing her face against Sophie's shoulder.

'I see she knows you,' said David drily. Damn, even his mare knew the chit!

'Yes, she was your brother's favourite. We often used to see him riding her,' said Sophie, petting the mare. 'I was sorry to hear of his death. He was a kind man and a good landlord.'

David nodded. Yes, that was James. Despite his

hurt over Felicity, he had never denied James's sterling qualities; he had been kind and undoubtedly he had been a good landlord.

'May I know your name, ma'am?' he asked politely.

'Miss Sophie Marsden. And—' seeing that the name conveyed nothing to his lordship '—I live at Willowbank House.'

'Then your parents are my tenants!'

'No,' she corrected him gently, '*I* am your tenant.'

'And may I enquire what Miss Marsden is doing on my preserves completely unattended?' At last he had managed to return to his original question.

'I'm not poaching rabbits, if that's what is worrying you!' she snapped, unaccountably annoyed by his continual harping on her solitary state. 'I'm not a green girl, you know. I am five and twenty and my own mistress. If you must have it, I am trying to retrieve a truant and—' this with a mischievous smile '—I have to admit it, he *is* probably tickling your trout.'

'Tickling my trout? How old is this poacher?'

'Ten,' replied Sophie.

'And you are responsible for him?' An incredible suspicion was forming in David's mind. He could not believe it at first. She seemed so sweet and innocent. But a boy of ten and she was only twenty-five! He stole a glance at her left hand. No, it was bare of rings, he had not misheard her. He was conscious of a sickening jolt of disappointment, swiftly followed by anger. And she had known his brother! Damn James! And damn women, they were all the same! First Felicity and now this one!

His voice, when he spoke again, was cold. 'I think, Miss Marsden, that you had better remain off my preserves in future. In fact, I suggest you remove yourself now and remember that any *game* I find on my land, I am apt to consider mine. Since I am riding towards the river anyway I will send your…er…*ward* home.'

Completely taken aback by the sudden change in his tone, Sophie stared at him in amazement. He had swung himself back into the saddle and was looking down at her with a faint air of hauteur. And his eyes were different somehow. They seemed to rove over her body in a manner which suggested that he…that he was stripping her with them. She felt a blush rising to her cheeks. No one had ever looked at her like that!

'Just so, Miss Marsden. I shall consider you warned. If I find you here again…'

He smiled at her in a considering way and she suddenly realised what he was thinking. Disbelief robbed her of speech for a moment and she stood positively gaping at him. Before she could recover enough to tell him exactly what she thought of his high-handed, insulting, overbearing character, he had pressed the mare into a trot and was riding away. Calling out to him that he was mistaken was unthinkable. Let him believe her a *bit of game*! She

hoped he would sink through the floor in embarrassment when he found out his mistake!

David rode away conscious of mingled fury and
disappointment, trying to forget the look of startled
surprise on Miss Marsden's countenance, which
had been replaced by embarrassment. The whole
thing was obvious enough. James, doubtless discovering Felicity's infidelities, had set up his own
mistress in Willowbank House. It was not a large
house, but quite commodious enough for a woman
and child. Curse it! No doubt James had signed the
house to the wench for a long lease on easy terms,
just so everything would look above board. Well, he
would have to do something about that. He was
damned if he wanted her living there!

The thought occurred to him that he could always
continue with whatever arrangement James had
made. Not a doubt but what she was a dainty
piece…and it would be deucedly convenient… No!
He didn't want James's leavings! He hadn't wanted
the scraps Felicity had been prepared to bestow
upon him and he didn't want this one! At least he
didn't think he did. She would be enjoyable though,
he thought to himself. Those soft, voluptuous curves
would nestle against him very comfortably…and
that temper hinted at a passionate nature…

Still considering the matter, he reached the oaks
and rode into the flickering shade at a walk. A
narrow path led through the trees. He knew it well

and tried to remember just how many times he had come this way as a boy in the evening or very early morning to catch a rise on the deep pool at the bend in the river. The mare's hooves made little sound on last year's leaves, damp from heavy rain overnight.

The trees eventually opened out on to the river-bank. On the far side the ground was marshy and bright with yellow flag irises. This side the bank shelved steeply, carved out as the river turned. Here in the deep, quiet backwater the trout lay up during the day. A demoiselle dragonfly skimmed across the water and he watched breathlessly, but there was no rise and the insect was gone again in a shard of blue. He looked further along and there in the long grass was a small boy lying on his stomach, peering over into the pool.

He dismounted and, dropping the mare's reins, walked quietly to where the boy was lying. His nankeens indicated that he had been sitting in wet grass and the soft brown curls were very familiar. A pile of books lay beside him. He had obviously not heard anyone approach.

David looked down at the child for a moment. There was something odd about the set of the child's shoulders which made him hesitate, but he cleared his throat warningly. The boy rolled over immediately and David saw in a flash that he had been crying and also from the surprise on his face that he had expected someone else.

Well, of course he did, you idiot, David casti-
gated himself. Heavens! He had the same black-
fringed hazel eyes, the same curls. It was uncanny.
Nothing of James there.

The boy had rolled back on to his stomach, 'Oh. I
thought you were someone else.' His voice was sullen.

'Your mother, for instance?' suggested David sardonically. And immediately regretted it. Those
hazel eyes were fronting him again with a sort of
suppressed anguish.

The small shoulders shook and a broken voice
said in a whisper, 'Yes, but it's always Aunt
Sophie!'

The riverbank heaved under David's feet. Aunt
Sophie? *Aunt* Sophie? *Oh, my God! And she saw
what I was thinking! Oh, hell and the Devil! What
did Peter say about carrying one's suspicions too
far?*

'Sophie Marsden is your aunt?' he asked gently
as he squatted down beside the small figure.

'Yes.'

'I see,' said David. 'The resemblance between
you is so startling I assumed she must be your
mother.'

The tear-stained face looked up, puzzled. 'But
how could she be? Aunt Sophie isn't married.'

How indeed, thought David ruefully. And to think
I was that innocent once. I've certainly made a hash
of this all right and tight! I must have been mad.

James would never have taken a fifteen-year-old as his mistress!

His new acquaintance continued, 'I know we look alike. Aunt Sophie and Mama looked a lot alike. I s'pose I took after Mama. I'm Kit Carlisle.'

David nodded, feeling his way. There was something here that he didn't quite understand. 'Miss Marsden was a trifle concerned about you. I met her coming this way and told her I'd send you home if I saw you.'

A sigh greeted this. 'Is she very angry?'

Well, yes, she probably was. But not with this youngster, thought David. 'Not very, I shouldn't think,' he said encouragingly. 'Did you have reason to think she would be?'

'It's the third time this week that I've given Auntie Thea the bag,' confessed Kit shamefacedly. 'She's my governess, you know. She left the room for a minute and put me on my honour not to leave my books...' He indicated the pile of books. 'So I...er...brought them with me.'

'Enterprising,' said David mildly.

'You're not cross?'

'Should I be?' asked David, surprised at the question.

'You don't think it was a bit mean?' asked Kit hesitantly.

'Well, since you mention it, I have to say it was not quite the thing to do,' acknowledged David.

'But I dare say I would have done it myself so there's hope for you yet.' He added feelingly, 'And if you never do anything worse to offend a lady then you'll be doing well!'

'I suppose I'd better go,' said Kit. 'If Aunt Sophie is looking for me…' His voice trailed off and he heaved himself to his feet.

'Why don't you wash your face first? It's a little dirty,' said David tactfully. He pulled out a handkerchief, reflecting that Miss Marsden was going to have quite a collection if this kept up. Reaching over to dip it in the pool, he asked casually, 'Any trout?'

Kit nodded as he scrubbed his face with the proffered handkerchief, 'Mmm. Three. But I put them back.'

'You tickled three trout out of there?' David was impressed. That rascally old poacher Twickenham had tried to show him as a lad how the trick was done without the least success. 'Who taught you that?'

Kit looked rather conscious. 'I s'pose I shouldn't say. They're your trout, aren't they?'

'What makes you say that?' Good God, the boy was as quick as his aunt!

'Well, I know Perdita and you look like Lord Helford a bit. Besides, I met your bailiff, Hurley, on the way and he said you were out riding, so it wasn't very hard,' explained Kit.

'I see,' said David, amused. 'Well, yes, I am Lord Helford and I suppose they are my trout, strictly speaking, and if you refuse to denounce the old scoundrel who taught you to tickle my trout I can only respect your discretion.'

Kit looked at him carefully. 'Does that mean you don't mind?'

'Mind? Of course I mind!' said David. 'I tried to tickle these trout for years and never caught one. Poor old Twickenham was ashamed of so clumsy a pupil!'

'Twickenham! But—' Kit stopped himself at once.

'You needn't tell me,' said David. 'If Twickenham's still alive I have no doubt that he was your master. You tell the old scoundrel I still can't tickle a trout when next you see him!'

A chuckle greeted this. 'You can't be as bad as Aunt Sophie. She fell in when I tried to show her.'

'Did she, indeed?' David tried to ignore the vision of Aunt Sophie in a wet and clinging gown, which promptly presented itself to his imagination for minute inspection.

'If you must be going, would you care for a ride home?' he asked. 'Since you and Perdita are acquainted I will presume on her good nature.'

'Is it out of your way?' asked Kit, obviously trying not to look too eager.

'Not in the slightest. You have reminded me that I have an errand to your aunts,' explained David, thinking that he certainly owed one of the lad's aunts an unconditional and grovelling apology.

'Auntie Thea isn't really my aunt, you know. I just call her that,' said Kit.

They walked over to the mare and David swung himself into the saddle and held a hand down to Kit. 'Put your foot on mine and up with you.'

Kit scrambled up easily enough and they set off back through the oak wood and across the meadows. Kit did not seem to be in the least in awe of a viscount and chattered away to David about the wildlife to be found around and about. To David's surprise he enjoyed the experience enormously. Children had not hitherto come much in his way. Naturally one had to have them to carry on the family name and title, but it had never occurred to him that they might be rewarding in themselves. Certainly the stiffly polite Miss Fanny Melville had not given him any such inkling.

Perdita's steady trot covered the distance very easily and as they pushed through the gap into the cow field behind Willowbank House a slim figure could be seen mounting the stile which led into the garden.

'There she is,' said Kit. He called out, 'Aunt Sophie, here I am!'

The figure turned at once and even at that distance David could see her stiffen in shock. 'Hold tight,' he said and pushed the mare into a canter.

By the time they reached her Sophie was standing on the lowest step of the stile, her face set and watchful. Nothing could have equalled her surprise at seeing Kit with his lordship. Her first assumption, that my lord must be taking the quickest way to remove an unwanted trespasser from his land, was quickly dispelled by a look at Kit's face. He was obviously quite happy with his company. A further look at Lord Helford's face told her that he was perfectly aware that he had made an appalling gaffe and was thoroughly ashamed and vexed with himself. Well, far be it from me to make it easy for him, thought Sophie savagely. Arrogant beast!

She was the first to speak. 'Thank you for the return of my *ward*, sir. As you see, I am off your preserves.' The icy politeness of her voice spoke volumes for all the things she would have liked to say, but was prevented from uttering by the circumstances.

Not for a moment did David delude himself that either her good manners or his own high degree were in any way cramping her style. The only defence between himself and another sample of Miss Marsden's temper was perched on his saddle bow.

'I'm…I'm awfully sorry, Aunt Sophie,' said Kit. And Lord Helford had thought she wasn't very angry! Kit had never seen his merry aunt in such a pelter.

Her face softened slightly as she looked at him, 'Very well. You had better go inside and repeat your apology to Thea. And after dinner you can help me with my accounts since I had to leave them to come after you.'

Kit slid to the ground with a grimace. Trust Aunt Sophie to come up with that. 'Yes, ma'am.' He grinned up at David. 'Thank you, sir. Goodbye.' He swarmed over the stile and ran off to the house. If Aunt Sophie wasn't cross with him, who was she cross with? It couldn't be Lord Helford. She'd only just met him. Besides, he was a great gun!

Miss Sophie Marsden was left confronting the man she couldn't possibly be cross with and said, 'Naturally I will remove myself from your side of the stile. Good day, my lord.' Those dark eyes were showing more green than brown and they were narrowed to blazing slits.

David swallowed and began his apology with all the air of a man leading a forlorn hope. 'Miss Marsden, I…er…I made a frightful mistake. And I beg you to accept my profound apologies for the—'

He was cut off sharply. 'Your apology is of not the slightest interest to me, sir!' snapped the lady. 'I have nothing but contempt for anyone with such a horridly commonplace mind as to assume…to assume…what you assumed. And furthermore, even if I were a bit of game, as you so obligingly implied, you are the last man alive to whom I would consider granting my favours!'

'How dare you say such a thing to me!' exploded David in outrage.

'No?' asked Sophie, a dangerous gleam in her eyes. 'Would you prefer me to tell you that I am very disappointed and should be charmed to entertain your dishonourable proposals? Have you never had a female refuse you before?'

David glared at her. 'Of course not!' He stopped, aware of her incredulous gaze. Bloody hell! What was he saying?

'How very gratifying for you, my lord!' she said, patently disgusted. 'I am delighted to think that I have enlarged your experience so easily!'

'Damn your eyes!' He was really furious now at having made such a cod's-head of himself. 'What I meant was that a young lady of birth and virtue, which I assume you to be, should not say such things! Not even know of such things! I have apologised for misjudging you!'

'And of course you would know a vast deal about proper young ladies, my lord,' retorted Sophie sarcastically. She snorted in a very unladylike way and continued, 'I've no doubt that you judged me on exactly the same basis as you judge your mistresses! And if you had any thought that I might be persuaded to join their ranks you can think again!'

This was of course exactly what he had done, but to hear it said openly, and by a delicately bred girl who should have known nothing of such things, was a salutary experience for his lordship. The outrageous little termagant! He told himself that he was shocked, or ought to be. But he was conscious of a ripple of amusement and, damn it all, admiration for the little spitfire ripping up at him.

'All I have to say,' continued Sophie, who had already said more than enough, 'is that your *mistake* says a great deal more about *you* than it does about *me!*'

'You little vixen!' said David, even more outraged. 'What does a chit like you know of my way of life? Well, I can see when I am outgunned! Miss Marsden, I will leave you to recover your temper and will call upon you in a few days' time. I trust by then you will be in a way to forgiving me and will deign to receive me.'

Sophie glared at him from the stile, a slender form fairly bristling with indignation, even down to the eyelashes. 'Since you are my landlord I can hardly refuse!'

He was turning the mare, but he stopped at that and held her furious eyes with his. 'On the contrary, Miss Marsden.' His deep voice was very grave. 'If you feel that you prefer not to receive me after the insinuations I made and the very improper way I spoke to you, then I will respect your privacy. You need have no fear that it will in any way affect your residence at Willowbank House.'

He rode away without giving her time to reply, but

stopped and looked back. 'Oh. Accept my compliments on your nephew. And tell him he needn't bother putting the trout back next time. He's a fine lad and you are both welcome on my preserves at any time. Without prejudice, of course.'

She stared after him in considerable confusion. Never had she been so puzzled by a man in all her life. From all she had ever heard of him he was the most dangerous of rakes but until he had considered her a…a *lightskirt*, to use a phrase culled from her military brother-in-law, she had felt perfectly safe with him. Unless, of course, you counted the fact that he had nearly run her over. Only when he had thought her a wanton had his manner changed and the way he looked at her. *As though I were a filly up for auction!*

She suddenly realised that she was still watching his lordship ride off through the cow pasture. Furious with herself, she jumped off the top of the stile into the garden and stalked towards the house. She wondered what he had thought when Kit had revealed their true relationship. Her ready sense of humour could not be denied and a choke of laughter had to be instantly suppressed. He must have been mortified! Served him right. Odious, arrogant… ooh! There were no words bad enough to describe him to her satisfaction!

And as for his insufferable charity in assuring her that she had nothing to fear in refusing to receive him! Had he threatened her with eviction she would have denied herself on principle. Now she would have to admit him!

Miss Marsden entered the house via the kitchen, where she found Anna industriously kneading bread dough. Anna took one look at her mistress's stormy face and decided not to comment. It was plain enough that Miss Sophie had had words with the gentleman. Anna had a good view of the stile through the kitchen windows and she had seen Miss Sophie on one of its steps and the tall gentleman on horseback who'd delivered Master Kit. Must be his lordship, surmised Anna. Looked like the old one, anyways.

'Miss Thea has took Master Kit into the bookroom to continue his lessons, Miss Sophie,' said Anna cautiously.

'Good,' said Sophie shortly and left the kitchen without another word.

The old woman smiled resignedly to herself. Not often Miss Sophie got into a tweak, but when she did all the storm warnings went up. Come to think of it, Anna couldn't remember when a mere man had managed to put her all on end. Miss Sophie took little enough notice of men one way or another. Which was a pity in Anna's opinion because if ever a better-natured, sweeter, prettier lass deserved a good husband, Anna had yet to meet her.

Her gnarled old hands automatically formed the bread into loaves and she put them by the fire to rise.

Ah, well. There was time yet for Miss Sophie to meet a real gentleman. One who wouldn't mind her having Master Kit to provide for.

Chapter Four

My Lord Helford rode home in a state of considerable vexation. Not only, it must be said, with Miss Marsden, but with himself. He could not think what had come over him to leap to such an unwarranted and insulting conclusion. The little vixen was right. It did say something about him. About his way of life and attitudes.

He wondered if she would receive him when he called. He wouldn't put it past her to have a servant deny her. And he wouldn't blame her either. Lord, when he thought of how he had allowed his eyes to run over her body, making it quite clear that he was assessing all her charms and possibilities! Little wonder she was so angry with him.

Still, it was the outside of enough that she should suspect him of wishing to make her his mistress now that he knew his mistake, even if that thought had briefly presented itself to him. Firmly he repressed the delectable fantasy this thought conjured up. For heaven's sake! He had caused enough trouble without indulging in erotic fancies which were not only insulting to the lady, but were also guaranteed to cut up his peace. He had to come up with some way to make his promised visit to her perfectly unexceptionable and demonstrate that he did not view her as a prospective mistress. It was a moot point as to who was in most need of the demonstration, Miss Marsden or himself.

Still annoyed with himself, he handed the mare over to Jasper when he reached the stables with barely a grunt of thanks. His henchman said nothing aloud, rightly assessing his master's mood as dangerous. But as he put the mare back in her stall he muttered to himself, 'On the fidget 'e is! Move over, lass. There'll be trouble over this 'ouse party, me girl. Mark my words. Can't see 'im settlin' down to a cold poultice for a wife. Not no how!'

With this very unflattering description of Lady Lucinda Anstey, he removed the saddle from the mare's steaming back and glared at the stable lad who had dared to peep over the half-door.

'And what might you be wantin', Master Nosey?'

'N…nothin', sir!' disclaimed the boy hastily. 'Thought you was callin' fer summat, that's all.'

It took Lord Helford time to hatch out a plan to make it quite clear to Miss Marsden that he was not planning to seduce her. When the solution finally occurred to him, he wondered where his wits had gone begging, it was so obvious. A dry voice in the back of his mind suggested that he might have thought of it all the sooner, had he been able to concentrate all his mind on the problem, rather than dwelling on the lady's fine eyes and pleasing form.

Accordingly, three days later, my Lord Helford rode out of the main entrance to Helford Place with his niece, Miss Fanny Melville, trotting beside him. In his brief acquaintance with her, Lord Helford had come to the conclusion that his ward was far from being the meek little girl he had originally thought. That was merely a façade for an abundance of mischief and energy. In David's opinion, she needed taking in hand by someone who would stand no nonsense. He had no turn for children, but he supposed that as the child's guardian he should take some responsibility for her—which was another good reason to marry a woman of birth and breeding as quickly as possible. Then *she* could superintend Fanny's upbringing!

He wondered how Miss Marsden would receive him. In the time since their last encounter he had managed to find out a little about her. His Great Aunt Maria had known all about Miss Marsden, of course. Even seemed to approve of her, which did not surprise him in the slightest. Lady Maria was one of the most outrageous women he had ever known.

'Sophie Marsden?' she had barked in answer to

his very casual query over the dinner table. 'Of course I know her. Good gal. None of your simpering niminy-piminy modern misses, that one! She and her sister took Willowbank House about two years back. Sister died last year. Sophie's got the boy in ward.'

'I see,' said David, understanding a great deal. No wonder young Kit had looked so devastated when he had suggested that his mother was looking for him.

'Got a bit of money,' continued the old lady. 'She don't lack for admirers, but I doubt she'll accept any of them. The way the money's tied up, her husband will assume control if she marries and she's determined to provide for the boy. That Garfield's dangling after her, but she'd be a fool to have him, boy or no boy. You may pour me another glass of wine.'

'Garfield?' asked David, obeying this last behest. 'Sir Philip Garfield? Fellow who called here yesterday? Good God, he must be forty-five if he's a day!' Somehow the thought of the gross Sir Philip making up to Miss Marsden revolted him. Nevertheless, he found it hard to believe that Miss Marsden would not eventually succumb to such an offer. What female in her position would not?

His distaste showed in his voice and expression. His great-aunt gave a cynical bark of laughter, 'What the devil has his age got to do with it? He's still a man, ain't he? And why should you worry? Besides, Sophie's not that stupid. She'll never take him!'

The conversation drifted on to the coming house party, Lady Maria only snorting disagreeably once or twice when she heard the projected guest list. It did not surprise her. She had her own sources of information. She at once realised the significance of the inclusion of Lady Lucinda and her mama, but forbore to comment. After all, she had set him on this path, even if he had taken her remarks about duty a little too much to heart.

And afterwards, when she retired for the night, she muttered to herself, So he's met Sophie Marsden. Well, she'd be a damned sight better than that pretentious chit of Stanford's! Not that Lady Maria had ever met Lady Lucinda, but the description she had dragged from her recent morning visitor, Penelope Darleston, had confirmed all her worst fears. Lord, what maggot had the boy taken into his head now? All these years he had avoided marriage and now he was setting himself up for the sort of union that would bore him senseless. And would do nothing to remove that expression of scornful cynicism that masked the daredevil, laughing boy she remembered.

Lady Darleston had tried very hard not to say anything derogatory, but her stilted replies and polite evasions to Lady Maria's searching questions had told their own story. The redoubtable old lady had ended by saying, 'Well, if she's anything like Aurelia Stanford I shall remove to the Dower

House. And my fool of a nephew has invited them here for a house party, you say? Lord! The end of it will be that he's been so particular in his attentions that he'll have to offer for the chit. What the devil possessed you to present him to her?'

Penelope had disclaimed all responsibility. 'I can assure you it wasn't my idea. He requested the introduction.'

'Damned fool that he is!' said Lady Maria roundly. 'Well, at least the Dower House is vacant. There's little enough I can do.'

She recalled this conversation as her maid readied her for bed. Sophie Marsden, eh? David might think to pull the wool over her eyes, but she'd seen the recoil of horror when she mentioned Garfield's interest in the girl. Hah! Like a dog with a bone! She settled herself into her enormous feather bed and blew out the candle, chuckling wheezily to herself as she thought of the dance Miss Marsden would lead her nephew. And wondered what she could do to further it. On reflection she concluded that she could do very little, except sit back and watch. And pray.

David took his niece around by the road through Little Helford to Willowbank House. He found it difficult to know what to say to her. She seemed outwardly quiet and self-contained, but David had already discovered that when she didn't get her own way the screams were earsplitting. From all he could discover her nurse usually gave in to her, a tactic David heartily deplored.

She rode well enough and David commented on this. 'You sit very well, Fanny. If you would care for it, I will take you to watch a meet next hunting season.'

'Can I follow the hounds?' she asked at once.

David groaned inwardly. Why the hell hadn't he seen that one coming? He said cautiously, 'You'll have to ask the Master. It's for him to say who may follow. Even I have to obey him on the hunting field.' He wondered if his niece would actually ask Sir Philip Garfield who was the local M.F.H.

'Why?' asked Miss Fanny. 'You're a Viscount. Sir Philip is only a Baronet. If you tell him I'm to follow, then he has to let me.' This was said with an air of calm certainty which took David's breath away. More than ever he was convinced that the child had to be taken in hand. There was something grating in her cool assumption of superiority. He hoped to God that his own children would not develop it.

He changed the subject neatly. 'Would you care to canter, Fanny? We will have to practise that if you are to follow hounds one day.'

Miss Fanny being pleased to fall in with this suggestion, the final half-mile to Little Helford was accomplished without further conversational quagmires. Mindful of the last time he had gone through the village, David slowed his unwilling charge down to a walk as they approached the first houses.

'Why must we slow down, Uncle David? Blossom isn't tired. We can canter for much longer than that.' Fanny was seriously considering kicking her pony into a canter to establish her independence when she encountered her uncle's level gaze.

'Fanny?'

'Yes, sir?'

'Don't even think about it.'

They walked their mounts through the village, responding to polite greetings and tugged forelocks. The villagers all knew Miss Fanny and quite a number remembered David from his youth.

In particular one gabby old fellow seated outside the inn hailed him with great pleasure, 'Well! If it ain't little Master David. An' they tell me ye still can't guddle a fish!'

'Twickenham! You old rogue, and you're still catching 'em too young by all accounts.' David leapt down from his saddle and held out his hand to the rascally old poacher.

"Tis a sight better nor not catchin' 'em at all, me lord!' Twickenham took the hand held out to him in a gnarled grip. Ah, it took him back, so it did, seeing this lad again! 'Makes me feel an old man seein' you all growed up.'

'Gammon!' said David. 'I must have been at least two and twenty when last I saw you.'

'Were ye now?' Twickenham grinned. 'I'll tell

'ee summat, lad. When ye're my age, two and twenty don't seem all that growed up!'

'Nor five and thirty, I dare say,' said David with a grin.

'Not so's ye'd notice,' chuckled the old man. 'Now you be off. Ye're keepin' the little lass waitin' an' that'll never do.'

David glanced at Fanny who had remained mounted. She had a remarkably wooden expression on her face. 'Fanny, have you met Twickenham before?'

'No.' She sounded startled.

'Well, he is a very old friend of mine and I should like you to know him,' said David firmly.

'How do you do?' said Miss Fanny, meeting a notorious criminal for the first time.

'Very well, missy,' answered the old man, lifting his cap to her solemnly. 'I kin tell fine *ye*'re a Melville.'

'How?' she asked in surprise.

'Same green eyes, same pretty hair, o' course. But ye sit a pony like ye growed there.' David watched in amazement as his stiff little ward actually blushed scarlet with pleasure at the old scoundrel's compliment. And Twickenham was right, the child was all Melville. He realised that he didn't find himself constantly reminded of Felicity by her daughter. And felt ashamed that this very fear had kept him from doing his duty to James's daughter for over a year.

'Thank you,' she said shyly.

'Come along, Fanny,' said David as he remounted, still reeling under the revelation of the old man's comment. 'We have still to call on Miss Marsden.'

Twickenham pricked up his ears, 'Callin' on Miss Sophie, are ye? Well, ye'll find her and the lad in the churchyard. Layin' flowers they are on poor Mistress Carlisle's grave. Saw 'em go in twenty minutes back.'

Armed with this information, David led Fanny along to the lych-gate which opened into the churchyard. Sure enough, there were Miss Marsden and Kit standing beside a small tombstone not far from the gate. A small posy of yellow flag irises and wild guelder rose lay on the grave.

He could hear Miss Marsden's voice reading softly from the book she held. *'Who shall ascend into the hill of the Lord and who shall stand in His holy place? He that hath clean hands and a pure heart. Who hath not lifted up his soul unto vanity nor sworn deceitfully...'*

David listened, entranced. The music of the words and the loving warmth in the girl's gentle voice washed over him in waves of peace. He thought guiltily that he had not yet even been to see his mother's tomb, let alone laid flowers on it. In fact, he had barely known his fashionable mother. He had gone to school at the age of eight and she and his father had frequently been away in his holidays. When he had received the tidings of her death six years ago he had been sorry, but not grief-stricken. He had long forgiven her for suggesting Felicity as a suitable bride for James.

A sudden pain shot through him at the thought that he had never cared for his mother as this boy so obviously had for his. Had never been given the chance. Ah, but then you can't be hurt, he told himself coldly. Or have the memory, another gentler voice said.

Miss Marsden had finished the psalm and was speaking to Kit. 'I think that one describes her, don't you?' David's heart twisted as he heard the love in her voice. 'And she will love the flowers— you gave them to her every birthday.'

David wondered what his mother's favourite flowers had been. Had he ever known? Had he ever gone out on her birthday and brought some in for her? Would she have appreciated a posy of flowers culled with love from the hedgerow? He found himself hoping that his children would love their mother with this depth. The vision of Lady Lucinda seemed to jar with this.

He watched dumbly as Kit nodded and slipped his hand briefly into Miss Marsden's. Suddenly he thought that this was an intensely private moment and that he should not intrude, but it was too late. The lad straightened his shoulders and turned to look directly at David and Fanny. Surprise, then pleasure, replaced the sadness in his eyes.

He came forward at once, saying, 'Good afternoon, my lord. Hullo, Fanny.'

Sophie spun around and nearly fell over. What was *he* doing here? She followed Kit through the gate, her thoughts in a whirl.

'Good afternoon, Miss Marsden,' said David with a smile which warmed his eyes. 'Er…may I present my niece, Fanny, to you? Fanny, this is Miss Marsden and her nephew Kit.'

'We've met before,' said Sophie with a faint smile. 'How do you do, Fanny?' She had previously thought his lordship's brilliant eyes rather cold. Now she perceived her mistake. They were positively glowing in a way which gave his chilly, handsome face even more charm.

David was surprised at the evident pleasure with which his niece greeted Miss Marsden and her nephew. Clearly she liked them.

He dismounted and handed his reins to Kit, saying, 'Perhaps you would oblige me by leading Perdita. I am going to escort you and your aunt home. Fanny, if you will promise me on your honour to stay beside Kit, then you may ride ahead of me. But you must solemnly promise to remain in a walk. Otherwise you won't ride for a week.'

Fanny had opened her mouth to protest but David said, 'Save your breath, child. Whatever may work with your nurse, it won't fadge with me. And if you start one of your vulgar displays here, I'll put you over my knee and spank you.'

Horrified at the thought of being publicly humiliated, Fanny gave her promise and rode off beside Kit.

Heaving a sigh of relief, David looked down at Miss Marsden, still with that glow in his eyes, and said, 'I was coming to call on you. I didn't intend to intrude like this, but once Kit saw us, well, I wouldn't like either of you to think I was cutting your acquaintance.' She did not reply and he continued, 'You may, of course, still prefer to cut mine, but I wish you won't.' He waited for her reply, amazed to find that it mattered enormously to him. For some reason he could not fathom, he very much wanted this outspoken chit to revise her first unfavourable impression of him.

The dark eyes glanced up at him briefly. Sophie was hard put to it to understand her reaction to this man. His deep soft voice was like a caress. She felt for all the world like a cat having its fur stroked at the sound. His eyes, which the other day had stripped her naked, now smiled at her understandingly, but she still felt wary. Something deep within her screamed that this man was dangerous to her. There appeared to be something seriously amiss with her lungs, which seemed incapable of performing their function with any degree of certainty. Anger at her own missishness steadied her. She would *not* behave like a silly fluttering debutante just because Helford chose to converse with her.

'I can't think why you should wish for my acquaintance, my lord,' she said bluntly. 'At least, I can, but since—'

He cut her short. 'Of course, I always present my niece to girls I plan to set up as my mistress.' There was an unmistakably teasing note in his deep tones.

Sophie glared up at him but reined in her temper. 'That was my "but", sir!' she said sweetly. 'Despite your reputation, which I am afraid I know all about, I never heard anyone describe you as quite that outrageous. So I feel moderately safe in your company.'

'Do you, indeed?' said David astringently. 'I suppose I ought to be flattered.'

'Not in the least,' said Sophie. 'I am merely doing you the courtesy of assuming that you can on occasion conduct yourself in a mode befitting a gentleman.'

'Why, you little hornet!' said David, amusement warring with outrage. 'I'll have you know that I always conduct myself as befits a gentleman!'

'Then my first impressions were quite off and I am perfectly safe,' said Sophie blandly. 'And since Kit seems to think you are, as he put it, *a...a right one*, I have not the heart to disabuse his mind of such an error of judgement.'

'I see,' said David wryly. He decided to change

the subject. 'Do you often lay flowers on your sister's grave?' He saw the solitary tear slip down one cheek to be hastily wiped and felt his guts wrench at the pain in her face. This, then, was what it was to care too deeply!

'Today was my sister's birthday,' said Sophie simply. 'Kit has been playing truant rather frequently and I thought that if we could do something to get him to talk about Emma it might help him to tell me what is bothering him.'

'I should have thought that was pretty plain to see,' returned David.

'Yes, I know he misses her,' said Sophie. 'But why has he suddenly begun to resent me?' She rubbed her nose thoughtfully. 'At least, not resent precisely. I can't quite describe it and I can't think why I am saying any of this to you at all!' She finished in a rush and walked on in silence, embarrassed to have burdened him with her concerns.

David said nothing. He was conscious of an odd desire to help Miss Marsden, who was far removed from the outraged girl he had insulted the other day. And he could not remember ever having wanted to help a woman before in his entire life! At least, not with a problem of this nature! Pecuniary problems were another matter. The only emotional problem his mistresses ever laid claim to was being in love with him. And that was definitely their problem to solve. Not his.

Strangely, he could understand her speaking what was on her mind. Obviously her softened mood was engendered by the circumstances and the feelings were too close to the surface to be hidden. But why the hell did he want to do something about it? It was none of his bread and butter. Stay out of it, he told himself firmly. You should have as little to do with this girl as possible!

Despite this excellent advice, something suddenly occurred to him. What had Kit said by the river the other day? Something about expecting his mother and...oh, come on...what did he say...expecting his mother and... and it was always Aunt Sophie!

'You look like your sister, don't you?' he asked at length.

She nodded. 'Yes. Anyone could tell we were sisters. Kit looks like both of us. Why?'

'I think it bothers the boy,' said David slowly. He told her what Kit had said.

There was silence while she thought it out. He noticed with an odd clarity that she again rubbed her nose in that appealing way.

'Then if he is pretending that Emma is still alive...' she said hesitantly, still working it through. 'And...and coming to find him...then there is that awful moment when he realises that she is dead after all...'

'And you look like her,' finished David.

'Which makes it worse,' said Sophie with catch

in her voice. 'Poor little chap. Well, at least now I know. Thank you, Lord Helford. I don't think I would have thought of that.' His understanding, the mere fact that he had remembered what Kit had said, amazed her. Well, he might be a dangerous rake but he had a kind heart.

David himself was startled at the ease with which he had seen the problem. He was even more startled at the fact that for a moment he had felt her anguish as a knife twisting inside him.

They walked on in a companionable silence for a while. It was rather pleasant, thought David, to be with a female who didn't strain every nerve to entertain him with vivacious chit-chat. If Miss Marsden had something to say then she said it, bluntly. Otherwise she seemed content to hold her peace.

Peace was the last thing that Sophie was conscious of. She found Helford's quiet presence by her side extremely disturbing. She had no illusions about what he had been thinking the other day. She supposed that, since he had acknowledged his mistake and apologized, she would have to forgive him. What she found far harder to forgive was the fact that his speculative glance had awakened all sorts of immodest and dangerous imaginings. What would it be like to…? No! She must not think of it! It was wrong! Quite improper! And it terrified her.

The sound of the children's voices floated back to them, rather stilted at first but becoming more and more vociferous as they found a subject in common. Horses. David grinned as he heard Fanny telling Kit how high she could jump now.

'She's exaggerating just a little,' he informed Sophie in a teasing undertone. 'My headgroom won't let her attempt anything over two foot six yet, so three feet is a distinct bouncer.'

'Kit is romancing a little too,' admitted Sophie, with a chuckle. 'That seventeen hand colt he's just mentioned is Farmer Gillies's new cart horse. I'm afraid he hasn't got his own pony. And Megs, the mare I have for the gig, is far too lively for a beginner. He's tried to ride her a couple of times and she puts him straight over her head. She's hardly ever ridden anyway and I only have a lady's saddle so he has to ride bareback.'

David thought that Miss Marsden's finances must be rather straitened, but said nothing. Sympathy would smack of patronage and condescension which she would resent mightily. He had the distinct impression that she was still not quite easy in his company. For some reason he could not fathom, he wanted her to feel comfortable with him.

'Would you like him to ride?' he asked cautiously, the seeds of an idea sprouting in his head.

'Naturally yes,' said Sophie wistfully. 'But I cannot afford the upkeep of another horse. At least I could, but I try to put money aside for when he must go to school and to add to our principal, you see. So, no pony, unless I sell Megs and buy another, but we are rather fond of her.' She clipped her lips together firmly. I'm doing it again! It's none of his business and he can't possibly be interested. All she could think of was that going to Emma's grave had released a need to talk, a need to share some of her burden. A need she had not hitherto recognised.

David nodded thoughtfully. 'Then that makes it easier for me to ask for your help.'

Sophie stopped and stared at him. 'My help? What do you think I could do for you?'

Quite a lot, thought David as he looked down at her upturned face. He tried not to imagine what it would be like to cup that face in his hands and kiss her, feel that soft mouth open under his and hold her in his arms as he deepened the kiss. He wondered what she would taste like and had to give himself a mental shake. *You have presented your niece to her! She is off limits!*

'My lord? Is something wrong?' Her concerned voice recalled him to reality. The black-fringed eyes were puzzled and a slight frown knotted her smooth brow.

Good God! What was he thinking of, that he wanted to smooth the frown away with a caressing finger? 'Fanny needs company of her own age and a woman of her own class to give her some much-needed guidance,' he explained. 'I wondered if you would consent to have her at Willowbank House for, shall we say, an afternoon a week?' He rushed on before she could answer. 'I realise that it is an appalling imposition, so what you say about Kit makes it easier. In return, I will bring Fanny this way for a ride once a week with her second pony and take Kit out with us.'

He waited for her reply, wondering why the devil he had made such a suggestion. Why on earth did he want to do something for Kit? Was it just to show this impossible chit that he could behave like a gentleman? Show her that she was wrong about him? That must be it. He ignored an ironic voice in his mind which assured him that Miss Marsden's pithy and unflattering reading of his character was not, after all, so very wide of the mark.

Sophie was stunned. What did he imagine she could teach Miss Fanny Melville? Why not a governess? What about Lady Maria? Why not find a little girl for the child to play with? All these questions and more whirled in her brain. In some confusion she tried to explain all this to him.

He cut her short. 'I know. But I want someone who isn't beholden to me in any way. Someone who will have no qualms in handing out a bit of discipline when necessary. Her governess, Miss Harris, is a meek creature and doesn't stand a chance, but I haven't the heart to dismiss her. She is old and would be unlikely to find another position. I could pension her off, but she tells me she would prefer to be working. Aunt Maria says herself that Fanny needs the attention of someone younger. As for finding a girl for her to play with, nothing could be easier, but I would like her to be with a child who won't take any of her tantrums. Kit won't.'

'I shall have to ask Kit,' said Sophie. 'After all, he is the one who will have to do most of the entertaining! Er…you do realize, my lord, that Kit's afternoons are spent mostly in such pursuits as fishing, climbing trees and playing cricket when he can persuade me to bowl. I have no intention of sitting him down to learn sewing or domestic economy.'

'Excellent.' said David. 'Do her the world of good. Ask Kit by all means.'

By the time they reached Willowbank House the details had been thrashed out. On Mondays Fanny would come over in the afternoon for two or three hours, and on Thursdays David would collect Kit after lunch and take the two children riding. He suggested that Miss Marsden might like to join them, but she declined firmly and refused to budge.

'It would start a great deal of gossip if I were to do that, my lord,' she said bluntly. 'You may be immune or indifferent to gossip, but as a single woman I am not!' He took her point. The last thing he wanted to do at the moment was stir up gossip. It would be fatal to his matrimonial plans.

By this time they were at the front gate. 'Would

you care for some refreshment, my lord?' asked Sophie politely. 'A glass of cowslip wine? A cup of tea? And I have little doubt we can run to a slice of plum cake.'

'Cowslip wine?' David blanched. 'Good heavens! Who makes it?'

'I do!' said Sophie stiffly. 'And it is perfectly palatable, if a trifle alcoholic.'

David laughed, 'Very well, the cowslip wine it shall be. Let's hope I don't end up in my cups!'

Sophie opened the front gate, saying, 'I shall give you half a glass just in case. Although,' she quizzed him, 'I should have thought you were well able to carry your wine!'

'Baggage!' he said in amusement, noting in some surprise that when she smiled, an utterly fascinating dimple peeped at the corner of her mouth, simply begging to be kissed. Why the hell hadn't he noticed the dimple earlier? He must be going blind.

Quite unaware of the temptation she was presenting, Miss Marsden merely laughed. 'Kit, why don't you take Fanny around to look at the new ducklings on the stream?'

'Are we stopping, Uncle David? What about the horses?'

'Yes we are stopping and the horses may be tied to the fence,' said David firmly. 'No one is going to steal them, so go and look at the ducklings. And,

Fanny, behave yourself. If Kit feels he can stand it, you are going to come here to visit on Monday afternoons. On Thursday afternoons we will come past with a spare pony and Kit can come riding with us.'

Sophie was not really surprised to see that Kit's face broke into smiles at this. What did surprise her was the undoubted pleasure on Fanny's face. She knew that Kit would be glad of a companion, even a girl, but the little she knew of Fanny had led her to think the child would consider Kit beneath her touch.

'Come on, Fanny,' said Kit. 'I'll show you the ducklings. We're going to eat one for Christmas!'

'Bloodthirsty little beast!' said Sophie feelingly as the children disappeared around the side of the house. 'I used to cry my eyes out when one of my ducklings got killed.'

David laughed as he followed her into the house. 'Never mind. Now come, where is the dreaded cowslip wine?'

'Oh, Thea,' said Sophie as Miss Andrews came out of the parlour into the hall, 'this is Lord Helford. Lord Helford, may I present Miss Andrews, who is good enough to lend me respectability and to act as Kit's governess?'

His lordship smiled and held out his hand to Miss Andrews. 'Ah, the lady who was given the bag by Master Kit. You will be relieved to know, ma'am, that he harboured grave doubts as to the duplicity of his action in taking the books. How do you do?'

Thea Andrews thought that she had never seen a more handsome man as she placed her hand in his. Her reply was somewhat flustered. 'Oh, my lord, I should have known better. After all the years I have been a governess! Especially for dear Sophie and Emma.'

'Did they give you a great deal of trouble, ma'am? I can well believe it and you have all my sympathy.'

'Come and have a glass of wine with us, Thea,' said Sophie, trying unsuccessfully not to giggle. 'Lord Helford is convinced I am trying to poison him, I believe.'

The dimple quivered again, giving his lordship the most peculiar sensations in the pit of his stomach. He had met dimples before, but never one that tantalised as this one did!

'Well, perhaps just one, dear,' said Miss Andrews. 'Your cowslip wine always makes me a trifle sleepy.'

Within a very few moments they were seated in the parlour with the sun pouring in at the window. David sipped his wine suspiciously. He had never tasted anything like it in his life, but was obliged to admit that it wasn't as bad as he had expected. Which was not, as Sophie pointed out, saying very much at all.

'Well, I wouldn't quite say that, Miss Marsden!' protested his lordship. 'I will grant you that it is perfectly potable.'

'Would you care for a second glass, my lord?' asked Miss Marsden in deceptively demure accents. Her eyes twinkled engagingly.

David rose to the challenge admirably. 'If only to drink to your eyes, Miss Marsden!'

'How...how very *heroic* of you, my lord!' achieved Miss Marsden with a delightful choke of laughter. 'I am rebuked indeed.'

'Rebuked?' Helford was amused. 'I meant to flatter you!'

Again that appealing gurgle. 'Then you must be losing your touch, my lord!'

'Sophie!' Miss Andrews was shocked. Or would have been if she were not used to her young charge making such outrageous remarks from time to time.

Helford blinked. The little baggage was actually daring to laugh at him! And at his reputation! Most women would have been cast into a flutter by a sally of that nature. This impossible female just giggled, setting not the least store by his gallantry. He was damned if he didn't like it! And why hadn't he noticed that dimple earlier? Ruefully he admitted to himself that their previous meetings had given Miss Marsden little cause to favour him with her delightful smile.

Through the window they could hear the faint sound of the children's voices.

Miss Andrews, seizing the opportunity to change the subject, commented on the fact that she could hear another child. Sophie was just explaining the arrangement she had come to with Helford when a splash followed by a loud shriek came to their ears.

Even before the yell of, 'Aunt Sophie! Hurry!' was heard, Sophie was on her feet and racing down the hall with her skirts hitched up. Taken completely by surprise, Helford was well behind her as she ran out a side door, across the garden and through a gate into the orchard. In fact, he was amazed that any woman could run so fast.

In the stream Kit was up to his shoulders trying to help Fanny who appeared to be in a state of complete panic. A small jetty jutted out into the water which Fanny had obviously fallen off. Before Helford could stop her Sophie had plunged in and was hauling the struggling child to her feet.

'Stop wriggling!' Sophie commanded sharply. Fanny continued to struggle and two sharp slaps rang out. Stunned, Fanny stopped, gasping and spluttering.

'Now, why don't you stand up?' suggested Sophie in matter-of-fact tones.

To her utter amazement Fanny found that she could do so and, still holding her hand, Sophie led her out on to the bank, closely followed by Kit, to stand dripping and shivering in the fresh breeze. All three of them were liberally festooned with mud and water weeds. Fanny's black curls were plastered around her face and Kit was probably the worst of the three, being covered in mud from head to toe, having slipped in it on his way out.

After one shocked glance at Miss Marsden, Helford set his jaw tightly and turned to survey his filthy and bedraggled niece. She was not meeting his gaze, a sure sign that she had been responsible for the disaster.

'Kit! What on earth were you thinking of to let her fall in?' asked Sophie in dangerously quiet tones.

Her nephew opened his mouth and then shut it again. 'Just looking at the ducklings, Aunt Sophie,' he said at last.

Sophie was about to favour him with a pithy description of his idiocy, but Helford forestalled her.

'Fanny. Would you care to tell us how you came to fall in?' His voice was deceptively bland, but there was an indefinable hint of authority in its depths.

Fanny hesitated for a moment, then said, 'I leaned over too far. Kit told me to get back but I…I didn't. So I sort of slipped. And Kit fell in trying to grab me, I think.'

Sophie stole a glance at Lord Helford. He was not looking at her and his face was icy. Oh, dear! He won't think this such a good place to leave Fanny now, she thought. She was rather surprised to discover how much she had been looking forward to Monday and Thursday afternoons. It would have been so good for Kit to have the companionship of a man, she told herself. Not to mention someone of his own age to play with and get into mischief with. The thought that it would be rather pleasant to see his lordship was ruthlessly suppressed.

She looked at the unrepentant Fanny. The child would take a chill, standing there in that soaking habit! She was getting a little cold herself.

'Perhaps we should get Fanny into some dry clothes,' she suggested tentatively.

'Good idea,' said his lordship curtly. He glanced at her briefly and averted his gaze at once.

Sophie flushed. He was obviously furious about the accident. Well, at least the child knew she could stand up in the blasted stream now! Even if she did fall in again she wouldn't drown! And he was the one who had suggested that Kit would be a suitable playmate. It wasn't my idea, thought Sophie rebelliously.

Miss Andrews, who had rushed out after them, said gently, 'I think, dear Sophie, that you had better change as well. And Kit, of course!'

'Yes,' said Sophie. 'Ask Anna to try and find some clothes for Miss Fanny. There are some of Kit's old ones in the chest on the landing and she can be bundled up in a cloak of mine so that no one sees her. And if his lordship takes her home across the fields they will be less likely to meet anyone. Kit, you may change in the scullery! Ask Anna to bring you some clean clothes.'

Having said this, she stalked off into the house and up to her chamber, leaving a trail of water and aquatic flora behind her from her sopping gown. Just before she began to strip her gown off she caught sight of herself in the looking glass and saw exactly what Lord Helford had seen.

No wonder he had refused to look at her! She might as well have been naked for all the good her light muslin gown was. It clung to her body in the most appallingly revealing way. And it was not only her form that was revealed! The material was rendered practically see through and the rosy tips of her breasts were quite apparent. Sophie blushed, a deep, hot crimson. He had no need to use his imagination to strip her now. There was not really a great deal left to imagine. How on earth was she to face him downstairs? What if he thought she had done it on purpose to gain his attention? How very mortifying!

When she did eventually leave her chamber it was still with heightened colour and in a very high-necked, long-sleeved grey gown which was a trifle too large for her and did not suit her in the slightest. There was no need to give his lordship anything more to think about, she thought as she went downstairs. Not that he could possibly be in the least interested, she admonished herself. With his reputation he must have seen hundreds—well, dozens anyway—of much prettier women without any clothes at all. Seeing Miss Sophie Marsden in damp…no, soaking muslin was hardly going to set his pulses racing.

David waited in the parlour while Miss Marden and her nephew changed their attire and while Miss Andrews and the maid rushed about finding clothes for Fanny. Not only were his pulses racing, but there was solid evidence that his lordship's carnal experience was not sufficiently broad to have rendered him immune from Miss Marsden's charms as displayed by a wetly clinging muslin gown. And the reality was every bit as delightful as the vision he had conjured up by the river the day he had met Kit.

He groaned audibly as he tried not to think about it. Unfortunately, that only made it worse. Her body was beautiful, so dainty and rounded. A slim little waist and those flaring hips! He could imagine his hands on them, holding her against him as his arousal throbbed between them. And, oh God, her breasts! He thought he would die at the memory of how the cold water had teased them into life. They would respond to his caress in the same way, springing up under the ministrations of his hands and tongue. His mouth felt dry at the very thought of cupping those breasts in his hands, of touching his tongue to those dainty pink morsels which had peeped through the soaking muslin.

And she would be his, all his! Never had he touched a virgin in his life. He had thought his preference was for experience. For a woman who knew how to entertain a man. A woman who would cry out in pleasure when he took her, rather than an untouched girl who would doubtless feel pain. The thought of teaching an innocent had always rather bored him.

Now he was burning with desire for a girl who would not have the slightest notion of how to satisfy his needs. And he didn't care in the least. He wanted to please *her*! He wanted to be the only one who had ever possessed her, heard her cries of passion. And they *would* be cries of passion when he was finished with her!

The only thing which acted as a lifeline in the sea of confused emotion and desire which threatened to engulf him was the knowledge that she would most certainly be hurt if he seduced her and not just physically! He couldn't do it! If it leaked out, she would be ruined and besides, she was not a woman of the world who could play the game for a time and then go on to the next lover. If she gave herself, it would only be because she cared for him. She was not the sort of woman he wanted to be his mistress. He did not wish to hurt her in any way. It would be best to see as little of her as possible. Thank God she had refused to ride with them! He could drop Fanny off and collect the boy with as little intercourse as possible.

He swore savagely as he paced back and forth, wishing to God that he too could go out and take a dip in the stream. For the life of him, he could not see how he was otherwise going to be able to ride home in any sort of comfort.

Fortunately for his lordship's peace of mind Kit, whose ideas on drying off and dressing neatly were rather rudimentary, was the first to make an appearance.

He came into the room, looking very embarrassed. 'I say, I'm awfully sorry Fanny fell in, sir. I should have dragged her off the jetty.'

'Never mind,' David replied. 'She's probably learned her lesson. Just keep her out of the river when she comes here.'

'You'll still let her come?' Kit asked in surprise.

David nodded. 'Oh, yes. If your aunt doesn't consider her too much of a liability after this.'

'What's a liar…liar…liarbilly?' asked Kit, very puzzled. 'That's what Aunt Sophie says about the open range in the kitchen because it uses so much fuel.'

By the time David had explained what he meant by a liability and decided to undertake a few improvements at Willowbank House, namely a modern closed stove, he was in a fair way to regaining control of himself. Miss Marsden's reappearance, camouflaged in an extremely unbecoming and voluminous gown, told him two things immediately. Firstly, that she was perfectly aware of how she had looked and, secondly, that she was very embarrassed by it. He acknowledged her very stiffly. He wanted to reassure her that she had nothing to fear, that he had not been in the least affected but, even if he could have lied convincingly, the presence of Kit and, a moment later, of Fanny, made any such thing impossible.

Fanny looked excessively improper in Kit's old clothes. David was highly amused despite his personal confusion, not least at the apologetic look on Miss Andrews's face as she shepherded the child into the room.

'So indelicate, my lord. I do beg your pardon but there is nothing else. All Miss Sophie's old clothes were given away years ago!' She held out the cloak over her arm, 'But I am sure you can contrive to bundle this around her and no one need know. None of us will breathe a word, you may be sure.'

David took the cloak with a charming smile. 'Miss Andrews, you are so calm about the whole thing that I can only assume that Miss Marsden and her sister must have given you almost as much trouble. Tell me—do you quail at the thought of being afflicted with my niece every Monday?'

'Certainly not,' asserted Miss Andrews. 'It would be very odd if I were to mind any arrangement Miss Sophie has made. Does that mean Fanny is still to come?'

'Most definitely,' said David without meeting Miss Marsden's eyes. She had looked thoroughly discomfited at his abrupt greeting and he did not dare to look at her lest his hard-won control deserted him. After making final arrangements to collect Kit two days later, he took his leave, firm in his conviction that the less he saw of Miss Marsden the safer she would be.

Sophie was heartily glad to see the back of him. Odious wretch! How dare he look down on her because she pulled his niece out of the stream! It wasn't as if she were used to having a man around to do things for her. Besides, he would not have cared to plunge into a muddy stream in his immaculate riding boots and leathers!

She wished she could refuse to have anything more to do with him, but it would be too infamous to deny Kit the opportunity to learn to ride, still more infamous to deny him the opportunity to be in a man's company. Even if he was a man whose morals and way of life she thoroughly despised, Sophie did his lordship enough justice to realise that he would not allow anything unfitting to come to Kit's ears. And besides, he had shown himself to be very understanding of Kit. Remembering what the boy had said and recognising its relevance to what she had said, suggested that he might be the very person to give Kit's thoughts a happier turn.

It was with this in mind that she went to bid Kit goodnight that evening. He put his book down at once when she came in and said, 'Shall you mind having Fanny here?'

'Not in the least,' she assured him. 'Will you mind

having to ride with her?' She sat down on the edge of his bed.

'Gudgeon!' he said affectionately. He was silent for a moment. 'Aunt Sophie?'

'Yes, love?'

'I'm sorry about all the running off and I've been rude to you…and…'

'Don't worry about it,' she said gently.

'But it's so silly,' he said. 'It's cos you look like her and I kept thinking you were her and then being sort of disappointed an' *angry* cos God took her an' not you. Remember how the Vicar said God wanted her an' loved her more than we could? Well, I just wanted to hit God for being such a skirter! I…I thought he could have taken you an' never known the difference.' He stopped, very embarrassed. 'An' then I'd feel awful cos you're so good to me.'

So Helford was right.

Sophie stroked the soft curls. 'Don't feel awful, Kit. I thought exactly the same thing when the Vicar said that! Believe me, I would have died happily to save you this! And I don't think God could possibly love your Mama *more* than you do. Differently, yes. But not more.'

They sat enveloped in a comforting silence as the house martins chattered under the eaves.

Eventually Sophie spoke again. 'What made you say all this?'

'Lord Helford,' said Kit slowly. 'It was when he

found me by the river and I thought it would be you behind me and I wanted…Mama…and he said she was looking for me. Before that I didn't really understand what was wrong, but I said it to him. I…I don't know why. Do you think he minded?'

'No,' said Sophie, reasonably certain that after some of the things she had said to his lordship, nothing Kit could say would startle him in the least.

Another long healing silence.

'Aunt Sophie, those flowers we took to Mama will die, won't they?'

'Yes.'

'Well, should we take some more? I mean, if they die, they won't look as nice.'

Sophie groped for an answer. She didn't want him to mope over Emma's grave. At last she said, 'I think, you know, that it is all right for the flowers to die. You see *their* souls will go to Heaven as well, so your Mama will have them there just the same. So perhaps we should just put them there on the days when you would have given her flowers anyway. You know—her birthday, Mothering Sunday, your birthday and also the day she died.'

Kit thought about it and said, 'I never thought of that. Of course the flowers have to die. Thank you.'

Sophie bent to kiss him and was half-suffocated by the enveloping hug. 'I like Lord Helford,' he said. 'I'm glad he likes you.'

'Likes me?' Sophie allowed her surprise to show.

'Well, he must!' said Kit logically. 'Why else would he take me riding?'

Faced with this undeniable logic Sophie went back downstairs to curl up in a chair by the fireplace with a book. After a few moments her rather battered volume of poetry was allowed to fall unheeded to her lap. Staring into the empty grate, she gave up the singularly useless attempt to banish Lord Helford from her thoughts. Why should he go out of his way to help her? And why did she feel so threatened by him? Because she did! His big powerful frame positively radiated danger of the most potent masculine variety.

And his reputation suggested that appearances were not deceptive. He was an acknowledged rake. Used to having his way with women at all times. Sophie had no doubts at all that he would be quite unused to being refused. She could understand why. His lazy smile held a world of temptation reflected in the wicked green eyes. And the thought of being surrounded and overwhelmed by that powerful, male body sent shivers of excitement wriggling up and down her spine… She caught herself up crossly. This would never do! He was just being kind to make up for his embarrassing gaffe.

He was a gentleman and would not pursue an un-willing female of birth and virtue. She could have no fears that he would allow his inclinations to obscure that fact. Reluctantly she faced the dawning knowledge that it was her own inclinations that she most feared. His lordship might be a gentleman, but he was no saint. The slightest hint that she might welcome his attentions would place her in the gravest danger!

Chapter Five

Two days later Lord Helford called to take Kit riding and return the clothes. Nothing could have exceeded the polite propriety with which he greeted Miss Marsden on this occasion unless it was the cool dignity with which he was received. He informed her that he wished to speak with her upon their return and promptly realised that his manner of doing so had well and truly set up her bristles.

'Do you indeed, my lord?' she asked in dulcet tones. 'Then naturally I will hold myself at your disposal. I shall give Anna instructions that I am at home to you.'

He glared at her. Curse the chit! He always seemed to say the wrong thing to her. What was it about her that made him such a clodpole? His mind sheered away from the obvious answer which was that never in his life had he wanted a woman this much. Especially one that he couldn't have. He told himself bracingly that if he had her in bed, it would break the spell. He could slake his lust for her and be done with it. He had never known a woman whose charms and skills did not bore him in the end.

Angry at the trend of his thoughts, he checked the girth on the pony he had brought for Kit and showed the boy how to mount. He swung himself into the saddle, raised his hat to Miss Marsden and rode off fuming with his youthful charges.

Sophie went back into the house to do a fair bit of fuming on her own account. After half an hour of savagely kneading bread, all the while pretending that she was wringing his lordship's arrogant neck, she calmed down enough to laugh at herself. Whatever would Emma think to see her little sister, who never took the slightest bit of notice of a man, so utterly furious over the opinion and overbearing ways of a comparative stranger?

By the time his lordship returned with the children, she had assumed a dignified and calm attitude towards him. This was dispelled by his first words to her after dismissing the children to the garden with a rider to stay out of the stream.

'I cannot see that your situation, Miss Marsden, is in the least eligible for either you or the grandson of an Earl. Why have you not enlisted the aid of Kit's paternal relations in your rearing of him?'

'What?' she gasped. 'How *dare* you imply that I am not capable of bringing him up as a gentleman!'

'Rubbish!' he said angrily. 'I meant only that Lord Strathallen should provide some assistance. Yet, from what Kit tells me, I should doubt of his even knowing that he has a grandson!'

'You can't possibly have got that from Kit!' said Sophie furiously. 'How dare you poke your nose into my affairs!'

'I have done no such thing! I was slightly acquainted with Jock Carlisle, though,' David informed her coldly. 'When Kit mentioned that his father died at Waterloo, I asked him what regiment. You may imagine my surprise when he told me the Scots Greys! Why the devil have you not been in touch with the Carlisles? Kit knows nothing of his birthright!'

The fury in her countenance made him take a step back. He thought he had seen the worst of her temper, but this was something quite different. Her eyes practically spat with rage and when she spoke it was in tones of the most bitter contempt.

'If Lord Strathallen had not refused to receive my sister when Jock was so ill advised as to marry her in the teeth of his father's threat of disinheritance, not to mention our own father's implacable opposition, then perhaps I might have done so!' blazed Sophie. 'As it is, since he did not even reply to my sister's letter informing him of Jock's death and, I might add, the birth of Kit, I feel I am absolved of any charge of denying Kit his birthright!'

'He disowned Jock? Why?' David could not believe his ears.

'Oh! Did you not know that?' Sophie was even angrier. 'Then might I suggest that you find out all the facts of a case before you pass judgement! Lord Strathallen is, as you may be aware, a Catholic. I understand many Scots hold to that still. He was affronted that his son chose to marry a Protestant and a Englishwoman at that. His family having fought at Culloden, he considered Jock doubly a traitor to have married south of the Tweed!' She paused for breath and to dash her hand across her eyes. 'As for my father, as a minister of the Church of England he took the gravest exception to Emma's marriage to a Catholic. She was also disinherited! The result is that I inherited ten thousand pounds, which I cannot touch except for the income until I am thirty-five. If I marry before that date, the money passes into the hands of my husband. My father did his best to ensure that I was powerless to help Emma and Jock.'

David was horrified. 'He did *that*? The bastard!' He caught himself up sharply. 'I beg your pardon. I had no idea and did not intend to offend you.'

'No! You just thought you would tell me what to do! Like Sir Philip, who would have me marry him and trust him to *settle a suitable sum on the lad*!' Her voice dripped with scorn. 'Well, he can take his offer and you can take your advice and—' She managed to stop herself right on the brink of saying something that would not have reflected at all well on her vicarage upbringing.

'Go to hell.' David finished the sentence for her. 'I don't blame you. No. I knew nothing of this. My acquaintance with Jock was of the slightest. I knew he was married, but I never met your sister. Miss Marsden, I apologise unreservedly, but I do feel that Strathallen ought not to be allowed to ignore his responsibilities. If you would like, I could—'

'No!' Sophie cut in. 'You are going to offer to write or see him and shame him into doing something for Kit. I would rather die than beg for his charity after the way he treated Emma. From all I saw, Jock's marriage was the making of him. He was the wildest, most spendthrift good-for-nothing! But he actually settled down with Emma and reformed all his appalling ways.' A tear ran down her cheek, unnoticed except by David who was conscious of an overwhelming desire to kiss it away. What had he done, unleashing all the hurt she obviously kept bottled up lest it should overwhelm her?

Sophie continued, in a hard little voice to hold back the tears which threatened to spill over. 'She…she used to write to me you know, through Thea. We were very close despite the seven years between us. So many things she told me. They were so happy and then Kit was born just before the peace in 1814. Papa was dead and it was all settled that they would come and live with me. But then Napoleon escaped and Jock died in that awful charge.'

'I'm sorry,' said David very gently. 'I will do nothing without your permission. But I will say that I do believe it is a matter not of charity but responsibility.'

Sophie looked at him unseeingly. In fact, he wondered if she had even heard him. She seemed to be miles away. In truth she was years away in the past, seeing the heartbroken agony of a widow who cared nothing for the fact that her husband had died a hero. A woman who held a fatherless child and wept over him in a despair that her young sister could feel but not fully understand.

At last she spoke in a husky voice. 'I'm sorry, my lord. I should not have spoken as I did. It is just that…I…I loved Emma and…and it was her birthday and…and…' Two more tears rolled down her cheeks unheeded.

'Damn!' David took two quick strides across the room and had her in his arms, her face pressed against his chest. There was nothing even remotely amorous in his embrace. He held her as he might have held Fanny or Kit to give comfort. Sophie accepted it as such, leaning against him trustingly, conscious of the sense of peace that seemed to radiate from his powerful body and the firm circle of his arms. One hand stroked her curls lightly.

Never had he known such a feeling of tender admiration. Her proud independence and determination to stand alone he found incredible. He knew that many women would have had no hesitation in forcing the boy's paternal relations to take charge while they used their inheritance to secure a good marriage. And with ten thousand pounds she could have done it easily. She was attractive enough to tempt any man.

Instead she had chosen to live in quiet obscurity, husbanding her money against the day when Kit should need it and refusing a more-than-eligible offer to ensure his future. Without conscious volition his arms tightened around her protectively.

They stayed that way for a moment before David released her. Even if his intentions were good, his unruly body was not capable of surviving that sort of abuse for long. He became agonisingly aware of the softness of her body against his, the silken feel of her curls under his caressing fingers. He knew it could not be long before he slid that hand under her chin and brought her mouth up to receive his kisses. And they would most certainly not be mistakable for mere comfort.

Feeling him pull back, Sophie stepped away at once, telling herself that it was the novelty of being held so intimately that made her heart pound, her knees feel wobbly and created that sensation of scorching heat that was melting her entire body. *He offered comfort, you little ninny! Comfort! Nothing more!*

She looked up and caught his green glance which

seared through her, causing a tremor to ripple up and down her spine. She had wanted to know what it would feel like to be held in his embrace. Well, now she knew. It felt simply wonderful! His embrace had engulfed her in its tender warmth. Never had she felt so safe or content.

'I beg your pardon, my lord,' she said carefully, not quite certain that her voice was to be trusted. Her breasts tingled at the remembered sensation of being pressed so firmly against a powerfully masculine body. 'You may be right about Lord Strathallen's duties but I would prefer not to be obliged to him in any way.'

He looked at her searchingly. Was she aware of how deeply he had been affected by their brief embrace? She seemed oblivious. At least she was calmer now.

Sighing, he said, 'I think I should leave you now.' *Because if I don't I will be embracing you again. And not for comfort this time.* 'Don't trouble yourself to see me out. I will find Fanny and go. Goodbye, Miss Marsden, and please don't fret yourself in any way.' He turned back at the door. 'I nearly forgot what I had to say to you. I have been considering improvements to the estate and have decided to install a closed stove in the kitchen here. I will arrange for the newest and most up-to-date model. It should arrive within a week or so.' With that he was gone.

She was only too relieved to see him go. Her own feelings were skittering here and there and it was difficult to think straight when the mere sight of him made her recall the sensuous motion of his long fingers tangled in her hair, the strength of his arms and the warmth of his powerfully muscled chest under her cheek. She sank into a chair as the door shut behind him. What was she thinking of? She couldn't be falling in love! Or could she? And why was he concerning himself with her old-fashioned, fuel-greedy stove? If he had ever so much as stepped into a kitchen in all his life it was as much as he had done! She was surprised to hear that he even knew what a closed stove *was*!

My Lord Helford's next few visits were remarkable for their brevity. He dropped Fanny off and collected her with dispatch, greeting Miss Marsden with punctilious civility. And when next they came to take Kit riding, he didn't even come into the house. Kit was waiting eagerly at the gate and Miss Marsden nowhere to be seen. Kit informed him that Aunt Sophie was out visiting in the gig.

It was a pleasant ride. The children, he was fast discovering, were amusing and delightful companions. They argued and teased each other, occasionally appealing to him to settle some point. As far as David could tell, there was very little they agreed on but this did not seem to disturb their friendship.

One thing they did agree on was their united affection for Kit's aunt, whom Fanny had taken to calling Aunt Sophie. As they rode Kit often let fall odd scraps of information about his aunt that told David just how hard she tried to make up to the boy for his orphaned state. He found himself thinking this afternoon that it was a pity Miss Marsden had set her face against marriage, since she would make such a wonderful mother. But the thought of Miss Marsden marrying was strangely disturbing, making him grit his teeth in anger. The idea that someone else should possess her was thoroughly unsettling.

They had just turned for home when Kit said, 'Oh. Look, there's Megs. Aunt Sophie must be visiting Mrs Simpkins and her baby.' He pointed to a little dappled cob harnessed to a gig tied up outside a farm labourer's cottage.

'A baby?' Fanny sounded interested. 'How old is it?'

Kit shrugged with typical male uninterest. 'Lord, how should I know? A week or so. I say, Lord Helford, could we stop and see if Aunt Sophie wants us to ride back with her?'

'Oh, yes!' Fanny was enthusiastic. 'And then I could see the baby!'

Standing at the open door of the cottage a few moments later, David could hear Miss Marsden's soft voice speaking in accents that made his heart turn over.

'Are you getting hungry, little pet? You won't find anything there for you!' Low and soothing, all of a woman's tender, protective love for a child resonated in her tones. 'Never mind, Mama will be out in a moment. She'll have something for you.'

Inwardly shaking, David stood stock still on the threshold. Miss Marsden was seated on a wooden settle with a tiny woollen bundle nestled in her arms. She did not even notice him, caught up as she was bending over the baby, who was nuzzling hopefully at her breast. The expression of yearning regret on her face tore at David's very soul. Clearly this was something she would have desired above all else but thought never to have.

Swallowing hard, he thrust away the longing to see her nursing a child of her own and tapped belatedly on the door.

She looked up slowly from her happy dream, hazel eyes soft and vulnerable. For a moment she could not think as that green look seared into her with unmistakable tenderness. She could not tear her eyes away from that regard, but stared back transfixed, conscious of her pounding heart and uncertain breath.

With difficulty she found her voice. 'My lord? Have you come to call on Mrs Simpkins? She is in the bedroom.' What on earth was he doing here? And why was he looking at her like that? As if he could see exactly what was in her heart and understood her pain! She was imagining things! How could he, of all people, possibly understand how she longed to have her own children? Not to replace Kit, of course, but the longing to hold and nurse a child of her own.

'Er, Kit saw your mare and thought you might like our escort,' explained David. He cleared his throat of an uncharacteristic lump and went on. 'And Fanny would like to see the baby, if Mrs Simpkins would have no objection.'

At this moment Mrs Simpkins came into the room and gasped at the exalted visitor. With practised ease David set her mind at rest, saying that his little niece would love to see her baby.

Polly Simpkins was only too delighted to oblige. Accordingly Fanny and Kit came in, and in a flash Fanny was on the settle beside Sophie, being shown how to hold the baby. David watched the two women instruct his niece with a strange feeling of growing emptiness. Never before had he been so conscious of a longing to have children of his own. Not heirs—children. The raw longing in Sophie's face had shown him something within himself, the existence of which he had never suspected.

Entranced, he watched them with the baby, the gentle, tender hands and protective arms. He knew, had any danger threatened, that they would have turned like tigresses to defend the child, whatever the cost to themselves. He had seen something of it in Sophie's reaction to his suggestion that she should contact Strathallen.

On the way back to Willowbank House Fanny and Kit cantered ahead while David held his mare beside the gig. Sophie seemed rather quiet and disinclined to conversation. David fell in with her mood, content to study her surreptitiously.

Her brown hair curled softly, drawn back into a simple knot resting on her nape, a few stray tendrils brushing her cheek, which made his fingers itch to tuck them back and caress the soft cheek himself. The greeny-brown eyes were faintly abstracted, an odd frown puckering her brow. The impertinent little nose still had that sprinkling of freckles over it. Freckles, he knew, were considered a blemish. These were enchanting.

The frown worried him, combined as it was with a pensive droop to the mouth. He knew beyond doubt what was bothering her. The baby. She had purposely gone to see another woman's baby, had cuddled it and loved it when she knew perfectly well it would set off all her own yearning for a child. Why did she court that sort of pain? Why not just avoid babies?

At last he could bear it no longer and asked gently, 'Why did you go, Miss Marsden?'

She negotiated a bend in the road before answering, giving herself time to think of an appropriate answer. How much had he seen? Just that she wanted a child of her own? Or had he seen that she had been pretending the baby was her own? That he might be pitying her was unbearable. He must be deflected at all costs.

Settling for face value, she responded with spurious brightness, 'Why, to see the baby, of course! Women like to do that, my lord.'

He was not to be deflected. 'Even when holding a baby is a reminder of all you cannot have? Surely you would be wiser to avoid such thoughts.'

Her hands trembled on the ribbons. What business was it of his how she chose to live? And how could he possibly understand how she felt? She knew it was foolish to pretend, but the joy of holding a baby was too precious to be denied, even if it hurt a little.

But she found herself struggling to explain. 'You see, I love babies and children. Even if it makes me a little sad, why should I lose the pleasure of holding a baby or looking after one? Why refuse little joys because the greater one is denied? That's not living. How can you even know what joy is unless there is some pain or risk of pain to temper it?'

'You see life like that?' he asked curiously. It was oddly at variance with his own decision to marry for convenience and avoid any risk of hurt. Sophie's way was so dangerous, especially for a woman. She could be hurt so badly. He didn't like the thought of that and tried stumblingly to warn her.

She interrupted at once. 'You were in the army! How can you possibly be so scared of life when you faced death and maiming almost daily?'

'A physical risk.' He shrugged. 'Perhaps because I faced them and grew to some degree inured. But I prefer not to lay myself wide open to the sort of pain you obviously felt back there. And all for an illusory joy.'

She flushed to think that her thoughts had been so apparent. Making a gallant recover, she said, 'We will have to agree to differ. My joy in Polly's baby was no illusion and I could not live if I had to avoid all the things that might hurt me or frighten me. It may not be wise, but it is how I am made.' She paused for a moment and then said, 'Emma felt the same. She told me once after Jock had been killed that their love had been, was still to her, the reality. That it was death that was the illusion. She said it was better to have known that joy than not. That even had she known the grief in store for her, she would still have grasped the joy. Lived every minute of it as though it might be the last.'

Her acceptance shook him to the core. In some odd way it made sense. She had enough courage to take what joy she could and accept the accompanying pain. Just as she had had the courage to leap into the path of his curricle to save a child's life. She was a risk taker, then. She would take the risk and reckon up the cost later. He shuddered to think of the sort of hurt she was courting.

The rest of the drive was accomplished in silence. David was trying hard to convince himself that the way Sophie chose to conduct her life was none of his business. He tried even harder to convince himself that his way was better. Far more sensible, far more practical and certainly safer. He tried to ignore the irritating voice that suggested his safe, comfortable existence might be a little dull.

He did not dismount to bid her farewell, merely saying, 'Goodbye, Miss Marsden, Kit. Please convey my regards to Miss Andrews. Come, Fanny.'

Sophie drove the mare around to the stables in a daze. Despite her avowal that she could not avoid everything that might hurt her, there were some things she would prefer to avoid. Having Helford read her heart and soul like a book was one of them. It was far too dangerous and there would be no joy to counter the hurt. She was literally playing with fire and it was her heart that was likely to be burnt. She would have to see as little of Lord Helford as possible.

Accordingly, the next time he brought Fanny, she greeted him briefly at the door, saying, 'You will not wish to keep your horses standing, I dare say.' Then she had swept Fanny into the house, the door closing firmly behind her. David was conscious of a feeling of momentary pique and then berated himself for an arrogant fool. She was not to be blamed for keeping a safe distance between them. She gave Fanny back into his care later in the afternoon with the same quiet dismissal.

It was the same when next he came for Kit. She was baking, she informed him calmly. Just as well, David told himself sternly as he rode away with the children. It would be most unwise to see any more of her than was absolutely necessary. Somehow she got under all his defences. Unfortunately he would have to speak with her when he brought Kit home. His house guests would be arriving from the following day and he would be unable to continue with the arrangement personally for the duration of the visit. It was, however, only polite to assure himself that Sophie had no objection to Jasper taking Kit out with Fanny.

He tried to ignore the fact that he wanted to see her. His efforts were not successful and he was irritated to realise that he resented the chit having to spend her time on such domestic drudgery as baking. She was just a child, he told himself, and ought to be having fun.

Unaware that his lordship intended to speak to her later, Sophie flung herself into the baking with a vengeance, just as she had flung herself into all manner of domestic activities in the past few days. If she kept busy there was little enough time to think—and thinking was a dangerous pastime at the moment. Whenever her thoughts were permitted to drift a tanned, aristocratic face invaded her mind and emerald green eyes seemed to peer into her soul, seeking out her innermost secrets. Night time was even worse. Then she found herself imagining his arms around her again and his hand caressing her hair. And not only her hair.

Bread was kneaded and set to rise. A cake compounded, the joint for tomorrow's dinner dressed, several pounds of plums were turned into jam. In this way did Sophie try to ward off the disturbing daydreams that plagued her. Dreams of tender kisses and powerful arms enfolding her to rest against a hard, masculine body. At this point her dreams broke down. She could not imagine what might come next. Or at least she could, but was far too shocked at the thought to allow it houseroom.

Curse it! You're doing it again! Sophie dragged her mind back to the pastry she was making for a raised pie and blinked at the soggy mass. Too much water, damn! The door bell pealed loudly as she was adding more flour and she frowned. Too early for Helford to have the children back. Besides, he wouldn't use the bell if he wanted to see her, he'd come straight in with or without the children.

The bell pealed again. 'You answer it, please, Anna. And I am not at home.'

'Aye, Miss Sophie.' Anna wiped her hands on a cloth and left the kitchen. She returned a few moments later. 'It's that Sir Philip Garfield, Miss Sophie.' She sounded annoyed.

'Well, did you deny me?'

'Aye, but he weren't takin' no for an answer,' replied Anna. 'Settled in the parlour like as how he owns it.'

Sophie used an expression which she had certainly not culled from her vicarage upbringing and stripped off her apron. 'Curse and blast the man!' she muttered. 'He never does take *no* for an answer! Well, I've tried being polite. This time I am going to leave him no room for doubt or hope or whatever he bloody well calls it!'

Anna was scandalised. 'Miss Sophie! You watch your tongue!'

Sophie stuck her tongue out and squinted down her tip-tilted nose at it. 'Hmm. Looks perfectly fine to me. Let's hope this time it can convince Sir Philip that I won't accept his offer and that he would be better off if I don't!' She was gone, leaving Anna unsure whether or not she ought to scold her highty-tighty young mistress or cheer her on.

One thing was for certain, Anna would be just as glad to see the back of Sir Philip. *Fetch your mistress at once, my good woman. You forget your place. Miss Sophie will not deny herself to such a trusted friend as myself!* Trusted friend! Bah! Miss Sophie would never take him! Good woman, indeed! She'd give him *good woman*, so she would!

Sir Philip, a large, florid man in his mid-forties,

rose to his feet as Miss Marsden entered the parlour and said, 'My dear Miss Sophie, you must allow yourself to be guided by one who is older and wiser. That servant of yours actually tried to tell me you were not at home. You should turn her off at once if she does not know her place better than that.'

'Anna was merely following out my instructions,' said Sophie, very much on her dignity as she went to stand by the chimney-piece. 'And I have no intention of dismissing a servant so much devoted to my interests.'

Sir Philip frowned at the unwonted sharpness in her voice. 'You must not resent the advice of another who is devoted to your interests, my dear. You need a servant who can distinguish when an unexpected caller is a close enough friend to be admitted.'

Miss Marsden smiled sweetly. 'Oh. Well, I assure you that Anna always does that, Sir Philip.' She waited with bright-eyed interest for her suitor to absorb the implications of this set-down.

'Now, now, Miss Sophie! You must not be naughty with me!' chuckled Sir Philip. He lowered his frame into a chair only to encounter a pair of raised black eyebrows from his hostess, who remained standing. Hastily he stood up again. What the devil had gotten into the chit? Always before she had received him with a deference which had encouraged him to think that her refusal of his suit lay in her natural modesty and the disparity between their estates. In his self-importance, it never occurred to him that Miss Marsden might find his advances repugnant.

Having decided at last to marry and beget an heir, Sir Philip was not the man to be put off by a little feminine coquetry. Sophie Marsden was as dainty a morsel as ever he'd seen and she'd warm his bed quite nicely, thank you very much! Her resistance to his suit merely added spice to the pursuit. The thought of overpowering her refusal was exciting. Doubtless he would have to overpower her in bed as well. All the better, for his money! He'd enjoy a struggle. Nothing worse than a wench who lay there like a corpse. Naturally one would not expect or wish one's wife to actually enjoy the business! That was for lightskirts and farm wenches one could tumble in the straw!

All this ran through his head as he stared at his unwilling hostess. No doubt she had forgotten to sit down. She'd do so at once now that she realised *he* wished to do so. To his amazement she did not. Instead, she remained by the chimney-piece, her dark eyes holding a faintly questioning look, as one who says, *Are you staying for long? Is there something I can do for you?*

Indeed, she was saying something very like that.

'I am very busy this afternoon Sir Philip. If there is something which you particularly wish to say to me I wish you will say it.' *And then get out of my house!*

Sir Philip smiled complacently. Aha! So she was going to listen sensibly at last!

'Well, well. I don't mind saying I think it is time that nephew of yours was taken in hand by a man's authority,' he said. 'Should be sent off to school by now! Won't do him any good to be tied to your apron strings, you know.'

'Might I remind you that my nephew is only recently orphaned?' snapped Miss Marsden. 'I consider sending a child to school at his age to be barbarous anyway and doubly so in these circumstances!'

'Oh, tush! Make a man of him!' said Sir Philip bracingly. 'Don't you worry. I'll take the lad in hand for you. He needs a man's authority.'

Miss Marsden was seized by a spirit of devilry. 'I am so much in agreement with you there, Sir Philip, that I have arranged for him to ride out once a week with Lord Helford, who has very kindly offered to mount him.'

Garfield stiffened like a wolf scenting the hunter. *Helford?* Mount young Kit? He'd warrant that wasn't the only thing his lordship was planning to mount! His colour rose in anger.

'I cannot think that to be an eligible arrangement,' he opined forcefully. 'Had I known you wished it, I would have taken Kit out myself!'

'I do not choose to be under any obligation to you, Sir Philip!' said Miss Marsden in chilly tones.

'Obligation? I wonder you will choose to be

under one to Helford! A young lady like yourself can know nothing of his reputation, but I assure you it will not do, Miss Sophie. I will not permit it in the woman I intend to marry!'

Miss Marsden had had quite enough at this point. 'Sir Philip, this has gone far enough!' she said in tones of unmistakable anger. 'You have no authority over me and I do not intend that to change! You have several times in the past offered me marriage. I have refused unequivocally on each occasion, but I have tried to avoid giving you pain by too blunt a reply. This time I will tell you plainly that the thought of marriage to you is repugnant to me and I would not consider it under any circumstances. You will please take my reply as final and cease to importune me with your suit!' That, thought Sophie, surely ought to be the end of it.

With any other man it probably would have been, coupled as it was with a look of frozen disdain from eyes which glared like chips of ice from under haughty black brows. Unfortunately Sir Philip was so far enthralled in his own conceit that he took Miss Marsden's declaration of repugnance as a challenge to his virility and acted accordingly.

Before she could so much as grab the poker, Miss Marsden found herself in a suffocating grip. One hand was at her throat trying to force her chin up and his wet mouth was fumbling clumsy kisses all over her averted face in an attempt to reach her lips.

'Stop it! What are you do—?' Her protest was smothered by his lips which at last reached their goal and forced greedy, rapacious kisses on her soft mouth.

Revolted, Sophie fought desperately, only to realise that in some horrible way her struggles were pleasurable to the brute beast assaulting her. Her very fear and anger seemed to spur him on. She tore her mouth free and was about to scream for Thea and Anna when a familiar voice ripped through the room in accents of blazing fury.

'That will be quite enough, Garfield! Release Miss Marsden immediately, unless you wish to sample my riding whip!'

A vice-like grip took Sir Philip, dragging him away from his victim and spinning him around. Something drove itself into his midriff with crashing force and its identical twin smashed into his jaw as he staggered backwards. Winded and stunned, he collapsed moaning on the floor. Sophie staggered slightly, dazed and confused. A gentle hand under her arm supported her to a chair and pressed her shoulder as she stared up gratefully at her rescuer.

My Lord Helford, who had been sitting outside on the garden seat under the open window waiting for Miss Marsden to get rid of her unwanted visitor, then turned to Sir Philip Garfield. He was still writhing ignominiously on the floor, a circumstance that David viewed with immense satisfaction as he said in a voice laced with biting scorn and a fine unconcern for the fact that Garfield was ten years his senior, 'In my day, Garfield, no *gentleman* would have dreamt of pressing his suit on a lady who had declared herself unwilling to entertain it. And he certainly would not have forced his attentions on her! I suggest that you get out of here before I am tempted to use my whip on you.'

Sir Philip regained his feet. He was brick red and said with some degree of physical difficulty, 'I…I am making Miss Marsden an…an…honourable proposal of marriage which—'

He was cut off coldly. 'Which she has refused. Now get out!'

For a moment Sir Philip looked ugly, but Helford's reputation with his fists was no less awe-inspiring than his reputation with the ladies of the Viennese Opera. And calling him out would be decidedly worse. He was reputed to be just as deadly with swords or pistols. Sir Philip decided that discretion was the better part of valour. He was a fair shot and a reasonable swordsman, but he knew that to challenge Helford on a matter like this was to sign his own death warrant. With a curt nod to Miss Marsden he left, one hand pressed to his solar plexus, the other cradling his fast-swelling jaw.

Sophie said nothing at first, but sat shaking in the chair Helford had placed her in. After taking a thoughtful glance at her David went to the side table which held that bottle of cowslip wine and poured her a glass. He could see that she was seriously upset and said, 'I think you need not worry, Miss Marsden. He is most unlikely to risk a challenge from me, you know. Here, take this.' His words and tone gave no clue to the turmoil of emotions raging within.

She looked up in white-faced horror. 'No! You mustn't!' A feeling of sheer panic shot through her at the thought of him courting such danger. A hideous vision of him dead or badly wounded rose in nightmarish detail before her.

He stared at her. Surely she wasn't going to feel sorry for the lecherous brute! Could he have mistaken her sentiments? Did she in fact plan to accept Garfield? The thought sickened him. That she might surrender herself to Garfield! To anyone!

Her next words as she took the glass showed him his error. 'I…I couldn't *bear* it if you were to be hurt for my stupidity!' She sipped the wine gratefully.

She's worried about me? David found the notion immensely interesting, not to say novel. On the only other occasion when he had challenged a man over a woman, she had been quite excited by the prospect of two men going out, each with the expressed desire of putting a period to the other's existence. After that, Helford had declined to offer challenges over women. They just weren't worth it—until he had heard Sophie Marsden struggling with that lecherous bastard! That had enraged him as nothing else had ever done. He had scarcely been aware of moving as he had leapt from the seat and hoisted himself through the window. He would have fought a dozen duels for her sake!

He tried to speak lightly to cover up his feelings, 'Very sweet of you, my dear, but you need not worry. I can assure you that if Garfield is fool enough to challenge me, it will be his corpse the surgeon has to deal with, not mine.'

Sophie managed a faint smile and said, 'I just wanted to make it clear to him that I wouldn't marry him! I thought that perhaps I had been too *gentle* on the other occasions when I refused his offer. So I told him that…' She hesitated. No matter what his crimes, it was scarcely the done thing to boast of Sir Philip's offer and then tell Helford how rudely she had refused it.

Understanding her sudden silence, David smiled, relief lightening his mood. 'You don't need to tell me what you said. I was right outside the window and overheard. I can only say that Sir Philip is a more conceited man than I, if he could possibly suppose, after a refusal like that, that he could change your mind by, er…*force majeure.*'

Sophie shuddered in disgust. 'No! I…I had no idea it was so *horrible*!' She continued without thinking, not realising how surely she was betraying her complete innocence, 'Why on earth do women get married? Ugh! How can they put up with it?'

David felt a surge of tender amusement at the inexperience evident in this. 'I am obliged to point out to you, Miss Marsden, that if the lady is willing it does not have to be a horrible experience for her. And not all men are as singularly inept and brutish as your erstwhile suitor. I trust I am not myself. And I certainly do not force my attentions on unwilling females!' A trace of indignation crept into his deep voice.

She looked up at him over the rim of her wine glass. How dreadful. She had offended him! 'I...I'm sorry. I shouldn't have said that. It was very rude. I am sure that you...I mean, that you wouldn't—' She stopped, very embarrassed. Better not to inform Helford that she was persuaded his attentions would have been far more acceptable to her!

'Never mind,' he said consolingly. 'It's far from being the rudest thing you've ever said to me. Now, to business.' *Probably better not to know exactly what she was about to say. And it would definitely be better not to think about correcting her misapprehension by a demonstration!*

He explained gently why he had wanted to see her. Sophie was silent. She told herself that she ought to be relieved that she would see nothing of him for a period. It would give her time to regain some measure of control over her thoughts. Especially after this afternoon. It would be all too easy to view Lord Helford as a gallant Perseus rescuing Andromeda and dream of living happily ever after. All he had done was to act as any man of honour would have done in his position. Yes, it would be as well if she were not to see him and the little stab of pain in her heart was undeniable confirmation of that.

'Very well,' she said at last. 'If you are happy to entrust Fanny to your tiger, then I can have no qualms about sending Kit with him. Thank you, my lord and…and thank you for your intervention just now. I am very grateful.'

She rose to her feet and held out her hand. It was taken in a warm firm clasp, but to her surprise Helford did not release it at once. Rather he held her eyes in his gaze and raised her suddenly trembling hand to his lips. He pressed a gentle kiss to her fingertips. He knew he should release her at once but then, unconsciously, her fingers returned the clasp and the dearest and shyest of smiles quivered on her lips. The dimple hovered uncertainly at the corner of her mouth, as if unsure of its welcome.

He wondered despairingly if she had the slightest idea of how devastating that wide-eyed look was, of what it did to him? It burnt its way into his very soul. And her fingers were still trembling in his suddenly tightened grip. Slowly, deliberately, he turned her hand over to caress the palm with his thumb. She stared up at him, her lips slightly parted in amazement at the shudders of pleasure that rippled through her at the implied intimacy of his action.

David was lost, all his virtuous resolutions forgotten as he drew her gently into his arms and lowered his mouth to hers. All the reasons why he should not kiss her were overwhelmed by the temptation of those softly yielding lips and the desire to show her what a kiss could be like. Her complete innocence was both spur and curb to his passion. He was very gentle, moving his mouth over hers in a tender caress as he marvelled at her sweetness, reining in his rapidly mounting desire.

Sophie, whose first kiss had left her shuddering in revulsion, was stunned at the difference. It seemed my lord was right when he said it made a difference if the lady were willing. She was of the opinion, though, that the skill of the man made a great deal of difference as well.

The seductive pressure of Helford's mouth was a far cry from the lustful slobbering of Sir Philip. Helford's lips were persuasive, exerting a subtle command to which she responded instinctively, her arms clinging to him for support as his tongue ran over her lips, seeking entrance.

With a little sob that shook David to the core, her lips flowered under his. Dizzy with passion, he plunged his tongue into her soft, vulnerable mouth, tasting and exploring in slow, sensuous strokes. *Oh,*

God! She's so sweet, so soft! He was racked with desire as he felt her body melting against him. One hand rose unbidden to fondle her breasts through her bodice. Even so he felt her nipples harden in response to his action, felt her sigh of pleasure, which his mouth absorbed.

The sensations coursing through Sophie's body robbed her of all power of thought. She had thought his kiss seductive enough before he deepened it, but when his tongue invaded her mouth she realised her mistake. Boldly sweeping and plundering, it hinted at all sorts of other intimacies.

She felt one compelling hand slide sensuously down to her hip, pulling her against his body in a way which should have shocked her. Beyond caring, she allowed herself to kiss him back, pressing herself against his powerful body, revelling in the hard muscles and glorying in the contrast between that and the gentleness of his touch.

Her breasts ached at the knowing caress of his large hand which was yet so gentle and she felt a strange tension building in her, which seemed to centre itself between her thighs. His kiss became more demanding, more intimately probing as her body's response set her trembling. And his loins moved back and forth against her in slow, erotic suggestion, telling her exactly what he wanted of her. No longer gentle, but fiercely possessive, his mouth and hands arousing her senses almost to the point of pain. And she acceded to his demands, surrendering totally to his mastery.

David was fast losing control of himself and it terrified him. His own arousal was pure agony. The sheer innocence of her response had set him ablaze with a desire stronger than anything he had ever experienced. A desire to have her nestled naked in his arms in bed, while he explored her body with ever-increasing intimacy. A desire to kiss and suckle her soft breasts and finally to take and possess her fully. A desire to make love to her until she cried out in the ecstasy of fulfilment. His loins were throbbing, positively screaming at him to do something—*anything!*—to relieve their torment.

With a groan of frustration he released her gently and, realising that her legs were unlikely to support her, put her back in the chair. What the hell was he doing? He looked down at her flushed face and swollen, trembling lips, bruised with his passion. Her eyes were dazed as she met his searching look and he felt a stab of appalling guilt. *I'm worse than Garfield! At least he was offering marriage! And who the devil is going to protect her from me?*

'I…I beg your pardon, Miss Marsden,' he said with difficulty. 'I did not intend…did not mean to take advantage…I…I hope you will not misconstrue…no insult was intended…I…I mean…' *Lord! What a meandering morass of rubbish! What the devil do I mean?*

Drawing a deep breath, Sophie Marsden reached for her tattered composure, draping it inadequately over her raw and naked emotions. It was better than nothing, even if it couldn't keep out the chilly reality which was seeping into her and quenching the fire which had raged through her body. *His kisses mean nothing, save that he wanted to kiss you.* All very well, but what was she to say?

Keep it light! Don't let him see how you feel! It was not that she feared he would take advantage, but she feared his pity if he saw how much he had affected her.

There was only a faint tremor in her voice as she said, 'It…it was most educational…my…my lord. You are indeed an improvement on Sir Philip.' *Oh, dear! Did I really say that?*

He stared at her in disbelief. *Educational? Educational, did she say? Good God!* He'd heard it called some funny things before, but that card took the trick! Then he saw the slight quiver of her lower lip, swiftly bitten down on, and realised how hard she was trying to control herself. *Help her, you arrogant fool!*

'If you can consider it as such, then I am obliged to you,' he responded, not feeling obliged in the least. He did not wish Sophie Marsden to consider him in the light of a passing stage in her worldly education. He was damned if he knew what he *did* want her to think of him, but it certainly wasn't that!

He went on smoothly, 'Naturally I am gratified that you found me an improvement.' *And I had best get the hell out of here before I improve on my own record!* He saw her mouth tremble again. *Damn! I can't leave it like this. It's too cruel!*

The door burst open and Fanny and Kit came tearing in.

'Aunt Sophie! I jumped a hedge! Truly I did!' Catching the quizzical eye of his mentor upon him, he grinned and said, 'Well, a gap in a hedge. And Lord Helford says I'll be a bruising rider!' He was absolutely ecstatic and went on charitably, 'Fanny jumped it quite well too, for a girl, of course.' Master Carlisle didn't dodge quite fast enough to avoid the thump Miss Melville landed on his shoulder.

'Uncle David didn't say it was good for a *girl*!' she said fiercely. 'And he said you'd be a bruising rider when you stopped riding fast at timber. Otherwise you'd be a bruised rider!' And she stuck her tongue out in a manner calculated to bring despair to the gentle soul of her governess.

Helford just laughed and said, 'Out, you revolting child! It is time we took our leave, and don't strike Kit again. It is not at all the thing when you know he is not permitted to hit you back.' *Damn the brats!*

Why did they have to come in just then? Not that I have the faintest idea what to say to her anyway.

Sophie rose to her feet. 'I will bid you good day then, my lord, Fanny. I hope you will enjoy your house party.'

She held out her hand to his lordship and he took it reluctantly. It was as though a knife twisted in his guts as he heard her dismiss him so coolly, but he had no choice but to accede. With a brief pressure of the fingers he was gone, pulling Kit's ear and telling him to be good to his aunt. Fanny paused only to bestow a hug on Sophie, of whom she was becoming very fond, and rushed out after him.

Kit went off about his own pursuits and Sophie was left alone. Why had he kissed her like that? Her fingers touched her lips in wonder. Never had she imagined a kiss could possibly make you feel like that. As though you were on fire and melting all at the same time! *Did he feel the same? Could he possibly kiss me like that without feeling anything beyond desire? Are men really that different?*

Suddenly exhausted, she sat down. Her muddled thoughts were interrupted by Anna.

'Miss Sophie. That Sir Philip, what happened? I saw 'im go. Did he try to make up to you?'

Sophie nodded. 'Yes. It…it was very unpleasant. Fortunately Lord Helford came in and…and…'

'Gave 'im a settler, I'll be bound! You be careful, Miss Sophie. You didn't ought to be receiving gentlemen alone. Mind you, his lordship's safe enough.'

Sophie did not feel it advisable to correct this false impression and Anna went on, 'Courtin' he is or so they say in the village.'

If Anna had dumped a bucket of cold water on her young mistress, Sophie could not have been more shocked. 'Courting? He is courting? Who?'

Anna shrugged, 'One of the young ladies comin' to stay up at the Place, I did hear. Good as betrothed to some Lady Lucinda.' She looked closely at Miss Sophie. Proper wore out she looked. 'You go an' have a rest, Miss Sophie. I'll look after things. Go on, now.' She shepherded Sophie out of the room like a large sheepdog with a very small lamb.

In the privacy of her bedchamber Sophie sat on the bed, staring blindly into space. He was courting. So what could he possibly want with her? At best he was amusing himself with a little flirtation, and at worst...at worst he would offer her a *carte blanche*, ask her to be his mistress. She shuddered to think that, after her disgraceful response, he could hardly be blamed for thinking that she would be a willing conquest. Well, he would learn his mistake!

At least she hoped he would. It was as she had known deep down at the start—if he wanted her and so much as suspected her willingness then she was lost. She would surrender herself even though she knew it would destroy her.

Chapter Six

All the next day Helford Place resounded to the rumble of arriving carriages and clattering hooves on the gravelled sweep of drive before the main portico with its lofty Grecian columns. Servants scurried hither and yon, conveying mountains of baggage to the various apartments assigned to the guests. The house echoed to the influx of new voices, footsteps and the whisper of silken skirts hushing over the floors.

Lady Maria viewed all this rather sardonically. Her eagle gaze had been quick to descry the tension in her nephew when he returned home the previous day. He had almost winced whenever Fanny spoke of Sophie Marsden, which she did very frequently, referring to her as *Aunt Sophie*. Well, not winced precisely. Frozen was more like it, as though he were trying to control or counteract some powerful emotion. And in Lady Maria's long and varied experience, there was only one emotion likely to bring out that sort of reaction over a woman.

So she waited with intense interest to see how he would greet the guests of honour. Snatches of conversation came to her ears when people thought she wasn't attending. 'Has he offered already?... forgone conclusion...probably announce it towards the end of the visit...'

Sometimes, thought Lady Maria, it paid to let people think you were a little deaf and more than a little senile. The irritation of being spoken to like a halfwit was more than amply compensated by the information you picked up. For example, Ned Asterfield would never have referred to Lady Lucinda as *a cold poultice* had he thought his hostess could hear him.

She sat in the Green Drawing Room, which was considered hers by long tradition, receiving the guests as Helford presented them to her, watching their approach across the empty expanse of carpet and knowing perfectly well that they found the experience singularly unnerving.

The old-fashioned, formal arrangement of the room assisted in the impression of approaching a throne. Gave you a chance to have a good look at the person. Humph! None of this new-fangled rubbish about cluttering up a room with furniture higgledy piggledy all over it. While she had breath in her body her apartments would be arranged in the old way with the furniture in its place against the wall. The way it was when a gown was a gown, thank you very much, and had a decent hoop to it! Not one of these scandalous modern muslin draperies calling itself decent attire for a modest female!

At length Lady Stanford and Lady Lucinda Anstey were announced and Lady Maria eyed her nephew's quarry as she made her way regally down the long room to be presented to her hostess. Tall and elegant, Lady Lucinda glided across the carpet to greet the old lady. *A beauty? Oh, yes, she's that, all right. The right girl for David? We shall see.*

She was demurely respectful, but Lady Maria was quick to detect a hint of patronage. And by the sudden frown in his eyes Helford had caught it as well.

Lady Maria responded to the young lady's greeting with a blunt, 'How d'you do?' Then she turned her fire on Lady Stanford. 'Good evening, Aurelia! How is Stanford these days? Still an eye to the fillies?' This enigmatic question left most of the assembled party in doubt as to whether the old girl referred to the absent Earl's sporting interests or other less respectable proclivities.

Everyone except Lady Stanford and Lord Helford, that is. The latter managed to disguise an unseemly crack of laughter as a fit of coughing, but Lady Stanford went purple with fury and barely returned a civil reply. Lady Lucinda was somewhat taken aback. Never had she seen her mama so put out by an innocent question. Lady Lucinda was one of those young ladies of birth, so recently extolled by Lord Helford, who knew nothing of a gentleman's reputation. Not even when the gentleman was her own father and carried on his amours with much the same regard for discretion as a stag in rut.

Oddly enough, his lordship was not delighted at her obvious ignorance. *Lord! What a pea-goose she must be! Stanford's peccadilloes are common knowledge!* Helford had, manlike, completely forgotten his dictum, so forcibly expressed to Miss Marsden, that young ladies should not know of such things. He found himself thinking that Sophie would have made some outrageous comment to put the old devil in her place. And Great Aunt Maria would have loved it!

Belatedly remembering his role as host, he strolled forward to rescue the seething Lady Stanford.

Fixing his outrageous relative with a look which would have wilted almost any other female and most men, he said, 'Perhaps you and Lady Lucinda would like to rest after your journey before you must change for dinner. It is after four now and we will dine at six. Country hours, you know.'

'Thank you, my lord,' responded Lady Stanford. *At least he knows what is due to me. Disagreeable old hag! When Lucinda marries, Lady Maria can retire to the Dower House or Bath. I'll see to that!*

She permitted Lord Helford to lead her from the

room and show the pair of them to the suite of rooms they were to occupy. The grandeur and appointments of these rooms went a long way towards mollifying her. These were the state apartments, their wainscoting lavishly gilded and the furniture luxuriously upholstered in gold silk damask. A large salon separated the two bedchambers, which boasted elegant and enormous beds surmounted by canopied drapes in gold and ivory silk.

It would be too much to say that Lady Lucinda was impressed by this display of ostentation, but she certainly appreciated it as her due.

'Lord Helford uses us with great respect, Mama,' she observed when she joined Lady Stanford in their private salon.

'Quite so, my love,' agreed Lady Stanford. 'And I am sure that he will not make a fuss about any little changes you may like to make.'

'Changes, Mama?' Lady Lucinda was surprised. As far as she could see the house was fitted up in the first style of elegance. Lofty rooms, a certain formal dignity. Some of the furnishings were a trifle old fashioned, but no doubt they could be relegated to less public rooms bit by bit. What could Mama be talking about?

'Yes, my dear. For example, I believe that Lord Helford's niece is living here at the moment. Understandably he has not had time to look about him and dispose of the child suitably. That will be a task for you, my dear. The child will be very much better off in a good school or with other relations. She must not be encouraged to think of this as her home now, you know. Orphans,' she spoke with a delicate shudder, 'can be sadly encroaching.'

Lady Lucinda nodded thoughtfully. Indeed, she did not wish to be troubled with someone else's child.

Lady Stanford continued, 'And, of course, Lady Maria is becoming quite peculiar. And she has been so used to ordering everything here just as she pleases. It will be very much better if she retires to the Dower House or even perhaps to Bath. Yes, Bath would be best. Her health, you know. I am sure the waters would be most beneficial.'

This point of view struck Lady Lucinda forcibly. Most certainly she did not want Lord Helford's Great Aunt interfering with her management of the house. She went down to dinner in a thoughtful frame of mind, determined to ask her mother's advice on how best to achieve these evictions.

By the end of dinner Lady Maria was determined on one thing. Her nephew was not going to marry that insufferably superior wench if she could stop it! And if he *was* fool enough to take her, then she would betake herself to the Dower House before the bridal trip was over. Never had she been more irritated by a female in her life, which was saying a great deal since most women irritated Lady Maria.

She made two exceptions. One was for Penelope Darleston, who was an impudent baggage, but at least kept that handsome rake she had married in *her* bed where he belonged. The second was for Miss Marsden, who was, she opined, a good gal and one who would give as good as she got. Not one of these mealy-mouthed modern misses who swooned if someone mentioned *breeches*. Lady Maria had had a soft spot in her heart for Miss Marsden ever since the day she had called upon her to find her chasing a piglet out of her parlour and using language which Lady Maria had not heard since one of the grooms had been kicked by one of her carriage horses.

By the end of the evening Lady Maria had added to her resolve about removing to the Dower House. She would take Fanny with her. The child had been brought down to the drawing room before dinner and Lady Lucinda had treated her with a mixture of condescension and patronage which grated on Lady Maria intolerably. *Damn it! This is the child's home, ain't it?* Not a doubt but that Lady Lucinda would be packing the child off to school faster than the cat could lick her ear. *Not if I have anything to say to it!*

By the time she retired and had heard Lady Lucinda assuring David that she would be delighted to see over the house on the morrow and give him the benefit of her advice in his plans for refurbishing the west wing, Lady Maria had heard more than enough. Lady Lucinda Anstey would marry David Melville over her dead body!

To this end she emerged from her bedchamber the next morning well before her usual hour. She wished to catch Helford before he began the day's entertainments which were to include a ride around the estate and a visit to Darleston Court. She found her nephew in the library just before breakfast.

He looked up in some surprise. 'Good God, ma'am! Has someone invaded the nation? What the devil are you doing up so early?'

'Don't you swear at *me* as if I was one of your troopers!' she snapped, secretly delighted at the easy, down-to-earth way he spoke with her. Hah! She'd like to see Madam Anstey's reaction if Helford addressed her like that!

Now, to be devious. 'Had an idea,' she said. 'Are you going to see anything of the Darlestons while you've got the house full of all these people?'

'Well, of course,' said David. 'In fact, I had arranged to call on them this afternoon while we are out riding. I sent a note over yesterday and Lady Darleston sent one back saying to bring as many as I liked.'

Lady Maria smiled in an odd way which made David feel very nervous. He remembered that look from his childhood and it always meant trouble for someone, generally the recipient.

'Why don't you suggest to Penelope that she calls

on Miss Marsden?' suggested Lady Maria. 'Those two should deal extremely well together. Not a hair's-breadth between them when it comes to speaking their minds and, as far as I'm aware, they've never met.'

David perceived that his memory must be at fault. He could detect no danger at all in this brainwave. Penelope Darleston would be just the right friend for Sophie. He was shaken to find that he thought of her as *Sophie* now, rather than *Miss Marsden*. There was something about kissing a girl which seemed to do away with such formalities. Especially when the memory of the girl's response haunted your sleep and left you feeling as though your bed were stuffed with nails. Damned chilly nails at that.

'Very well, Aunt Maria. I'll suggest to Lady Darleston that she calls on So...Miss Marsden. Good God! Look at the time. I'd best get to breakfast. If you can be out of your room this early, I can make it to breakfast on time.'

Lady Maria permitted him to escort her from the room, not betraying by so much as a quiver of her lips that she had caught his telltale slip. *Sophie, indeed! Once that impudent creature Penelope gets wind of this, I can trust her to do something about it without my having to say a word.*

True to his word Helford showed Lady Lucinda around the house after breakfast.

Lady Lucinda had reminded him that she was all eagerness to give him the benefit of her advice. 'Indeed, it will be a pleasure, my lord. You must know that Mama recently had several rooms done up at Camberley in the Chinese style. I fancy that the result is not just in the common way and I should be happy to assist you.'

David was conscious of an unexpected twinge of pure fright, since it was evident from her arch comments that Lady Stanford had no intention of accompanying them on this expedition. He was at a loss to understand his dismay since, logically speaking, it should be just what he wanted. A chance to become acquainted with his prospective bride. *It looks so particular! You'll have the entire party gossiping by noon if you take only her. Think now, some camouflage is called for.*

'Perhaps Mrs Asterfield might care to come along as well,' he said, smiling in the direction of a young matron who showed every sign of having a *tendre* for him.

'Why, I should be delighted, my lord,' responded Kate Asterfield, a faint smile curving her lips. She was no fool and understood exactly what his lordship was at. Perfectly happy with her husband, an old friend of Helford's, she was nevertheless quite happy to spend a morning in the company of a man who was the most handsome thing God ever put in breeches. Especially if it would annoy that in-

sufferable Anstey chit. Not that Lady Lucinda
would ever do anything so human as to show annoyance, but she must surely be conscious of a little
chagrin that she was not the sole recipient of this
signal honour.

The tour was a mixed success. The two ladies
had enjoyed themselves enormously. Mrs Asterfield
was not a woman who had to be the centre of attention to be happy. On the contrary, she was quite
content to stand back and observe the foolishness
of others. She derived no small satisfaction from listening to Lady Lucinda instruct his lordship in the
principles of modern taste, consigning several obviously valuable heirlooms to the attics in the
process. She was relatively sure Helford had been
quite shocked at some of the suggestions put forth,
but he was the soul of tact, merely saying quietly
that he had a liking for this piece or that and would
prefer it left in its place.

Blissfully unaware that she was not showing to
advantage, Lady Lucinda gave full rein to her ideas
and was tolerably certain that Lord Helford was
much struck by her understanding and taste. With
her mama's advice in mind she even ventured to
enquire when 'dear little Fanny', as she described
the child, would be off to school.

'Surely a wise move, my lord. It must be painful
for the child to be constantly reminded of all that

she has lost,' said Lady Lucinda with an air of sincerity which made Mrs Asterfield long to smack her.

David merely replied, 'Indeed, I am of the opinion that she has lost so much that I prefer not to remove her from her home while she is so young. I must say I can see little need for her to be sent away to school at all. Her governess appears to me to be doing an admirable job.' It was said quietly and in the friend-liest of tones, but Mrs Asterfield was convinced she had seen a flash of anger in those green eyes.

Oblivious to her blunder, Lady Lucinda said, 'Oh, but she would benefit from companionship.'

David inclined his head, 'Just so, ma'am. I have arranged for her to visit a friend of my aunt's once a week so that she may play with Miss Marsden's nephew. And I even take the pair of them riding so that Miss Marsden does not feel imposed upon.'

He was startled at the pang of longing which shot through him in just mentioning Sophie. He thought of the way in which she had taken on the responsibility for her orphaned nephew and wondered at Lucinda's lack of understanding. It suddenly occurred to him to wonder how Lucinda would deal with Fanny. He was coming to have a fondness for the child and felt a stab of uneasiness at the thought that his bride might not wish the child to remain with them.

Mrs Asterfield was speaking. 'Besides, dear Lucinda, Helford will be setting up his nursery one

day and will no doubt provide lots of companionship for Fanny.' It would be too much to say there
was a glint of mischief in the lady's eyes. She had,
his lordship judged, a perfectly straight face. Which
was more than could be said for Lady Lucinda, who
actually glared at her.

With a strange tightening of his throat David
found that all he could think of was Sophie with that
tiny infant cuddled to her breast, her tender voice
as she dreamed over it. And with a jolt he realised
that it was that that had started him thinking of her
as *Sophie*, not merely kissing her.

'And, of course, so many little girls become positively maternal where babies are concerned,' continued Mrs Asterfield with, David considered, malice
aforethought. The look of extreme distaste on Lady
Lucinda's face had obviously not been lost on her.
'Why, I did myself after my eldest sister was
brought to bed with her children and I was not so
much older than Fanny is now, being the youngest
of twelve. I believe it all kept my parents shockingly
busy.'

They were standing in the Round Parlour in the
South Tower at the time and Mrs Asterfield caught
sight of a Gainsborough over the chimney-piece
depicting the wife and very numerous progeny of
the fourth Viscount.

'I am sure another picture of that nature would
gladden his lordship's heart,' she said sweetly, in-

dicating the painting with an airy wave. The children surrounded their mother, the youngest nestling on her lap, her arms curved around him protectively.

'Quite so, ma'am,' responded Helford drily, as visions of Sophie surrounded by children assailed him. He wondered whether Ned Asterfield would accept a plea of extreme provocation when his wife was found strangled.

Lady Lucinda was looking absolutely outraged at the impropriety of this conversation. Lord Helford could not help thinking that Sophie would in all likelihood have succumbed to giggles by now and probably would have said something just as outrageous. It clearly behoved him to bring the tour to an end as quickly as possible, which he did by suggesting that the ladies might like to repose themselves before partaking of a luncheon prior to their ride over to Darleston Court.

Entirely satisfied with the morning's activities, Mrs Asterfield took this gentle hint. She retired in good order, reflecting as she did so that poor Helford deserved *some* time alone with the chit if he really was desirous of making her an offer.

David found himself left alone with Lady Lucinda, giving him the chance to say, 'You may not know that I spoke to your father before leaving town. Naturally I feel it to be of the first importance that we are both quite sure of our own minds before coming to any final agreement but…' He smiled at her meaningly.

'Of course, my lord,' said Lady Lucinda without the slightest trace of coyness or embarrassment. 'There is no need to be hasty over such an important matter.'

Telling himself that he ought to be pleased that she so obviously viewed the match with the same cool propriety that he did, Helford escorted Lady Lucinda back her bedchamber. As they went he tried to imagine her with children, a baby snuggled in her arms, and failed dismally. The image just didn't fit. He took his leave of her very formally and departed to think over his morning in the solitude of the library.

The visit to Darleston Court was very pleasant. The Earl and his Countess received the party with great hospitality, and if Lady Lucinda thought that the presence of Lady Darleston's extremely large dog was inappropriate she left her opinion unvoiced.

Helford noticed, however, that she avoided Gelert assiduously and wondered how she would react to dogs in the house. He had every intention of selecting a couple of puppies from his keeper's current litter of springer spaniels. Dogs always made a house seem…well…more like a home. He had not kept a dog since leaving England and was looking forward to it very much.

He took the first opportunity of suggesting to the Countess that she might care to make Miss Marsden's acquaintance.

'Great Aunt Maria thought you would be pleased with her,' he said in explanation of his request as he absent-mindedly fondled Gelert's ears.

'Did she, indeed?' asked Penelope. 'Then, of course, I will do so. Willowbank House? Oh, yes, I know it. Very well. I shall call in the next day or so. I often ride out that way.' *What now is Lady Maria up to?* Penelope was far too well acquainted with his lordship's aunt not to detect a distinct whiff of rodent in the seemingly innocent suggestion.

Thinking Kate Asterfield and Lucinda might well be tired, Helford took the party back by the shortest route which led them straight past Willowbank House. For the preceding mile the temptation to stop briefly and visit Sophie warred with the knowledge that to see her would be extremely unwise. Positively dangerous, in fact. He could place no reliance on his ability to keep the line with her now.

As the house came into view he decided firmly that he would ride straight past and resist temptation. Therefore he was understandably stunned to hear his own voice say, 'Please ride on ahead. I must stop and speak to my tenant here about some improvements I have in hand for the house. I will catch you up in a very few minutes.' *Where the devil did that come from?*

He dismounted, rather dazed at the lack of control he seemed to have over his behaviour, and tied the mare's bridle to the gatepost. All the way up the path he issued mental instructions to himself to keep his hands and mouth off Sophie, that she was his tenant, a lady of breeding and un-doubted virtue, and as such should be treated with respect. And also that he had as good as offered for Lucinda Anstey, who had every qualification he had demanded of his bride. She was beautiful, titled, well behaved and well dowered—a ve-ritable paragon.

To his mingled relief and chagrin Sophie received him with Thea Andrews in attendance. If she was surprised to see him again so soon, it did not show in her demeanour.

'Good afternoon, Lord Helford. It is very pleasant to see you again.' Her voice was quiet and dignified, giving no hint of the turmoil raging within. *Why is he here again so soon? What does he want? Surely he is not going to…to offer a…carte blanche. Stop it! Stop it at once! He can't do so with Thea in the room. And if he is, it doesn't matter! Unless you are fool enough to accept!* But it did matter. She knew she would be immeasurably ashamed if he thought that her disgraceful response to his kisses meant that she would consider such a connection. And she would have no one but herself to blame. She should not have talked in that indelicate fashion about marital duties. Of course a man of his reputation would be unable to resist such a challenge.

She indicated a chair to his lordship, 'Please be seated, my lord.'

'I…I should not stay, Miss Marsden. I…I wished merely to say that I have been calling at Darleston Court this afternoon and I mentioned you to the Countess. She… er…intends to call upon you in the next day or so. I…I hope you do not mind?' *Good God! Stop stammering like a lovesick schoolboy!*

Miss Andrews was all a-twitter. 'Why, how very kind of you, my lord. I am sure that Miss Sophie could not possibly mind. Indeed, why should she? Sophie, dear, you say nothing?'

Sophie was staring at Helford in complete confusion. Her eyes met his with a look of puzzlement. At last she spoke. 'It is certainly very kind in you, my lord. But I can think of no reason why you should do such a thing. What can I have in common with a Countess?'

She undervalues herself so dreadfully. Aloud he said, 'Well, my Aunt Maria approves of both of you. In fact, it was her suggestion that I should mention you to Lady Darleston. I am quite sure that you will like her, you know.' He continued reassuringly, 'She is not in the least top lofty or condescending and I don't think she cares in the slightest about rank or degree or any of that nonsense. So don't tease yourself on that head. Now, I must be going. I am supposed to be escorting my house guests home. They are riding on ahead.'

Sophie rose gracefully to her feet. 'Then I will escort you to your horse, my lord, and thank you for your kind offices. I shall look forward to meeting Lady Darleston.'

Helford bid Miss Andrews a polite farewell and held the door open for Sophie to precede him from the room. The soft fragrance that hung around her hair drifted past him teasingly. He shut the door behind them, wondering just what the scent was.

'Miss Marsden. I hope you will forgive my behaviour the other day…it was infamous of me—'

'You need not consider it, my lord.' Her voice was cold. 'I am well aware that I ought not to have received Sir Philip alone. I would not have done so had I not intended to refuse his offer in such blunt terms. And you have certainly demonstrated the folly of receiving you alone. The responsibility is mine.'

She was blaming herself for his behaviour? Damn! *She* shouldn't feel guilty because he had behaved like a cad! He knew that many people would assume that she had asked for it in some way or another, but such attitudes stuck in his gullet. A man should not hide behind such cowardly untruths. He had kissed her because he had not been able to help himself, but the fault was not hers. Unless she was to be blamed for being too lovely, too appealing.

'The fault was not yours, Miss Marsden,' he said

gently. 'It was mine. You are not to be blaming yourself or thinking that I will read anything into your…er…into what happened.'

Into my response? Into the inescapable fact that I kissed you back? That I did not merely permit but encouraged the liberties you took? That I enjoyed it? Sophie did not answer as she went down the path to the front gate. She did not know what to say.

'Goodbye, my lord. I will expect Fanny on Monday.'

He nodded, accepting his dismissal. 'Farewell, then.' He held out his hand. She looked at it for a moment and then placed hers in it hesitantly. The long fingers closed around it in a light grip and before she could withdraw he raised it swiftly to his lips to drop a kiss on the inside of her wrist.

Her eyes widened in shock at the ripple of delight that ran through her. 'No,' she whispered. 'This must stop. I am not for you, my lord. Look else-where for your amusements and leave me in peace!' She wrenched her wrist from his grasp, her cheeks stained scarlet.

'My amusements?' David was shocked. Was that what she thought? *What else could she think?*

'What else can this be?' asked Sophie fiercely, echoing his thought. 'I do not know whether you are simply indulging in a little flirtation or something more serious, but I tell you this, Lord Helford: I want none of it! Goodbye!'

She nearly ran back into the house, leaving David wondering what the devil had possessed him to do such an addlebrained thing. He'd only just apologised for the previous day's familiarities and there he was doing it again. Always with other women he had been in full control of himself. Oh, he had desired them right enough, but he had always been in command of his actions. Never had he felt so completely powerless to restrain himself.

It's because I can't have her. If I could have her in bed, then she would cease to have this power. Ah! But you can have her. She responded yesterday. How much effort would it take to—?

No! Horrified at the turn his thoughts were taking, Helford spurred his mare into a brisk canter. He couldn't, he simply couldn't take advantage of her in that way. Had he only defended her from Garfield's mauling to destroy her himself? It was unthinkable. Or it ought to be. She deserved better than that. Why the hell was he interested in her, anyway? She had no extraordinary degree of beauty, her connections were no more than passable and she had a tongue on her like a wasp when she was annoyed.

And her mouth had opened under his in the sweetest, most trusting way, her body melting into his embrace as no woman's ever had. Her very inexperience and shyness set his senses blazing. But through it all was this inexplicable urge to protect her, even, or rather especially, from himself.

Stay away from her. It's the best thing you can do. Unless you are prepared to offer marriage. And the last thing you want is marriage to a woman you care for...a woman who can hurt you.

The thought seared itself into his mind just as the tail end of his guests came into view around a bend in the high hedges and he cantered up to them, a terrible suspicion forming in his mind that he might have made an appalling mistake. That he might have all unwittingly fallen into the very trap he had sought to avoid. While he made polite conversation to Kate Asterfield and Lady Lucinda, a remark Peter Darleston had made on the subject of love pounded mercilessly in his brain.

I didn't even recognise it.

He gritted his teeth. If he had fallen in love with Sophie Marsden, then there was only one thing to be done about it. Avoid her. Like the plague.

Sophie ordered herself to forget about Lord Helford. She knew now why she had instinctively recognised him as dangerous. He wielded a power over her that no man ever had. A few more interludes like that, she thought, and I won't be able to refuse him. No matter what he asks. His mouth and hands robbed her of all ability to think rationally. She lay in her bed that night for hours, waiting for sleep, trying to convince herself that this madness would pass.

It's just a physical attraction. You can't be in love. You hardly know him. What do you like about him apart from the fact that he kissed you out of your senses?

But there were many things she liked about him. His kindness to Kit and his understanding of the boy's problem. The way he had actually taken some time to acquaint himself with his niece. Kit was full of things that Helford had said to him in the most casual way which told Sophie that she could not have found a better man to influence him. And he had seen unerringly to the heart of her make-believe with Polly Simpkins's baby.

She cursed and thumped her pillow. *Damn! Try and think of things to his discredit, you little fool. His reputation for a start. And what about the way he nearly ran you over? Thought you a bit of game? Accused you of keeping Kit from his family? Arrogant, interfering oaf!*

Her natural sense of justice was no help at all.

But he apologised for all of those things, unreservedly owning himself at fault.

It only made her love him the more. For it was love, she could not lie to herself, even if she did manage to preserve a cold front with Helford. And she would have to preserve a very cold front. She knew he would never press her if he believed her unwilling. She must take care never to be alone with him again. It was the only way to be safe from her own weakness which would surrender to him at the first opportunity.

Elusive sleep came at last but brought her no peace, haunted as it was by his voice and tender caresses. She woke several times, her body trembling as it had in his arms, her heart pounding and that strange tension building in her belly. The dreams were so real that each time she sank back into sleep, confused to have found herself alone.

Chapter Seven

After dinner the next day Sophie dismissed Kit to his afternoon pursuits and Thea went to her usual afternoon rest. She knew that the best thing she could do was to keep busy, so she fetched the beeswax from the scullery and set about polishing the furniture in the parlour. Most of the pieces were very old with no pretensions to fashion. They had belonged for the most part to her father's family and showed signs of wear and aging. Nevertheless they glowed with care and lent the small room an air of home for her. She had lived with this furniture all her life. To her they spelled safety and security.

She flung open the casements, allowing the fresh air to flow into the room. The garden was full of flowers and their scent drifted through with the light breeze. Humming a soft air to herself, she went about her work.

Piece by piece she moved around the room, applying the wax sparingly, knowing that a small amount of wax to a large amount of elbow grease was the best combination. As she went the hum became a song and her rich, warm voice floated out to mingle with a whistling blackbird. After she had waxed several pieces she judged that the first one, a small drop-sided dining table, would be dry enough to buff and returned to it, still singing.

I will give my love an apple without ere a core,
I will give my love a house without ere a door.
I will give my love a palace wherein he may be
And he may unlock it without any key.

The visitor coming up the path with her dog stood as though petrified as she heard the plangent air and the poignant intensity of the voice. She waited for a moment, and then walked up to the door. She had been very nervous about calling on a complete stranger, but she just had to know what that song was.

Just as Sophie picked up the clean cloth the door bell jangled loudly. She frowned. Who on earth— surely, surely not Helford again? Anna's footsteps were heard in the flagged hall and the sound of the door opening. A charming, feminine voice was heard inquiring if Miss Marsden were at home.

Before Sophie could so much as stuff the jar of wax and the cloths in a drawer, Anna was opening the door and announcing, "Tis Lady Darleston, Miss Sophie.'

Sir Philip might have had a point, thought Sophie in horror. A Countess comes to call on me and Anna has to show her in before I even have time to tidy myself. Horribly conscious of untidy hair, a streak of wax on her cheek from pushing a curl out of her eyes and a shabby old gown, Sophie came forward to greet her exalted guest.

Her first impression was one of extraordinary beauty. A tall, slender figure in an elegant dark blue habit, the skirt looped up gracefully over one arm. Glowing auburn curls nestled under a charming hat with one curling feather and set off a delicately fair countenance.

Sophie drew herself up proudly. *I have nothing to be ashamed of!* A second glance revealed the caller's laughing grey eyes and merry smile. Suddenly Sophie was reassured.

This was confirmed by the first thing Lady Darleston said. 'Oh dear, I am interrupting you. Should I come another time? I…I…don't mean to intrude, but when Helford said Lady Maria wanted me to meet you…we are to dine with them, you know, and she is bound to ask me how I liked you.'

Despite herself Sophie started to laugh and her extraordinary guest joined in. 'Oh, good! You looked so dreadfully stern for a moment that I was quite scared. It didn't fit in at all'

'Fit in with what?' asked Sophie.

'That lovely song you were singing. You're going

to sing it for me again so I can learn it,' explained the impossible Countess.

'Won't you sit down, Lady Darleston?' asked Sophie, still smiling. 'Anna, bring some cakes and sandwiches, please, and tea.'

'Yes, Miss Sophie, and what should I do about the dog?'

'Dog? What dog?' Sophie was puzzled.

'Her ladyship's dog what's taking up the entire hall.'

'Can he come in, Miss Marsden?' asked Lady Darleston. 'He's enormous, but very well behaved. Or I could leave him outside with my groom.'

'Bring him in,' said Sophie. 'And, Anna, tell Lady Darleston's groom to take the horses around to the stable. He may put them in the spare boxes.'

Lady Darleston gave a soft whistle and Sophie stared as the largest dog she had ever seen came in and sat beside his mistress.

'Good God! Do you *need* a groom with him to escort you?' The question was out before she could stop it. Oh dear, that probably wasn't the right way to address a Countess. But this particular Countess did not seem to have the slightest notion of fitting into any of Sophie's preconceived ideas.

'Of course not. Gelert would simply savage anyone who accosted me. But you know what men are!' she said with an infectious chuckle. 'Darleston insists if I am off our own land. On our estate I never bother with a groom.'

Sophie laughed and said, 'It must be nice to have someone fuss about you that much. Please sit down. I am glad you called. Lord Helford warned me that you might, but I didn't think it would be so soon.'

Lady Darleston grinned as she sat down with the dog at her feet, 'How well do you know Lady Maria?'

'Not terribly well,' admitted Sophie. 'She used to call here once in a while, but she doesn't get out much now, I believe.'

'And you don't call on her?'

'N...no. I...er...I didn't think...' Sophie didn't quite know how to tell Lady Darleston that she would not dream of presuming that she was welcome to call at Helford Place. Although the previous Viscount had been kind enough, his wife had certainly never indicated that she wished for any sort of intimacy.

'You didn't want to be thought encroaching?' Lady Darleston smiled understandingly. 'Next time I'm calling on her I shall come in the carriage and take you up if you would care to come. She likes visitors, even if she does always give one a tremendous scold for not coming next or nigh her for months. You should have heard what she said to me after I didn't visit for a month when my twins were born.'

Sophie was fascinated. She found it hard to believe that this slender creature could be the mother of twins. 'I had heard you had twins,' said

Sophie shyly. 'How lovely for you.' She felt a pang of envy for this girl who had everything she would never have. A husband, who by all accounts worshipped the ground she trod on, and children of her own.

At least I have Kit. She pushed away the thought of Lord Helford. Whatever he might offer, she did not think love would come into it. At least not love as she understood it.

Lady Darleston was speaking again, 'What were you singing when I was walking up the path? I had never heard it before. It's very old, isn't it? It sounded lovely.' She hummed part of the melody.

'One of our maids taught it to me when I was a child,' said Sophie. 'It's just a country song, but I like it.'

'Will you play it for me?' asked Lady Darleston, indicating the harpsichord in the corner.

Sophie shook her head. 'I play very badly.'

Lady Darleston stood up and went to the old instrument. She lifted the lid and sat down, twinkling at her hostess. 'Very well. Sing. I have to learn this song. Darleston would love it.'

Slightly self-conscious, Sophie sang the old air and was amazed when her guest joined in with a light accompaniment on the second verse. Her touch on the keys was sure and light and she played with a delicate sensitivity. 'Again,' she commanded at the end. This time she played the whole way through, adding an improvised interlude between the verses.

Penelope Darleston had never heard a girl sing like this one could. The voice was so warm and vibrant and there was that peculiar aching quality. It made Penelope's heart contract to hear it, as though the singer's soul was bared. Enough to break your heart, she thought as she struck the final chords.

Their eyes met and held, the song's spell still holding them in thrall. In that moment friendship was born as each recognised in the other the power of music to stir them and express all the things that could never be spoken.

At last Penelope spoke. 'I hope you will come to dinner one evening and sing that for Darleston.'

'Oh, I couldn't, Lady Darleston!' said Sophie in horror.

Penelope laughed. 'Oh, yes, you could. He'd love it. And I think since we are going to be friends that you had better stop calling me Lady Darleston. Everyone I like calls me Penny.'

'You want me to call you Penny?' Never had Sophie imagined that a Countess could be so unaffected and charming. No, not charming. Warm, friendly and yet there was a dignity about her that would preclude anyone taking liberties with her.

Penelope nodded. She definitely liked this girl with her soft brown curls and greeny-brown eyes.

She had an oddly taking face with its impertinent freckled nose. Far more welcoming than Lucinda Anstey's aristocratic countenan— Good God! Is that what Lady Maria is up to? Does she think that Sophie Marsden can cut that insufferable girl out with Helford? Well, if he ever hears her sing! But from all I hear he's as good as offered for Lucinda. How the devil can he get out of it now?

'Please do,' she went on aloud. 'Now we have met I would like to be friends. And if Lady Maria likes you that's something we have in common. She's terribly choosy.'

'Well, I can't imagine why she does like me,' confessed Sophie. 'The first time she called here to see how we were settling in I nearly knocked her flat, chasing a piglet out of this room and the language I was using was not precisely…polite.'

Penelope burst out laughing. 'I can imagine. The little beasts can run so fast and they are so *slippery*! Nothing at all to get hold of. That wouldn't bother Lady Maria. She can't bear people to be what she calls mealy mouthed!'

'I certainly wasn't that,' said Sophie with a grin. 'Quite the opposite.'

'Good for you. Tell me, do you know Helford well?' She watched carefully and saw the slight stiffening of Sophie's expressive face.

'Not very well,' said Sophie lightly. 'He brings Fanny over once a week to play with my nephew and he takes them out riding another day so I…sometimes see him when he calls. He has been very good to Kit.'

'I see,' said Penelope thoughtfully. Why on earth should Helford do that unless he was interested in Sophie? And if he was interested, why was he still pursuing Lucinda Anstey? He couldn't possibly be intending to offer Sophie a *carte blanche*. Surely not if he brought his niece here and had suggested that she should befriend the girl. Besides, she was not the sort of girl whom a gentleman *would* set up as his mistress. She was plainly of good family and Helford would have to be an utter scoundrel to ruin her. Penelope couldn't believe that of any friend of Peter's.

She chattered on about Helford and came to the conclusion that Sophie was very uncomfortable. Her voice, thought Penelope, was a complete giveaway. Too expressive to hide her feelings.

Tactfully she changed the subject to children, asking Sophie about Kit. 'Is he dreadfully naughty? Or do they really grow out of it? My two-year-olds are frightful at times!'

By the time Penelope left she was convinced that Sophie Marsden was not at all indifferent to Lord Helford. Whether it was love or not Penelope had no idea, but she was sure of one thing: Sophie Marsden would be a far more popular choice than Lucinda Anstey with Helford's friends and his aunt. With the child too, thought Penelope suddenly. She could not for the life of her see Lady Lucinda Anstey permitting the residence of another woman's child under her roof.

'Goodbye, Sophie,' said Penelope. 'Now we have met at last I shall call again and, if you are coming past, please call and see me. I shall send a note over to Lady Maria telling her how much obliged to her I am.'

Her groom put her up into the saddle as though she were made of porcelain and said, 'Best be quick, me lady. Master don't like it if ye're too late.' He swung himself into his saddle and raised his cap to Sophie.

'Oh, pooh!' said Penelope. 'His lordship worries if I'm five minutes late. Come along, Gelert!'

They trotted off and Sophie went back into the house, feeling as though a ray of light had broken through heavy clouds. In her straitened circumstances she had held aloof from most of the local gentry, not wishing to be thought encroaching.

Except for Lady Maria, none of the women had bothered to call on them more than once and there had been no suggestion that they would welcome any further acquaintance. Several of them had sons of an impressionable age and they had made it quite plain that Sophie would not be acceptable. Until, that is, they had found out after Emma's death that she did have some money. Then one or two had called with their younger sons in tow. One lad had gone so far as to offer for her and had been told gently that she would require him to settle half her fortune on Kit.

He had hummed and hawed. Like Sir Philip, he had thought it quite unnecessary. The lad did not need the half of such a sum, surely. He did not know what his mama would think of such an arrangement!

Sophie had suggested sweetly that perhaps he should discuss it with her and renew his offer if the lady approved. He hailed this idea with obvious relief and had not called since. Nor had anyone else, except, of course, Sir Philip, who had tried on several occasions to turn her polite refusal into an acceptance.

She reflected on all this rather sadly as she went back to her polishing. Even as the furniture glowed under her vigorous rubbing so too did the dull ache in her heart deepen. Why had fate put Helford in her path, if only to torment her? *Ah, but he sent you a friend. No doubt he is trying to be a good neighbour.*

For the next week it rained without ceasing. The countryside lay dripping under a grey, sodden sky, an apt reflection of Sophie's depression. She longed to get out of the house and go for a long walk to burn off some of her fidgets, but Thea would not hear of anything of the sort.

'Dear Sophie, you would catch an inflammation

of the lungs, I am persuaded, or a putrid sore throat!' she protested. 'It cannot rain forever after all, and then you may go out again.'

Sophie forbore to comment on the likelihood of its raining until at least Christmas and submitted with a docility which made Thea wonder if she were sickening for something. She had fully expected her erstwhile pupil to don a heavy cloak and boots and be off into the meadows.

Fanny came to play with Kit and they nearly turned the house upside down with their chasing and romping, which served to cheer Sophie up insensibly. Helford's tiger, Jasper, ensconced himself in the kitchen and held Anna spellbound with his tales of the army and Vienna.

He viewed with equanimity little Miss Sophie's presence in the kitchen. She was as good as ever twanged, she was and asked as many questions about his foreign travels and army days as what Mistress Anna did. He noted sapiently that she never asked about the master, but if he happened to enlarge on the more respectable exploits of his noble employer she listened with great attention. A shame and a pity it was that his lordship seemed not to have noticed what a good 'un Miss Sophie was, but had settled with that Lady Lucinda.

The new closed stove was installed with the maximum of confusion and upheaval, but afterwards Anna was like a child with a new toy, hardly daring to cook on it lest its gleaming newness should be sullied.

'Never seen nothin' like it, Miss Sophie, Miss Thea, not in all me days. Why, the fuel it saves on! An' when you think it was his lordship's wood we was buying—well, I can't see where 'is profit's comin' from!'

It occurred to Sophie briefly that perhaps his lordship was trying to ingratiate himself, but it didn't match her knowledge of him. He was not the sort to entice a woman with anything except himself. *He wouldn't have to.*

The rain finally stopped the day before Kit was due to go riding with Fanny and Jasper. He was in tearing spirits all morning, barely able to concentrate on his lessons until Thea had the bright idea of practising French conversation and picked the subject of horses and riding.

'I was surprised at how much he knew, dear,' she confided to Sophie later. 'It just goes to show! He really did very well.'

'Aunt Sophie,' said Kit suddenly over his apple dumpling, 'Why don't you come with us this afternoon? You could ride Megs. She needs exercise. Jasper says she is as fat as butter!'

'Ride Megs?' Sophie laughed. 'She hasn't been ridden for ages. She'd have me off in no time.' Megs was notorious for her dislike of being ridden.

'Oh, do come,' he urged. 'If she is too awful, you could swap with Jasper. He wouldn't mind. He said last week he didn't know why you didn't come.'

Sophie was sorely tempted. She had given up riding the little cob because it seemed so unfair to ride her when Kit could not. In fact, before Helford's offer she had been seriously considering selling her and buying something Kit could handle despite her fondness for the lively little mare. But buying a horse was such a risky business. Unless you really knew what you were doing it was so easy to be cheated. She had turned her back very firmly on the insidious suggestion that she might ask Lord Helford for advice.

There seemed no reason not to go. Helford would not be coming. She could go out with the children and enjoy herself. But not on Jasper's mount. Nothing would induce her to ride one of Helford's horses. If Megs got rid of her, that would be her bad luck.

Kit watched her breathlessly. She was thinking about it! He could tell by the way she rubbed her nose. Aunt Sophie always did that when she was undecided. 'Please?' he said in tones that would have moved a sterner guardian than Sophie.

'Very well, Kit,' she said, smiling, unable to resist his obvious desire for her to share the treat. 'I'll come, but I'll expect you to rub arnica into my bruises later on.'

'Hurray!' yelled Kit. He bolted the remains of his

dumpling and leapt up from the table. 'I'll ask Grigson to get her ready!'

The sound of his flying feet dwindled into the distance.

Thea looked at Sophie. 'Do you really think you should, dear? I mean, if Megs is too lively for you…'

With a wry smile Sophie said, 'I have no doubt at all that I will return with a muddied habit, but the ground is so wet after all this rain that I am more likely to drown than break anything.'

She was not quite so sure when Jasper and Fanny arrived and the little dappled mare was brought around from the stables. Megs had not been out at all for several days and had not been ridden for months. The unaccustomed saddle was obviously annoying her and she was in what might have been charitably described as a fidget, with her nervously flickering ears and rolling eyes.

'Goin' ter join us, are ye, Miss Sophie?' asked Jasper with obvious pleasure. He ran an expert eye over the restless cob. Too much for a lady. 'Better swap saddles, Miss Sophie. I'll ride the mare an' you have old Ben. He's a nice ride.'

'Certainly not, Jasper,' said Sophie firmly. 'If Megs is too resty it's my fault for not keeping her exercised.' She was damned if she'd let Helford have the mounting of her. In any way!

He shook his head, 'Master won't half kill me if'n you gets hurt…'

'Are you going to put me up or not?' asked Sophie crossly. 'Megs will settle once we get moving.' How dare he suggest that Lord Helford had anything to say to which horse she rode!

Jasper bowed to the inevitable and put her up. He had to own that she handled the cob well. Kept a short rein on her and never gave her the least chance to get her head down and buck. And them short-backed cobs could really put you down if they got half a chance. He'd like to see that Lady Lucinda manage as well. Looked good on a well-bred, mannered horse but he'd lay she'd be in trouble on this 'un. Lor', she'd be off so fast it 'ud make yer head spin. That is, if she had the gumption to get on at all!

They set off across the fields towards the river and had a wonderful ride. Megs, after her initial carry on, was so pleased to be out of her stable that she seemed to overlook the shameful circumstance of having a rider and behaved herself so well, only fidgeting with the bit and plunging very occasionally, that Sophie was moved to comment.

'Megs must be getting old. I thought she'd have me off in the mud by now.'

Jasper snorted his disapproval. 'I'd say she's a proper varmint, Miss Sophie! An' if the master could see us he'd have me hide! Still, you handles her proper, I'll say that fer ye.'

They had just turned for home when a series of

hunting cries from the other side of a tall hedge told them that they were about to have company. Jasper pulled up at once. He knew one of those voices at least.

One after the other, half a dozen horses came sailing over the hedge. Most of the riders would have galloped on but one, on a familiar chestnut mare, seeing the little group, pulled up.

Helford was delighted to see his niece and Kit. He had half suggested that they might join his riding party, but Lady Lucinda had been quite taken aback at the idea. She had seemed to think that it would be far too much for the children. They could all ride back together now, that would be quite unexceptionable. Their horses were tired after a long ride. Jasper could escort Kit home and…and *Sophie*!

He had spent the last week trying not to think about Sophie Marsden. Trying to ignore the voice in his brain which whispered her name incessantly. Trying to convince himself that what he felt for her was just a passing fancy and would die as swiftly as it had been born. For a moment he was tempted merely to greet them and then ride on, but his party had followed him over and Kate Asterfield was speaking.

'Hullo, Fanny. Are you going to ride back with us? Do introduce your friends.'

And Fanny was doing the honours, 'Aunt Sophie, this is Mrs Asterfield and Mr Asterfield and Lord Mark Reynolds and Captain Hampton and this is Lady Lucinda Anstey.' She paused for breath. 'And this is Miss Marsden and her nephew Kit Carlisle and Uncle David's tiger, Jasper.'

She looked at Helford a little nervously. 'Did I get that right, Uncle David?'

'Perfectly right, sweetheart. But you didn't need to introduce Jasper. They already know him.' Helford's friends had all managed to keep straight faces at being introduced to his tiger as their social equal. In all conscience he could do no less, even if Lady Lucinda was looking daggers at the child, whether in fury at being introduced to Jasper or being left until last he wasn't sure.

Ned Asterfield was saying, 'Well, we do, of course, but I can't recall that you ever introduced him so politely. Delighted to make your acquaintance at last, Jasper. And yours, Miss Marsden.' He eyed her with an unmistakable approval, which made David's hackles rise. 'I call it most unkind that you four didn't join us this afternoon, don't you, Tom?'

'Very shabby indeed,' said Captain Hampton, smiling at Sophie and Kit. Sophie warmed to him at once. He had a kind face, not precisely handsome, but pleasant and distinguished by smiling grey eyes. He looked more closely at Sophie with a little frown. 'Have we ever met, Miss Marsden? Your face is familiar, but I don't recall your name... Wait! Did not Fanny say this was Kit Carlisle?'

'Yes, sir,' said Sophie quietly. 'If you find my face familiar, then I think that you must have been acquainted with my brother-in-law, Major Carlisle, and met Kit's mother, my sister Emma. We were very alike.' Megs began to sidle and toss her head restlessly, impatient at the delay in returning to her comfortable stall. Sophie soothed her with a gentle hand and murmur.

'Of course! Jock's wife.' Captain Hampton slapped his thigh. 'And this is their son! How amazing to meet you like this.' He rode up to Kit and leant down from his saddle. 'Kit, I am delighted to meet you. Your father was a very close friend of mine and I am proud to meet his son. And how is your mama?'

Kit held his head up proudly and said very steadily, 'I am sorry, Captain, but my…my mother died last year. Aunt Sophie looks after me now.'

Hampton grimaced. 'I'm sorry to hear that. She was a lovely person. Please accept my condolences.' He turned to Sophie. 'So you have him in ward. Surely Strathallen has made some provision, though, in the circumstances.'

David held his breath, but it seemed that Sophie saved her temper for his benefit. To do her justice, Hampton had touched upon the subject far more tactfully than he had.

'Lord Strathallen,' she said calmly, 'has never shown the least interest in Kit's existence. I believe my sister wrote to him and informed him of her husband's death and that they had a child, but he never replied. He did not approve of the marriage.'

'I see,' said Captain Hampton slowly. He looked as though he would have said more, but then exclaimed, 'Well, this is indeed a coincidence. I shall look forward to meeting you again, Miss Marsden. Perhaps you would permit me to ride over one day to call upon you?'

Sophie smiled and said, 'I would be happy to welcome any friend of Jock and Emma's. Lord Helford can direct you to Willowbank House.' Again she steadied Megs, who was beginning to pull at the bit in an attempt to get her head down. Firmly Sophie brought it up again, wondering if she could politely go before the mare really got annoyed. Stopping for any length of time with Megs under saddle was always risky. Besides, she was beginning to feel decidedly nervous about Helford, whose glittering green gaze was boring into her in a very uncomfortable way.

'I'll do better than that,' said David, by no means sure he liked the way Sophie had smiled up at Hampton and aware that he was being ridiculous. All the more so since he had decided to ignore his own inclinations. 'We'll escort you and Kit home now and Fanny and Jasper can ride back with us. It is only a couple of miles further. If that is agreeable to everyone?' He glanced around questioningly, not really expecting anyone to mind.

That was quite enough for Lady Lucinda. How dare Helford suggest that they should go out of their way to escort a shabby, little provincial nobody mounted on a badly mannered farmer's cob? It was beyond anything. And the effrontery of announcing that Helford could direct anyone to her house! Besides which, she did not at all like the way Helford looked at the creature. There was something most unbecoming in such warmth.

'I must confess I am really rather weary and would much prefer to ride straight back, Helford,' said Lady Lucinda in the fragile tone of one who holds herself in the saddle by will power alone.

David looked his amazement. Only moments before she had been challenging them all to jump the last hedge. Good manners forbade him to say anything and he was about to agree to escort her home when Kate Asterfield spoke up.

'I'm a little weary too, Helford. If Miss Marsden will assure me that she does not believe me to be cutting her acquaintance, then I will accompany Lucinda and the rest of you may extend your ride as much as you like.' This was said with a convincing sweetness and gave no hint of the annoyance she felt. *Little cat! Of all the snobbish, ill-bred things to do! If Helford marries Lucinda I wash my hands of him. Ned can visit by himself!*

'Oh, but we should never find our way!' protested Lucinda. Kate Asterfield, she thought, was in need of a good set-down. The only problem was that giving Kate a set-down had a nasty tendency to backfire. As when her mama had commented on the flightiness of so many of the younger matrons and Kate had smiled in that *insincere* way, agreeing that her grandmama had said just the same only the other day.

'If I might make so bold, me lord,' said Jasper. 'If'n you and the other gentlemen is to escort Miss Sophie an' Miss Fanny, there baint no need fer me to come along of ye. I dessay I kin guide the ladies back safe.'

Before Lady Lucinda could open her mouth, Kate had said, 'Heavens! What an honour for us. Helford's tiger to escort two lowly females, neither of whom is a Melville. Come, Lucinda, not even my grandmama could accuse us of impropriety with that escort.'

Helford had the oddest feeling that something he didn't understand was going on here. Kate was looking as though butter wouldn't melt in her mouth, almost as big a danger signal as that peculiar smile Great Aunt Maria had been wearing recently. Lucinda, on the other hand, was glaring at her, the blue eyes hard as ice and a decidedly pinched look about her mouth.

Very embarrassed, Sophie said rather more sharply than she intended, 'There is not the least need for anyone to escort us. If Fanny is to ride back with you, Helford, I am sure that Kit and I will find our way home.'

It was plain to her that Lady Lucinda considered

a little dab of a country nobody far beneath her exalted touch. As for Sophie, she wished Helford joy of his courting. She felt an ache inside at the sight of Helford's chosen bride. Lady Lucinda was the most beautiful girl she had ever seen and only a ninnyhammer would continue to indulge dreams which left her weeping on her pillow each night.

Little fool! Why would he look twice at you when he has her?

Something of her irritation must have communicated itself to Megs, who suddenly flung her head up and down in annoyance. Sophie was quick to get her head up again and shorten the rein before the mare could give more than a token buck.

'Jasper!' said David sharply. 'What the devil do you mean by letting Miss Sophie out on this little varmint? Why did you not swap mounts?'

His tiger did not get a chance to reply. Sophie said rather breathlessly as Megs swished her tail and lashed out, 'Jasper offered and I refused. I am perfectly capable of managing Megs, thank you, Helford! And now it is time Kit and I were getting along. Good day! It was so nice to meet you all. Captain Hampton, Kit and I will be glad to welcome you if you care to visit us.'

'You are not riding back alone on that mare,' said David firmly. 'I at least will come with you.' He felt suddenly nervous at the thought of Sophie riding the flighty mare with only Kit for escort. Anything might happen! He told himself glibly that his concern arose not for personal reasons, but from motives of the most disinterested chivalry. *And since when has disinterested chivalry had anything to say to your dealings with any woman?*

Lady Lucinda bridled angrily, but was careful not to show it. What was Miss Marsden to Helford that he should be so concerned about her safety and offer to mount her? If she could not handle her own cob, then she was certainly not fit to ride one of Helford's well-bred horses. And how dare she give such an intemperate reply to a lord of the realm! Especially after such a forward invitation to Captain Hampton! Brazen little hussy! Obviously her mama's dictum that she must turn a blind eye to his lordship's vagaries held force before as well as after marriage.

Observing her, Kate Asterfield was moved to murmur to Lord Mark that a little temper did wonders for dear Lucinda's looks, did it not? Beautiful, of course—but ever so slightly…inanimate? Lord Mark's imperfectly concealed choke of laughter earned him a chilly blue stare. He straightened his face at once and informed Kate in a pithy undertone that she was born to be strangled, and the sooner Ned attended to it the better.

'Oh, well, then,' said Lady Lucinda, 'let us all go. I am sure I would not care to go home early if you are all set on a longer ride.' She brought her horse up beside Megs and addressed Sophie directly for the first time. 'I vow you are a famous horsewoman. Myself, I prefer a *well-bred* horse to give me a comfortable ride. My papa, Lord Stanford, you know, is always so careful to choose for me.'

Sophie met the faintly patronising blue eyes and replied, 'How very fortunate you are. As a parson and the son of a bishop, mine was always more concerned with selecting an appropriate psalm for me to memorise.'

Lady Lucinda's blue eyes widened. Outrageous! The little hussy had actually dared to imply that the Earl of Stanford was not as good a father as some provincial clergyman! And daring to claim a connection with her betters! A bishop, indeed!

Captain Hampton, riding on the other side of Sophie, chuckled. 'Did he? So, too, did mine, although he wasn't a parson. Tell me, Miss Marsden, when did your sister die? I meant to keep in touch after Jock's death, but with one thing and another I lost track of her and the boy.'

Captain Hampton was being sadly taken in by her airs, thought Lady Lucinda scornfully. She looked Sophie over coolly, noting the well-worn habit and unfashionable hat. No pretensions to beauty either. The nose was decidedly unpatrician. And such dull brown hair! It was curly enough, no doubt owing more to art than nature, but brown! And as for her eyes! Well, if you could decide what colour *they* were, you would be doing better than most. No doubt those preposterous lashes and brows were darkened. Altogether Lady Lucinda could not understand why Helford or any other gentleman should take the slightest interest in this bumptious little provincial.

She dropped back slightly to ride with Helford and was annoyed to see him move up beside Miss Marsden. But before she could push forward to ride on his other side Lord Mark, deserted by Kate, brought his mare up and said, 'Do you care for another gallop, Lady Lucinda? Asterfield and I are going to have one. Do join us.'

'Why, certainly, Lord Mark,' agreed Lady Lucinda and then, as an idea occurred to her, 'Do go on. I shall have to adjust my stirrup.' She bent down and reached under her flowing velvet skirts to fiddle with the leather. 'I will catch you up directly.'

'Can I assist you?' asked Lord Mark politely.

'No, no. *I* am well able to manage for myself,' said the lady, continuing to fiddle. Lord Mark nodded and cantered off to join Asterfield.

Lady Lucinda cast a quick glance around. Kate Asterfield, who obviously had a taste for low company, was actually riding slightly ahead with the groom. How *could* she, thought Lady Lucinda with a slight shudder.

No one was watching. Still bent over, she put a

hand to her hat and drew out a hat pin. Captain Hampton had ridden forward to catch some comment thrown him by Kate. Lady Lucinda saw her chance and spurred her mount as she straightened up. Drawing level with the little cob's hindquarters, she reached over to jab her hard in the rump and quickly swung her own mount out of the way, dropping the pin as she did so.

Chapter Eight

Megs went absolutely mad. With an outraged squeal she leapt forward, got the bit between her teeth, flung her head down and began to buck. Taken completely by surprise, Sophie tried in vain to get the mare's head back up.

'Sophie! Look out!' cried David in horror as he watched helplessly. Swearing, he forced his mare up beside the cob in an attempt to grab her bridle. He was not in time. Sophie had sat the first few bucks firmly, but Megs had taken quite enough for one afternoon. On the sixth buck she gave a peculiarly malicious twist which unseated her rider.

Sophie went straight over her head, landing on her bottom with an audible thump and then lying motionless on the wet grass. Having achieved her goal, Megs took off across the meadow, still bucking and plunging.

David's cry of alarm was almost drowned by the scream of childish terror from Kit who had been trailing behind with Fanny. White with fear, he flung himself from his pony and ran to Sophie. David was already beside her, feeling for a pulse in her wrist. He looked up at the boy and his heart lurched at what he could see in the blanched face and those great hazel eyes. This, then, was what it meant to love someone!

'Aunt Sophie! No!' Kit's voice was shaking and small trembling hands groped for the wrist Helford wasn't holding. Not Aunt Sophie! She couldn't be! God couldn't be so cruel! It was because he had wanted God to take her instead of Mama. God was telling him how wicked he had been to think such a thing.

Under David's suddenly nerveless fingers a pulse beat strongly. 'Thank God!' he whispered huskily. Kit's eyes flew to his face, hope flaring. I have never cared like that about anyone, thought David, as he saw the tears on the boy's cheeks. The thought hit him like a body blow that he did now. He cared about Sophie Marsden in a way he had never even imagined and it was the most frightening thing he had ever known.

He reached over and ruffled the boy's curls, wishing he dared caress those other curls which were now very muddy.

'Just stunned, I think, Kit. All the wind knocked out of her too, I shouldn't wonder.' His voice cracked slightly and Kit stared at him. He nodded.

'Oh, yes. I thought the same as you. My heart nearly stopped!'

He began to pat Sophie's cheeks gently, trying not to think about how soft her skin was. A movement at his elbow made him look up.

Tom Hampton was holding out a silver flask. 'Never move without it, dear boy. Not since the night I got caught out in the rain with a lame horse ten miles from anywhere. Take it and welcome.' David took the flask in a shaking hand and tried to avoid Tom's puzzled eyes.

He could almost hear Tom thinking, wondering what had got into him to be so upset over a fall. She was all right, just stunned, her eyes would open in a moment...so why was he still feeling as though his stomach had parted company with him? As though the whole world had tilted under him, leaving him dizzy and...frightened.

Conscious of Tom's steady gaze, he looked up and said, 'Thank you...I...think she's just winded... I...I...'

His voice trailed off under the dawning comprehension in Hampton's clear grey eyes. The startled disbelief. He reached for control. He didn't want this!

The rest of the party had come up. 'Tom, what happened?' asked Kate.

'Don't know,' said Hampton slowly. 'That little cob went absolutely berserk. Miss Marsden did well to stay on as long as she did. I think she's just stunned.'

Kate went on in a low voice, 'From the look on David's and the boy's faces, I should say they expected the worst.'

'Surely there is no need for dramatics over a paltry tumble,' said Lady Lucinda in rather bored accents. 'Although I do quite see now why Helford felt she should be escorted home. Why, that bad-mannered animal nearly kicked my poor Rufus!'

Kate did not waste subtlety on her this time. 'Lucinda,' she said quietly. 'Hold your tongue.'

At this point Sophie opened her eyes to find Helford and Kit bent over her, the latter with tears on his cheeks.

She smiled up at him. 'Gudgeon! I told you Megs would have me in the mud!'

'It's my fault!' said Kit pitifully. 'Because I was so angry with God!'

Sophie cut him off. 'Fustian! I should have kept a shorter rein on her.'

'Can you sit up, Sophie?' asked David gently, without realising that he had used her Christian name, so used was he to thinking of her that way. 'The ground is very wet. You shouldn't lie here too long. Come. Drink some of Tom's brandy and we'll take you home.'

She blinked at the tender note in his voice and the merest suspicion of unsteadiness in the deep tones.

Why should Helford be so upset? Surely, surely he didn't care for her? And he had called her Sophie, something he had never done before.

While she was still puzzling over his behaviour, Helford slid an arm under her shoulders to support her as she tried to get up but she cried out as pain shot through her. 'My back!'

Suddenly terrified again, David lowered her to the ground, unable to meet Kit's eyes.

'Wiggle your feet!' he commanded harshly. She did so. 'Thank God!'

Ned Asterfield said diffidently, 'Not an expert, of course, Helford, but did you happen to see where she landed?'

David looked at him in withering scorn. 'Right here, of course, you cod's-head!'

'Not what I meant at all, old chap. Which bit of herself did she land on?' explained Ned patiently.

'Oh.' David thought hard. He was so shaken he couldn't think straight.

Fanny answered for him. 'On her bottom, Uncle David. I saw everything!' She cast a fuming glance at Lady Lucinda as she said this. She was sure she had seen her hit Megs as she passed. Not quite sure enough to accuse, but sure none the less. She couldn't understand. Surely grown-ups didn't do mean spiteful things like that?

'Did she, now?' Asterfield nodded. 'Then I should say she's jarred up all the muscles in her back.' He got down and removed his coat. 'Excuse me, young man.' Kit made way reluctantly. 'Lift her up again, David.' He did so and Asterfield put the coat under her. 'Right. Turn her over. Going to feel your back, Miss Marsden. You tell me if it hurts anywhere I touch.'

David watched in mounting possessiveness as Ned's hands moved firmly over Sophie's body. *Don't be a fool! He's only doing what a doctor would do!* He gritted his teeth and clenched his fists in the effort not to strangle his well-meaning friend who was taking such unpardonable liberties with a woman he considered *his* and his alone!

What a fuss about nothing, thought Lady Lucinda scornfully. She might have known the girl would make a to-do over it. Hurt back, indeed! And Ned Asterfield as foolish as Helford!

'Hurt there?' Ned was speaking.

'No.'

'Here?'

'No.'

'Here?'

'No.'

'You can start breathing again, David. Like I said, jarred all the muscles. Did it myself once. Miss Marsden, you'll be stiff and sore for a while. Stay lying down rather than sitting and move around as much as you can without tiring your back muscles. If you must sit, put a cushion behind your back to support it. Er…no riding that cob for a few weeks. You see that she don't, young Kit!' He cuffed the boy's head lightly.

'Not at all!' David struck in. He lifted her carefully to a sitting position.

'Me lord?'

'Yes, Jasper?'

'I've caught the mare—which horse should I put her saddle on? Should be gettin' Miss Sophie home now an' the mare's mighty upset.'

David nodded but said, 'She's not riding. At least not alone. I'll take her up before me on…Ben… isn't it? He's quiet enough.'

Completely ignoring Sophie's protests, he forced her to drink some of the brandy before carrying her to the horse. She was lifted up by Asterfield and Captain Hampton and found herself nestled in Helford's arms, leaning in a position of appalling intimacy against his chest. She tried to sit up straight, but the throbbing ache in her back defeated her; anyway, the brandy that Helford had poured into her so liberally was creating a delicious feeling of warmth and lassitude.

Helford said gently, 'Lean on me, my dear. We'll have you home directly.'

Tears stung her eyes at the unconscious endearment uttered so softly in her ear. How lovely it would be if he truly cared for her and were not just being kind because she had so foolishly allowed

Megs to get away from her. She could feel the hardness of his powerful chest under her cheek, the easy strength of his arms as they held her there. His big frame was a strangely tender cradle for her aching body. She had never felt so safe or cosseted in all her life.

The little group set off at a walk, chatting soberly.

To take her mind off the agreeable sensation of being held in such a tender embrace Sophie smiled down at Kit, who was riding as close to them as he could.

"I'll be all right, Kit. Why don't you and Fanny ride on ahead and ask Anna to draw a bath for me? That will help the stiffness.'

Kit nodded, his voice still too wobbly to use, and looked around. Where was Fanny?

She was off her pony looking at something on the ground.

He trotted back to her and jumped off. 'What are you doing? Hurry up, we have to get Aunt Sophie home!' he said impatiently.

Fanny looked up at him and asked, 'This is where Aunt Sophie fell off, isn't it?'

'Pretty much. Come *on*!' Kit could hardly bear to see the torn-up ground where Megs had bucked.

'Well, look at this!' Fanny held up a long shiny hat pin. 'That Lady Lucinda went past Aunt Sophie just before Megs started bucking. I thought she might have hit her, but maybe…maybe it was this!'

Kit stared in disbelief. 'Why should she do that? Aunt Sophie might have been killed! Are you sure? Why didn't you *say* something?'

'Because I *wasn't* sure!' Fanny flashed at him. 'And Lady Lucinda doesn't like me. If Uncle David marries her it's going to be simply horrid! I'm sure she means to pack me off to school!' She pushed the hat pin into her own hat and said, 'Help me mount, please, Kit.'

Kit was astounded. 'Lord Helford's going to marry her? Why would he want to do a bacon-brained thing like that?' He jumped down and made a stirrup for her with his hands.

'For an heir,' explained Fanny as she vaulted into the saddle. 'I heard the servants talking about it. None of them like her either!'

Kit remounted. 'Then why on earth would Helford bother marrying her? If no one likes her, it's silly!' Kit could not imagine why any sensible chap would want to marry anyone. Except Aunt Sophie, perhaps, or Thea if she wasn't so old. They didn't nag at a fellow. If you stepped out of line they told you and made sure you stepped back in and there was an end of it. And they didn't make spiteful, cattish remarks at other people. Like that Lady Lucinda did to Aunt Sophie.

'Come on,' he said. 'We'd better hurry. Aunt Sophie asked us to ride on and have Anna get a bath ready.'

They pushed their ponies to a canter, quickly

catching and passing the other riders. Kit was thinking furiously. He'd sneak out later to look at Megs's quarters, and if Fanny was right then he'd pay Lady Lucinda out if it was the last thing he ever did. He ground his teeth in rage. How could anyone do such a beastly thing?

Helford watched them go. Kit's face was bleak as the pair raced by them. A nasty shock for the lad, thought Helford, unconsciously tightening his hold on Sophie. He knew exactly how Kit had felt. Never had he felt so helpless in his life, always excepting the afternoon he had met the wretched chit and nearly run her down. His heart was still pounding at the memory. At least he hoped that was the cause.

Gradually, however, he could no longer ignore the fact that his heart was not just pounding because of Sophie's fall. His body was becoming increasingly aware of the glorious sensation of holding Sophie nestled trustingly in his arms. The temptation to rest his cheek, even briefly, against the soft, disordered curls was almost irresistible. His arm about her slender waist longed to hold her in a more intimate embrace, feeling the texture of her skin, not just her shape. Somehow he knew she would be silky smooth, pliant… Oh, God! Yielding! *Stop thinking about it!*

Riding was nigh on unbearable, the pain of his arousal like nothing he had ever experienced. *Think about something else!* He spared a glance for Jasper leading Megs who, if her flattened ears and switching tail were anything to go by, was still upset. What the devil could have set her off like that? He forced himself to consider it. Despite his own reservations about Sophie riding a horse that tricky, he had to admit that she had been handling the mare with great skill. He had been taken by surprise just as much as Sophie when the mare started bucking.

Hampton came up alongside. He cast a knowledgeable glance at Helford, noting that he appeared to be in almost as much pain as his fair burden. Most interesting! He would have a little chat with Kate Asterfield in the near future.

'How are you, Miss Marsden?' He smiled at her kindly. White as a sheet, poor child, he thought.

'A bit sore,' she admitted, understating the matter very substantially. *But terrifyingly comfortable apart from that. Stop it! It's just the brandy! Now you know why Papa disapproved of spirits!*

'Never mind,' he said comfortingly. 'Funny how the mare went off like that. Has she ever done it before?'

'Not like that,' said Sophie, who had been puzzling over it as she lay in Helford's arms. 'I mean, she does buck from time to time. She doesn't really like being ridden. We keep her to draw the gig. But I've never known her to go off like that without a bit of warning. I hope she isn't going to make a habit of it.'

'You don't mean to say you'll ride her again?' This from Kate Asterfield, who had ridden up.

'Like hell she will!' growled David and felt Sophie stiffen in his arms. The thought of Sophie riding the mare again sent extremely unpleasant sensations shooting through his entrails.

'Since she is the only horse I possess, naturally I will ride her again,' she said defensively. 'Something must have alarmed her. Maybe a bee stung her or…or something. Anyway, it is quite my own affair.'

'The devil it is!' exploded David, before he could stop himself. His arms tightened visibly around her, protective, possessive.

Oh, bloody hell! He saw Kate's eyes flicker to Lady Lucinda, riding a few yards away with Lord Mark. Outwardly she appeared to be engrossed in conversation, but she would have to be deaf not to have heard his outburst. Would everyone know what a fool he was making of himself by the time he got Sophie home? First Tom, and now Kate Asterfield and his intended bride?

He went on quietly. 'Sophie, I mean, Miss Marsden, if you could have seen Kit's face! He thought you had been killed for a moment.' *As I did!* 'Think of what the boy will suffer every time you mount that mare.'

Sophie was silent. He was right, of course, but she couldn't bring herself to condemn Megs out of hand. After all, she had never behaved quite that badly before.

Hampton added his mite. 'You must consider that you know, Miss Marsden. Helford does not mean to sound dictatorial. It is just a bad habit that he has picked up somewhere!'

Sophie had to stifle a giggle, despite the pain in her back.

Helford was speaking again. 'Will you at least agree to a swap? Send her over to Helford Place for a while and let Jasper exercise her. See if she does anything like it again. I will lend you a pony to draw the gig. There will be no obligation.' He knew what she was thinking, that people would talk, draw conclusions. 'If you were to call on Great Aunt Maria every so often I think that might silence any wagging tongues. And she would enjoy it.' *As I would.*

'I should accept, my dear,' said Kate quietly. 'There can be no objection to you swapping horses with Helford for such a reason and, if Megs turns out to be too unreliable, then I dare say Helford can put you in the way of replacing her without being cheated.'

David shot her a look of heartfelt gratitude and she smiled slightly before turning to Lady Lucinda. 'What do you think, Lucinda? I should merely think that Helford was being a good neighbour, but of course there is no telling what the minds of the vulgar will invent.'

Lady Lucinda froze. Was Kate Asterfield actually daring to insinuate that *she*, an *Anstey*, could be classed as vulgar? Somehow she managed to bite back the very unladylike response which rose to her tongue and said merely, 'Oh, it is his own business after all. Myself, I should have the horrid brute shot out of hand. I dare say it will come to that in the end.' *After all, the animal must be a dreadful commoner to behave like that over a little prick.*

'No, it won't!' said Sophie fiercely, firing up in defence of Megs. 'If Helford considers her unsafe to ride, then I shall take his advice and not ride her. She is always perfectly well behaved in harness so there is no need to have her destroyed.'

'Then I am satisfied,' said David equably, determinedly ignoring Lady Lucinda's uncharitable remarks. It struck him for the first time that Lucinda's high degree did not necessarily render her an agreeable companion. 'She would not be the first horse to be perfectly reliable in harness and useless as a saddle horse. Would she, Hampton?'

'Hardly!' answered Hampton with an unholy grin. 'When, I should like to know, was the last time anyone put a leg across your chestnuts?'

'Silence, Rattle!' Kate admonished him in mock severity. 'You blaspheme. A leg across Helford's chestnuts, indeed! Why, the mere thought is sacrilege, is it not, Helford?'

'Something very like it.' Helford's deep chuckle rumbled in his chest, sending some very peculiar sensations rippling through Sophie's belly.

'What's that?' asked Ned Asterfield, who had not really been paying attention for several minutes. 'Ride Helford's chestnuts? I wouldn't do that, Kate! Probably react like the cob!' He went on cheerfully, 'Tell you what, Miss Marsden! You swap horses with Helford for a few weeks. Let one of his lads ride your mare. See how she goes. Helford's got more horses than he knows what to do with anyway. He can very well spare one until your mare is sorted out.'

'What an excellent idea, Ned.' Helford's voice was very dry. 'Where would we be without you?'

'Where, indeed?' asked Ned's undutiful wife. 'You great oaf! We decided that ages ago!'

Sophie gave a choke of laughter. It seemed she had little choice. Everyone was taking it for granted that Helford should lend her a horse and undertake to vet Megs for her. The notion of someone taking care of her for a change was immensely appealing. You'd better enjoy it while you can, she thought sadly. Lady Lucinda was simply beautiful with those gleaming curls and sapphire blue eyes. So tall and elegant, too. Why should Helford, who could doubtless have his choice of brides, look twice at a poor little dab of a girl with dull brown hair and eyes which even their owner stigmatised as muddy? *Stop dreaming and get on with your life. You are intended for a spinster aunt, not a wife and mother.*

Helford glanced down at the brown curls resting

against his chest. The little spurt of suppressed laughter gave him a dizzying sense of intimacy. He had a vision, instantly throttled, of those curls resting against his naked shoulder and spreading over his arm, of running his fingers through them and…his overactive imagination had no trouble filling in the rest of the scene.

Looking around for someone to speak to and distract his thoughts, his eyes met Lucinda Anstey's hard blue gaze. A faintly supercilious smile curved her rather thin lips.

'Poor Helford,' she said sweetly. 'Your chivalrous nature must be such a burden to you.'

Kate Asterfield squashed her at once without compunction. 'Dear Lucinda, has no one told you yet that men like to feel chivalrous! It panders to all their baser instincts! And since earlier heroes have accounted for all the dragons, Helford will have to content himself with reforming Miss Marsden's mare for her. A far less dangerous proceeding, especially since Jasper will undertake it.'

'Quite so, Lady Lucinda,' said Helford with another grateful look at Kate. 'At the moment I am feeling a veritable Sir Galahad.' He reflected ruefully that if the legendary Sir Galahad had ever felt like this, then he had been sadly misinformed.

By the time they reached Willowbank House and Sophie had been carried upstairs to her bedchamber by Helford, he was in such a state of frustrated desire that he could barely speak without gritting his teeth. The worst of it was that he was quite certain Tom Hampton had a very fair idea of what he was going through. Not that he would say anything. But that quizzing look was the outside of enough.

Having deposited Sophie on her bed in the fussing care of Thea Andrews and Anna, David gave an inward groan of relief. Never again, he thought. There was a limit to what he could be expected to endure and he had definitely reached it. In future he would avoid Sophie Marsden. For both their sakes.

All he said was, 'I'll leave you in safe hands, Miss Marsden.' *Safer than mine at all events.* 'I'll send another horse over with Jasper and Fanny on Monday. Goodbye. We won't stay now. It is time I got the others home.'

Sophie looked up him gratefully. 'Thank you, my lord. I…I hope this has not caused you any…well… trouble. I think some of your party were a little put out. I…I should not like to be the cause of any un-happiness.' Even if she did dislike Lady Lucinda ex-ceedingly, the girl was apparently as good as betrothed to Helford and could not be expected to like him paying attention to another woman.

Perfectly aware of what she meant, David said firmly, 'You need not concern yourself in the slight-est. The only thing of any consequence is that you rest quietly as Ned recommended. Goodbye.'

He left very quickly, consumed by the knowledge

that he had indeed fallen in love with Sophie Marsden. Had done the very thing he had sworn he would never do. He could almost be glad he was practically honour bound to offer for Lucinda Anstey. If he didn't have to offer for her, he would be in serious danger of committing the crowning folly of offering for Soph—Damn it! Miss Marsden!

He groaned inwardly as he went back downstairs to find his guests awaiting him in the parlour. They were chatting quietly amongst themselves, except for Lucinda, who was wandering about the room, casting a disparaging eye over everything.

'So quaint,' she was saying to Lord Mark as she glanced at the harpsichord. 'I had not thought anyone still possessed such a thing!'

David clenched his teeth. Despite his growing distaste for the idea, he had better offer for Lucinda as fast as possible. In that way he could escape the worst consequences of his idiocy. Being shackled to a woman who could, if she ever so wished, deal him an even crueller lesson than the one Felicity had so generously taught him.

'Is everyone ready?' he asked abruptly. 'Miss Marsden is in safe hands now. We should be going.' Before he was tempted to rush back upstairs and beg her to resign herself to his hands. Before he offered his own heart again for a woman to break.

Chapter Nine

By the following Monday Sophie was feeling a great deal better. Her back still ached like the devil if she tried to do too much and, as Ned Asterfield had predicted, she was more comfortable standing or lying down than sitting, but it had improved. Kit had been rather subdued for a couple of days, but he seemed to have recovered his spirits and had even protested at the idea of selling Megs.

'Sell Megs? But, Aunt Sophie, she's never done that before! At least not like that.' His face was flushed and earnest. 'I'm sure she won't do it again. Please don't sell her!'

Sophie was startled. 'Lord Helford has offered to have Jasper ride her for a few weeks and lend us another horse. If Jasper thinks she is safe, then I shall keep her.'

'She *is* safe!' said Kit.

The discussion was dropped and when Fanny arrived on the Monday she was immediately dragged out to the stables after barely being permitted to greet Sophie and thrust a note into her hand, telling her it was from Lady Maria.

Captain Hampton, who had brought her over in Helford's curricle, laughed as the two children disappeared. 'Some mischief they are brewing! Fanny is up to something, if you ask me. She barely spoke two words on the way over and I thought myself quite a friend of hers. God alone knows what it is and I can only be grateful that I have not been admitted to His confidence. The thought of being implicated in any plot of Fanny's hatching fills me with dread.'

He sat down by the sofa where Sophie was resting. 'How is your back, Miss Marsden? And I should mention that I brought a pony over behind the curricle. Helford insisted. We are to take Megs back with us.'

'Oh, dear. Very well,' she said, putting Lady Maria's letter down unread on the little sewing table beside her. 'It is very kind of you all. I cannot think why you and the Asterfields should have been so concerned. Or...or Helford for that matter,' she went on, flushing slightly.

'No, well, it was only sensible,' said Hampton dismissively. Not for worlds would he have informed Miss Marsden that he and the Asterfields were desperately hoping that Helford could be brought to his senses in time to realise that just because he'd suffered one disappointment in youth, did not mean he had to condemn himself to a loveless match if something better offered.

'Is it?' she asked with a smile. 'I think it is very kind indeed and especially kind of you to come all this way to ask after my back, which is much improved.'

'Not at all,' he said. 'As a matter of fact, there was something I wished to say to you. About Kit.'

'About Kit?' she echoed. 'What do you mean?'

He was silent for a moment. 'How much did you know about Jock's family?'

'Very little,' said Sophie. 'I was only ten when Emma eloped with him. All I knew was that he was a younger son of the Earl of Strathallen and very wild. At least that was what Papa said. And I only heard that because he had forgotten that I was in the corner learning Psalm 51 as a punishment.'

The captain nodded. 'He *was* wild. Strathallen was a fool to disown Jock over his marriage. It was the making of him. Your sister was very good for Jock. He cared for her so deeply that he actually settled down.' He paused and then asked, 'Are you quite sure Strathallen knows about Kit? You may say that Kit is none of his business, but I do have a reason for asking!'

'I believe Emma wrote when Jock was killed,' said Sophie slowly. 'Well, I know she wrote to let him know something about Jock's death. Quite a number of his friends wrote to her, you see, to tell her how it had happened. She…she thought that his father ought to know how they had thought of him…read for himself that Jock had died a hero.' Sophie's eyes filled with tears. 'She actually copied extracts from those letters for that hateful old man and it…it took her *ages* because she wept over them! And he never even acknowledged the letter!'

Angrily she blew her nose hard. 'I am sure she mentioned Kit in the letter. Thea might remember better, you know.'

'I hope you won't think I am interfering,' said Captain Hampton thoughtfully, 'but I believe you should contact Strathallen and remind him of Kit's existence. You see, his eldest son Alastair died two months ago and, as far as I can recall, Jock was next in line, which would mean, of course, that Kit is his heir.'

Had he struck her in the face Sophie could not have been more devastated. 'But that…that means they would take him away! No! Emma would not have wished for that!'

Hampton looked at her white face compassionately. 'Would she have wished him to be denied his birthright?'

'I'm sorry,' said Sophie after a moment in which she regained control of herself. 'That was a foolish thing to say. And selfish.'

'Not at all,' said Hampton gently. 'After all, you have stood as a mother to the boy. Known him from infancy and cared for him. It is hardly surprising that you should view any thought of losing him with abhorrence.'

'What should I do?' asked Sophie. 'How should I go about it? Can you advise me?'

Hampton said diffidently, 'If you wish it, I will discuss the matter with Helford and we will write to Strathallen on your behalf. I did indicate to him today that I intended to mention Kit's grandfather to you. He…er…seemed to think I would be in some danger by doing so.'

He grinned understandingly as he took in Sophie's blush. 'He is a trifle dictatorial, but I assure you there is no one who can be kinder. No doubt he expressed himself badly.'

'If you and Lord Helford would not mind doing so, I would be most grateful,' said Sophie, not feeling in the least grateful. The thought that his paternal relations might assume responsibility for Kit when they had totally ignored his existence for ten years hurt abominably. But it was as Captain Hampton had said, she could not stand between Kit and his birthright even if it were possible.

In the meantime, the subject of their discussion was seated on a pile of hay in the hayloft with his little playmate, doing enormous discredit to his upbringing.

Fanny was staring with undisguised horror at the wooden box he was proudly displaying to her. 'A *rat*! Ugh! Is it alive?' A loud scrabbling from the box informed her that the inmate was very much alive.

'Of course it is! What use would a dead rat be to us?' asked Kit impatiently.

Fanny gave him to understand in no uncertain terms that, whatever his own requirements, a rat was of not the slightest use to her, dead *or* alive.

'Don't be such a nodcock, Fanny! It's not for you!' said Kit, seeing that she was about to decamp down the ladder. 'It's for Lady Lucinda.'

She stared at him, her mouth open. 'For…for Lady L…Lucinda?' She sat down again. 'Why? Do you mean that—'

She got no further. 'Because I looked at Megs the other night after she calmed down and you were right!' said Kit savagely. 'I could see where she had been jabbed with that hat pin! So I caught the rat to put in her bedchamber!'

'H…how?' Fanny was awed.

'Used a sticky trap. Glue, sugar syrup. Made an awful mess of one of Anna's old pots. I had to catch it alive, you see,' explained Kit.

'Er…that wasn't quite what I meant,' said Fanny nervously. 'How are you going to put it in her room?' She had a sinking feeling that she really didn't want to hear the answer to this question.

'Well, you are, of course!' said Kit in surprise, confirming her worst fears. 'You aren't actually scared of a rat, are you?' He conveniently forgot the unaccountable squirming sensation which had assailed him in the region of his belly when he saw the large and ferocious rodent struggling in his sticky trap.

'No, but I'm scared of Uncle David!' lied Fanny.

'Why should he think it was you?' asked Kit.

'Well, who else would do it?' she asked impatiently. 'One of the servants? My great aunt?'

'I wouldn't put it past Lady Maria,' said Kit with a grin. 'She's a great gun! No, really, Fanny. Everyone knows that old houses like Helford Place are always teeming with rats. Why should anyone suspect you?'

'We are *not* teeming with rats!' said Fanny indignantly, justifiably incensed at this slur on her home.

'You must have a few!' argued Kit. 'I'll tell you what. Suggest to a few of the maids that you've heard some scuttlings and squeakings. Ten to one half a dozen of them will have seen a big rat within a couple of days. Then, when no one will be at all surprised, you sneak into her room one night while she's at dinner or something and put it on her bed with a half-eaten apple. With a bit of luck it'll still be there when she comes to bed!'

Fanny thought about it. It was true. Mention a possible rat to even one maid and they would all be seeing things within a few hours. And she did want to pay Lady Lucinda out for hurting Aunt Sophie.

The thought of her face when she was confronted with a large, revolting rat in her bedchamber was simply irresistible.

Seeing her wavering, Kit said cunningly, 'Just think, Fanny, if you're scared of it, she'll be even more scared!'

'She will?' Fanny found the idea that anyone could possibly be more scared than herself hard to swallow.

'Well, of course!' said Kit. 'To start with, she's a coward. Only a coward would have played that trick on Aunt Sophie. And she won't be expecting it!'

Nothing, thought Fanny, could be more certain than that! But she rather liked the implied compliment that Kit didn't think her a coward.

'Besides,' said Kit on a note of inspiration, 'If she thinks the place is teeming with rats, she won't want to marry Helford!'

Even if Fanny hadn't already made up her mind that would have taken the trick. 'Can you catch a few more?' she asked hopefully.

Kit grinned. 'I knew you'd do it! Have you still got the hat pin?'

'Yes, I thought I'd better keep it as evidence,' said Fanny.

'Good. Give it back to her.'

'Whatever for?' Fanny was very surprised.

'To let her know you're on to her,' explained Kit. 'Then even if she does suspect you, she won't dare say anything to Helford. Give it to her in front of as many people as possible and say she dropped it the other day. No need to say when. Just say you saw her and kept forgetting to return it.'

'You think of everything!' said Fanny, simply lost in admiration.

Kit had the grace to blush. Never before had a female gazed at him in quite such approbation and it was really rather nice, he was rapidly discovering.

'Well, I don't want you getting into trouble,' he said roughly. 'Now mind, if they do bubble it, you tell Helford at once that it was my idea and that I gave you the rat!'

'We Melvilles,' said Miss Melville in lofty tones, 'don't rat on our allies. I mean, we don't give them away!'

'And we Carlisles,' said Master Carlisle in even loftier tones, 'don't leave our allies in the lurch!' He looked at her seriously. 'If Helford does work it out, don't you dare try to stand buff! I won't have it! That's *my* rat and I won't have you pinching all the credit! Promise!'

Immensely moved by this touchingly expressed concern for her safety, Miss Melville gave her word, reflecting as she did so that Great Aunt Maria could be counted on to stand her friend in an emergency. Especially if it involved a rat in Lady Lucinda's bedchamber. Fanny was tolerably certain that Great Aunt Maria liked neither Lucinda nor Lady Stanford.

The sound of hooves on the cobbled yard made the pair of them scramble to the edge of the loft and peer over. A strange groom was leading in an old black hunter.

'Hullo,' said Kit.

The groom looked up and grinned at the two faces. 'Afternoon, young master and mistress.'

'Whose horse is that?' asked Kit.

'Lady Darleston's horse.'

'Oh,' said Fanny. 'She's nice. Even Great Aunt Maria likes her.'

Quite unaware of the high approval bestowed on her, Penelope Darleston was greeting Sophie. 'I only heard this morning. Are you all right?' She looked at Sophie questioningly. 'It must have been a rattling fall. You're still terribly white.'

Sophie hesitated for a moment and then said, 'It's not just that.' She turned to Captain Hampton. 'I would like to tell Lady Darleston if you have no objection.'

'None at all,' he said.

The news made Penelope's jaw drop in surprise. 'Goodness! How amazing! And that wretched old man has ignored Kit's existence? But that's impossible. If the estate's trustees find out, he would be liable for an action at law. He can't be that vindictive, surely! You'd better find out quickly, Captain Hampton.' She smiled at Sophie, 'Well, that's good news, then. Why the long face?'

'What if Strathallen decides to remove Kit from

my care?' asked Sophie miserably. 'I…I know it's selfish but…but…I just can't—'

Penelope interrupted, 'Of course you can't! Did your sister leave a will?'

'Yes,' said Sophie. 'She left everything to Kit.'

'Did she name a guardian?' asked Penelope intently.

'Well, me, of course,' said Sophie. 'There was no one else. I…I have a deed of guardianship.'

'That's that, then,' said Penelope triumphantly. 'I doubt there's anything Strathallen can do to remove Kit from your charge. If he tries Helford would support your claim, I'm sure, and I think I can safely guarantee that Peter would also back you up.'

Sophie heaved a sigh of relief. 'I never thought of Emma's will. And now I think of it, Jock's will named her as Kit's sole guardian. He specifically cut his family out at the time.' Her lovely smile transformed her face. 'Thank you, Penny. I…I never thought to find such good friends.'

'Now,' said Penelope, 'I heard about your accident because Lady Maria sent a note over this morning inviting us to dinner next week. Apparently Helford is inviting quite a number of locals.' She grinned at Sophie. 'Quite apart from saying you had taken a tumble, she also wrote that she is inviting you to dinner the same night.'

'*What?*' Sophie felt as though she had been invited to her own execution rather than a dinner party. 'No! I couldn't possibly go!'

Penelope nodded, 'I see.' With an inward smile she recalled Lady Maria's note,

No doubt the silly chit will refuse to attend. I'm relying on you to nip any such intention in the bud...

There was no need, of course, to tell Sophie that so she just asked, 'Could you tell me why not? I mean, Lady Maria will be terribly disappointed.'

Captain Hampton said thoughtfully, 'That must be the invitation there.' He indicated the forgotten note Fanny had thrust at Sophie before being hustled out by Kit. 'Lady Maria gave that to Fanny just after breakfast and told her to be sure not to forget it. Maybe you should read it.'

Sophie picked up the letter, broke the seal and read.

My dear Miss Marsden,
Take pity on a poor old woman beset with a lot of boring house guests and accept an invitation to dinner on Tuesday next. We are inviting a number of residents, including that rake Darleston and his baggage of a wife Penelope so you will not lack for agreeable company. We will expect you at 5:30. I am sorry to hear that you parted company with your mare. Fanny was very put about by it, as was Helford.
Your affectionate friend, Maria Kentham

Despite herself Sophie was tempted by the invitation. But it was not to be thought of. The less she saw of Helford the better and if, as was likely at a dinner party for the locals, he announced his betrothal to Lady Lucinda that night she did not wish to be in the room. It would be unbearable.

Resolutely she looked at Penelope and said quietly, 'No, I would very much prefer not to attend. I…I have nothing suitable to wear and, besides, I refuse to drive myself up to Helford Place for dinner in a gig. Old Grigson who looks after Megs for me is not up to driving at night.'

Unfortunately Penelope demolished these very cogent reasons in no time. 'Oh, pooh! We shall go up to your chamber presently and look something out and as for driving up in a gig; it would be most ineligible! Darleston and I shall be delighted to take you up.' She turned to the Captain. 'Please tell Lady Maria that Miss Marsden is delighted to accept her kind invitation and is looking forward to it very much.'

Left with no room to retreat or manoeuvre, Sophie capitulated. She could not bring herself to tell Penelope, even privately, her real reasons for not wishing to attend, so she permitted herself to be whisked upstairs. She even became mildly enthused as Penelope opened her armoire and chest to find an old gown of Emma's in amber silk, which she held up against Sophie with a cry of triumph.

'This is it! It will look lovely. Just the right colour for your eyes and hair.'

Sophie flushed scarlet. 'If anyone could tell what

colour my eyes are, I might agree with you,' she said drily.

Penelope grinned wickedly. 'It never hurts a man to be kept wondering. Even if it's only over the colour of your eyes.' She giggled, a naughty, chuckling ripple. 'Besides, if he can't decide what colour they are, he'll gaze into them all the longer!'

Before she could stop herself Sophie said, 'Lady Maria refers to you as a *baggage* in her letter. I begin to see why!'

'Does she?' Penelope giggled again. 'You should hear what she calls Peter!'

'That rake Darleston..?' quoted Sophie with a twinkle. Penelope nodded and they collapsed on to the counterpane in fits of laughter.

The gales of laughter which echoed through the chamber were faintly audible downstairs. Anna, chopping vegetables in the kitchen, smiled grimly to herself. That Lady Darleston certainly had a way with her. And thank God one of the local ladies had decided to give Miss Sophie a bit of a hand. Bout time it was.

Tom Hampton, idly flipping through a book in the parlour, smiled as well. Do the poor girl good to have a bit of fun. He wondered what Helford would say when he heard that Miss Marsden was invited for dinner. Tom had a sneaking idea that Helford was more than a little confused. He had decided he wanted one thing and gone all out to get it. Now he was presented with something else and he wanted that too. Well, he'd have to make a choice because he certainly couldn't have both. At least he could, but Tom Hampton didn't think David Melville the man to take a girl like Sophie Marsden if he wasn't offering marriage. Too shabby by half that would be!

Lady Lucinda would be very put out, thought the Captain. He grinned to himself. He found that he could bear the prospect of Lady Lucinda's discomfiture with great fortitude. It occurred to him that, if he and Kate Asterfield handled things carefully, they might be able to ensure Helford had no opportunity to offer for Lucinda Anstey or in any way commit himself before that dinner party.

Seeing the two women together in company and realising that all his friends, not to mention his aunt, liked Sophie, might just tip the balance, he mused. He was fairly sure that in issuing an invitation to Miss Marsden, Lady Maria was sending a clear signal of approval to her unexpectedly obtuse nephew.

At this point in his cogitations Sophie and Penelope returned. They chatted away merrily until it was time for Captain Hampton to take Fanny home. She and Kit were extracted from the stables where they were found admiring Penelope's horse Nero, a hero of Waterloo, the groom had told them.

'Home, young lady,' said Hampton sternly.

'Before your uncle has a search party out after us and accuses me of kidnapping you. Miss Marsden, I will see to that business for you as soon as possible. Lady Darleston, your most obedient servant. Kit, I shall look forward to making your better acquaintance on another occasion.'

He swung Fanny up into the curricle and drove out of the stable yard in fine style with Megs trotting behind, and if he had had reason to complain of his companion's lack of conversation during the drive over, there was no cause for complaint on the way home. If asked, he would have said ruefully that he had never realised Fanny could be such a little bagpipe. To do him credit, though, he studiously avoided inquiring about the large and highly suspicious bundle upon which she was resting her feet. It was none of his business after all.

When their visitors had left, Sophie and Kit walked back to the house together after duly admiring the little Welsh grey Helford had sent over to take Megs's place.

'He's complete to a shade,' said Kit reluctantly. 'But I'd rather have Megs. Even if she does misbehave. It… it…wasn't her fault, Aunt Sophie!' He stopped, unwilling to say more. It would never do if she found out about the rat.

Sophie looked at him closely. 'You sound very certain, Kit. Is there something you aren't telling me?'

'Yes,' he admitted.

'And you are convinced that it wasn't Megs's fault.' There was no question in the way she spoke.

He nodded.

'Then I'll keep her no matter what Helford says,' declared Sophie.

Kit stared at her. 'Just because I said so. Without even telling you why?'

Her eyes quizzed him gently. 'But of course. Your word is good enough for me, Kit. Just as your father's or mother's would have been.'

His heart swelled with pride to think that his word was believed in this way. Trust Aunt Sophie to know how a fellow liked to be treated. She was as good a gentleman as Helford, who had never pressed to find out who had taught him about tickling trout. He told her so in gruff tones which imperfectly concealed the depth of his affection.

Even the best of aunts, however, is prey to the complaint that killed the cat. Sophie Marsden was no exception. She spent quite a long time that night wondering just what Kit, and, by implication, Fanny, knew. That they were plotting something she was sure. It had not needed Captain Hampton's remarks to tell her that.

What could they have seen? Carefully her mind went back over her fall. Where had everyone been? At last she had it. The only person right behind her had been Lucinda Anstey. If Kit swore that Megs had not been at fault then…the idea was ludicrous…why should she do such a thing? *To make you look no how!*

The answer presented itself with startling clarity. Lady Lucinda, if she had somehow caused Megs's explosion, must have meant for her to look a complete fool. Which confirmed that she resented the attention Helford had paid to her. She must have been as cross as crabs when it backfired, thought Sophie with a reluctant grin. She couldn't possibly have anticipated that Helford would end up carrying her victim home.

Drat the man! Why couldn't he have just left her alone and stayed out of her life? Dismally she thought that the sooner Helford took himself back to London where he belonged, the better. It occurred to her that he might decide to live at Helford Place for much of the year. That she might have to live with him as a neighbour. She couldn't do it. Perhaps if the Carlisles wanted Kit, she could go too. That would be better than seeing Helford and his wife constantly. There would certainly be no joy to alleviate that pain.

Later that evening Helford sat in his library, listening to what Captain Hampton had to say with increasing concern.

'You think Kit is the heir?' He was incredulous. 'Are you sure?'

Hampton shrugged. 'Of course I'm sure. You don't think I would have told Miss Marsden if I weren't, do you?' He poured himself a brandy. 'Look, David, Jock Carlisle was a very close friend of mine. I stayed with his family once or twice and I'm as sure as I sit here that Kit is Strathallen's heir.'

'Good God!' said David blankly. 'What did Sophie… Miss Marsden say?'

'She was horrified,' admitted Hampton. 'Seemed to think Strathallen might try to remove the boy. Which is very possible. He disinherited Jock for marrying Emma Marsden, after all.'

'He might try, but he won't get away with it!' said David fiercely.

Hampton grinned. 'That's much what Penelope Darleston thought,' he said. 'She felt that you could be counted on to support Miss Marsden and even pledged Peter's backing.'

David nodded. He couldn't stomach the thought of Sophie losing Kit to a vindictive old man who had refused to acknowledge the lad's existence all these years.

He sipped his brandy. 'You told her we would write to Strathallen? Good. I'll do it now and you can add your signature to mine in the morning. Have you got the old man's direction?'

Hampton was rather taken aback. 'Er…aren't you joining the ladies in the drawing room?' He had pulled Helford aside as they left the dining room after the port.

'No,' said David in a tired voice. 'Make my apologies, Tom. Say something urgent came up and that I must get this letter off first thing. It's true enough. Besides…well…I need to do a bit of serious thinking.'

Hampton looked at him sharply, but said nothing beyond, 'Just as you like but, you know, Lady Lucinda won't like it!'

'No, I don't suppose she will,' agreed David, still in that weary tone.

Hampton left him, but turned back at the door to say, casually, 'I like your Miss Marsden, David. She's as gallant a lass as you'd meet, isn't she?'

David just nodded with a rueful smile. The door clicked shut. *Trust Tom to spot it!* He wondered how many others had realised his attraction to Sophie Marsden. Kate Asterfield, no doubt. Ned? Lord Mark? Most unlikely. That pair rarely noticed anything beyond their dinners and horses. Well, that was a little unfair. Ned certainly noticed his wife. But that was probably because she made quite sure he remembered her existence.

Lucinda? Certainly. That would account for the way she had behaved, although he was surprised to find that she could feel jealousy. Justifiably expecting an offer from him, she had no doubt been miffed at his behaviour. He couldn't blame her.

At last he faced the fact that he had been trying

to avoid for over a week. He had to offer for Lucinda quickly before his passion for Sophie led him into the snare he feared. Before he lost control of himself and rode over to Willowbank House and begged her to marry him. And what he felt for Sophie was a far cry from the youthful infatuation he had succumbed to with Felicity. This was the most terrifying emotion you could possibly imagine. That appalling fear when he had thought her dead. The fury that consumed him when Sir Philip's importunities recalled themselves to his memory. More than ever it confirmed his notion that to care too deeply was dangerous. That he would be better off, safer, if he never saw her again. If he allowed his passion to die a natural death.

A marriage of convenience, wasn't that what he had wanted? A well-bred wife who would cause no scandal. A wife who would make no demands on him, who would turn a blind eye when he sought his amusements outside her bed.

And, after all, Lucinda was a very attractive woman, he told himself. One who conducted herself with the right degree of maidenly modesty. With breeding. She had been brought up to know his world and her place in it. There would be no surprises there. She'd certainly never rip up at him about his morals as Sophie had!

But she's so...so cold. He could not dismiss the thought, and groaned. Surely once they were wed she would thaw out somewhat. Surely with all his skill and expertise he could…seduce her?

Perhaps. If you wanted to… Frankly, the idea left *him* cold. Somehow the words *seduce* and *Lucinda* did not seem to belong in the same world, let alone the same thought.

For the first time he wondered just how Lady Lucinda would take to her marital duties. Unfortunately, his imagination was not even remotely interested in speculating on the possibilities. With difficulty he conjured up an image of her elegant figure, white skin and silky black curls. He was rewarded with not the slightest twinge of desire. Determinedly he thought about kissing her, but again his imagination refused to cooperate.

That might have been due to the fact that it was unceremoniously thrust aside by his memory, which interposed the remembrance of Sophie melting in his arms and that little moan as her mouth opened under his… For a moment Helford allowed himself the pleasure of this recollection and felt more than a twinge of desire and guilt. He was tolerably certain that Sophie was not in the least indifferent to him. She was not a wanton, could not possibly have responded to him like that had she not cared.

Worse than his own misery was the knowledge that he had hurt her. That she would continue to think he had amused himself with her innocence. That she had been nothing to him.

Grimly he faced the fact that for him his memories could hold no joy, only a bitter cynicism. He had recognised love far too late. He told himself that, had he been able to gaze into the future after their first meeting, he would have ensured that he never saw her again. Because now he would have to banish Sophie Marsden from his thoughts completely.

Perhaps, he thought in resignation, I should try kissing Lucinda. Maybe that would banish these... these fantasies. *Tomorrow, then. Surely she won't be too shocked. After all, she must be expecting an offer.*

It occurred to him that she might reasonably expect the offer first and the kisses later.

Or not at all.

Resolutely he thrust his cogitations aside and concentrated on writing a letter to an elderly Scottish peer which combined tactfulness with clarity of expression and in no way hinted at the writer's opinion that Strathallen was a curmudgeonly old fool.

Chapter Ten

Having made his bitter decision, David found that over the following week he had no opportunity to be alone with Lady Lucinda Anstey. Tom Hampton and both the Asterfields seemed to be afflicted with an incredible lack of tact. Kate in particular appeared to have a hitherto well-concealed predilection for Lady Lucinda's company and sublimely ignored all hints to make herself scarce. Nearly all hints, anyway. On the few occasions when David managed to get rid of Kate, Aunt Maria turned up and was impossible to shake.

Tom Hampton and Ned were also extremely demanding of his time. Both of them had developed a bloodthirsty urge to rid his estate of rabbits and were constantly dragging him out to shoot at the hapless creatures with the result that rabbit was appearing on the menu rather frequently.

By the time he was dressing for dinner on Tuesday night he had not had even the smallest opportunity to kiss Lady Lucinda. Nor had he offered for her, which he had told himself he ought to do.

To the immense disapproval of his valet, David dressed for dinner with unseemly haste. It was not that the result was anything less than perfection, thought Meredith grudgingly. It was just that these things ought to be done properly and haste could lead to slovenliness, a tendency to be heartily deplored. He firmly suppressed his horror as his master even hurried over his cravat, taking twenty minutes where usually half an hour was considered quick.

The reason for this callous assault on Meredith's sensibilities and professional pride was simply that David had asked Lady Lucinda to meet him alone before dinner. He was starting to suspect that he was being outmanoeuvred. When the thought first flashed into his mind he had dismissed it, but then all the little things started to add up. Tom and Kate had been as thick as thieves for days past and they had been extremely attentive to Aunt Maria. Ned, he decided, was simply along for the ride. Such strategy was beyond the scope of his kindly, but limited, thought processes. He would, however, be only too happy to fall in with whatever devilry his wife might be plotting. He was terribly proud of Kate's quick brain and hardly ever called her to order.

David reflected on this grimly. Yes, he began to see now. Kate and Tom were orchestrating the whole thing, but why? The answer was not long in

coming to him. They didn't want him to offer for
Lady Lucinda. Now he thought about it, that was
fairly obvious. Damn it all! Did they think he didn't
know his own mind?

So, as he escorted Lucinda upstairs to change for
dinner, he had said, 'Would it be too shocking of
me, Lady Lucinda, to ask you to come down, shall
we say…fifteen minutes early? I should very much
like some private talk with you.'

She had inclined her head graciously. 'I think I
may safely agree to that, my lord, in our situation.'
She accorded him a gracious smile. 'I am sure
Mama will see no harm in it.'

David started. Damn! He didn't want Lady
Stanford to know. Irritably, he realised that this was
precisely what he had wanted in his bride. A well-
bred and virtuous damsel above all gossip. He went
away to his own chamber to violate unthinkingly all
his valet's cherished notions of the way in which a
gentleman should dress for dinner.

Entering her chamber, Lady Lucinda found her
maid there waiting. She glanced at the clock and
realised that she would have to hurry. Her bath was
unwontedly swift, and the maid was shocked at the
haste with which her ladyship arrayed herself in
the gown of jonquil silk laid out for her. Neither did
Lady Lucinda change her mind half a dozen times
over which pieces of jewellery to wear. Her pearl
necklace and matching earrings were chosen

without the least hesitation. Kid slippers and a silk reticule completed the ensemble.

'I will ring for you when I come up to bed, girl,' said Lady Lucinda coldly. She had the greatest dislike of her maid waiting for her in the evenings. Why, once she had found an impertinent servant actually asleep on her daybed. Without even waiting for Betsy's respectful curtsy, she sailed through to her mama's bedchamber.

Lady Stanford was still in her petticoat and chemise.

'Not that dress, girl! Lilac, I said! Cannot you see that one is mauve? Stupid wench!'

In very different tones, 'Lucinda! You are very early!'

Her daughter looked significantly at the hapless maid who was clutching two dresses of identical colour with a countenance devoid of all expression. Lady Stanford took the hint at once.

'Take yourself off, girl. I wish to speak to Lady Lucinda. Wait in the sitting room!'

The maid bobbed and removed herself, wondering if she could get another position. She'd gladly take a drop in status and wages to find a more pleasant mistress.

'Helford has asked me to come down early, Mama,' explained Lucinda. 'You do not object?'

Lady Stanford gave it some thought. No doubt Helford wished to offer for Lucinda privately. That was not how it had been done in her young days, but one must move with the times. It was not surprising that he should wish to see her alone. She could depend upon Lucinda to keep the line.

'No, my dear. You may do so. But I would be failing in my duty as your mother if I did not drop a word of warning in your ear. He may well attempt to kiss you! You must not repulse him. Nothing could be more fatal! I say this only to warn you not to allow your instincts as a lady to rule you. Nothing could be more natural than that you should find it excessively distasteful, I do myself, but you must not flinch. Such a thing would be very bad! A lady does not shrink from her duty and you would not wish to give Helford any cause to think you would be less than dutiful.'

'No, indeed, Mama,' agreed Lady Lucinda and after some more of her mama's advice, all of which made it perfectly plain why Lord Stanford had, since the moment of his marriage, sought the consolation of a string of mistresses, Lady Lucinda Anstey descended the stairs to the Green Drawing Room.

David was before her and he looked up with raised eyebrows as she entered the room. It would not have surprised him in the least if Lady Stanford had been with her daughter, but to his relief Lady Lucinda was alone. As she came across the room he told himself that she really was very lovely—those blue eyes were quite extraordinary and her figure was excellent.

'At last, Lucinda,' he said with a forced smile, dropping her title for the first time.

Her eyes widened, but she reminded herself that it was quite the thing for a gentleman to assume a more informal manner with his intended, at least in private. The way Darleston always used his wife's Christian name among friends was, she considered, most unseemly.

'Good evening, Helford,' she responded to his greeting.

He held out his hand to her with a slight lift of his black brows. With all the dignity of an aristo going to the guillotine, she placed her hand in his and allowed him to draw her into his arms. It was not too distasteful, she thought. He had put one finger under her chin and was pushing it up slightly. His mouth covered hers and moved in a very peculiar way while his free hand moved over her back and urged her to stand closer. Obediently she did so and was rather surprised when he moved one of her arms to encircle him. Surely he did not expect her to embrace him! She did not move the arm, but certainly its fellow did not join it.

David was finding Lucinda's lack of response most disconcerting. It was not merely a lack of response, he thought, as he moved his lips over hers as seductively as he could. It was a complete lack of interest. Even disgust would be better than this ice-cold submission. At least that would be something with which to work. To make matters worse his body, which had ignited just holding Miss Sophie Marsden, categorically refused to work up the slightest spark of enthusiasm for the far lovelier siren he was providing for its pleasure. He thought whimsically that if his body could have yawned, it would have!

Determined to try a little harder, he allowed the hand caressing her back to move around to the front, or rather, since it had showed no interest in doing so, he put it there and cautiously essayed to sample one breast. That did get a reaction. Lady Lucinda opened her mouth, to which David responded by reluctantly pushing his tongue inside and sweeping it across the roof of her mouth.

Unfortunately Lady Lucinda had only opened her mouth to request Helford to keep his hands to himself and his disgraceful invasion revolted her to the core. Her blue eyes opened wide in shock and she could not repress a shudder of revulsion. It was only with great self-control that she did not break away from his hold. He was releasing her anyway and seemed about to say something when the door opened to admit Lady Maria.

Lady Maria cursed mentally as she saw the two alone by the fireplace. *Damn! Hope I'm not too late. Might have known he'd try to get down early. Thank God Kate told me Lucinda was down.* By the look of things she'd interrupted something. That chit was looking as close to discomposed as she'd ever seen her.

'Good evening, Aunt Maria,' said David awkwardly. He was not sure whether he was furious or relieved at her appearance. Having kissed the girl, he had intended to offer for her, but his aunt's arrival had put paid to that.

'Helford, Lucinda.' She stalked across to her accustomed chair and her nephew at once handed her into it. Sitting down, she said, 'I beg your pardon for not being down before you, Lucinda. I trust Helford has kept you tolerably well entertained.' Her eagle gaze did not miss the way Lady Lucinda stiffened as she responded.

'Yes, I thank you. But I was early. You must not blame yourself, Lady Maria.'

'And where's your mama?' she continued. 'Not at all the thing for a chit to come down alone with a rake like Helford. Lord, girl, don't you know his reputation?'

The look of utter distaste frozen on Lucinda's lovely mask was balm to Lady Maria. She'd lay anyone handsome odds that Helford had been kissing the girl and she hadn't liked it above half. Good! That would put Helford off if nothing else did. He was the sort of man to like 'em willing. He wouldn't like the idea of sharing his bed with a wench who only entered it on sufferance.

'Thank you, Aunt Maria,' said David coldly. This

was going too far! 'Perhaps we could leave my reputation out of it.' What the devil was the old lady up to? Anyone would think she was trying to put Lucinda off. Which seemed, he thought, to be a work of supererogation. Not that Lucinda had repulsed his advances exactly, but he had received the distinct impression she would have liked to do so.

Perfectly satisfied with Lucinda's reaction to her comment, Lady Maria went on as though no one had spoken. 'Well now, who's coming this evening? Let me think. The Darlestons, of course, and Sir Philip Garfield. Someone else…oh, yes, the Vicar and his wife…now, who else…ah, here is Mrs Asterfield. Good God! Does she call that thing a gown?'

Lady Maria raised her quizzing glass the better to survey Kate Asterfield's nearly transparent pink silk gown. It was plain that whatever she was wearing beneath it did not constitute any protection at all against the chill of the room.

'Humph! Well, it may not warm her,' observed Lady Maria acidly, 'but I can guarantee it'll warm Asterfield! Wouldn't you say, Helford?'

Lord Helford, completely forgetting his company, was moved to reply in tones of great appreciation, 'Not a doubt of it, Aunt Maria!' There was a slight movement beside him. Lady Lucinda had taken a very definite step away. He looked at her and surprised a look of utter scorn on her face.

He frowned slightly. Kate's gown was outrageous, he supposed, but damn it! She and Ned were his friends and it was as plain as a pikestaff that Lucinda disliked her intensely. And that was another thing that concerned him, apart from the fact that Lucinda had relished his attentions not at all. It would be deucedly uncomfortable if she disapproved of all his friends. *Oh my God! It's a bit late to think of all this now!*

Kate's greeting interrupted his thoughts. 'Really, Helford! Why can't you keep your rooms properly heated?'

He grinned at her and said most improperly, 'We do. Would you like me to find you some clothes? I'd give you my coat, but then Aunt Maria would accuse *me* of being indecently garbed.'

Lady Maria gave a crack of laughter, but Kate just twinkled up at him.

'Never mind, Helford, I can assure you that I won't remain cold for long!'

Disgusting, thought Lady Lucinda. The woman was shameless! No doubt she was trying to ensnare Helford! Well, if it kept him from taking those foul liberties with her more often than was necessary for the begetting of an heir, then she would gladly look the other way when he strayed!

Lady Maria was speaking again. 'My memory's not what it was, Mrs Asterfield. I can't remember who's joining us tonight.'

'Oh, the Darlestons, didn't you say?' responded

Kate helpfully. 'And the local Squire, Sir Philip Whatsit? Did you say something, Helford?' A disgusted snort had erupted from her host. 'Now let me think. Oh yes, that charming girl who fell off her mare last week.' She smiled brightly at David. 'Miss Marsden, is it not?'

David stared from her to his aunt and said in a constricted voice, 'Sophie Marsden is coming tonight, Aunt Maria?' He was aware of Lucinda Anstey's gasp of shock from behind him, but Lady Maria's reply was lost as the gentlemen of the house party came in together with Lady Stanford.

Ned Asterfield lived up to everyone's expectations by exclaiming when he saw his wife, 'I say! That's a devilish pretty gown, m'dear. I like that!'

Lord Mark and Tom Hampton merely looked their appreciation at Kate, who ignored them as she bestowed a glowing smile upon her husband.

'Dear Ned, you always say the right thing! Helford practically told me to go and put my clothes on.'

Ned Asterfield just grinned and said, 'You leave me to worry about my wife, old boy. Time enough for you to tell a wife what to do when you've got your own.' Clearly unconscious of having said anything in the least untoward, he looked around and said, 'No one else here yet?'

At this moment the door opened and the butler announced, 'Sir Philip Garfield. The Reverend Mr Henshaw and Mrs Henshaw.'

David eyed Garfield with disfavour and pointedly greeted the Vicar and his lady first. He had not been able to veto Sir Philip's inclusion in the dinner party without telling his aunt just why he had taken such a dislike to the man. Any other man, he thought disgustedly, would have politely declined the invitation.

Not Sir Philip, who entered the room with a slight swagger, sure of his welcome. He had come to the conclusion that Helford had been under the mistaken impression that Miss Sophie would accept a *carte blanche*. By now he would have discovered his mistake. Miss Marsden's unwillingness to receive his own suit he put down to her expectation of a more respectable offer from Helford. She was far too unworldly to realise that a man of Helford's rank did not offer marriage to a little country nobody. Even if he wasn't betrothed to the daughter of an earl. By gad, the wench was lucky *he* was prepared to offer marriage.

So he greeted his icy host with all the bonhomie of a man who had not recently been laid low by the host's punishing left. 'Ah, Helford. We meet in more gracious surroundings. I fancy our little misunderstanding is all cleared up?'

David permitted himself a frosty smile. 'I am afraid any misunderstanding of the situation was on your side, Sir Philip.'

Before anything more could be said the door opened again to admit the final guests.

'The Earl and Countess of Darleston, Miss Marsden.'

David moved forward to greet them, scarcely able to take his eyes off Sophie. Shimmering amber silk clung to her lissom body, the perfect foil for her creamy complexion and complementing golden highlights in the simply arranged curls. It was years out of fashion with its crossover bodice and raised waist and, compared to the jewellery worn by the other women, her ivory beads were mere trumpery, but she carried herself proudly as if she were dressed like a princess.

His greeting to Peter Darleston and his wife was disjointed to say the least, which brought a twinkle of amusement to the Earl's eye. Resignedly David wondered just *who* had told Peter *what*. It didn't bear thinking about. Gritting his teeth for control, he turned to greet the woman he both wished miles away and, at one and the same time, locked irrevocably in his arms.

Sophie felt absolutely terrified. Never in her life had she been in a room like this. Its grandeur and formal elegance overwhelmed her. She wished desperately that she had not come. There was Lady Lucinda looking as scornful as ever and an older lady who must be her mother.

She dragged her attention back to Helford. He was greeting her.

'What a pleasant surprise, Miss Marsden.' His

voice cracked slightly. Seeing her like this just as he was about to offer for Lucinda was shattering. His heart was like lead in his breast, all his resolution destroyed.

'A…a surprise?' A puzzled frown creased her brow. 'Did…you…did you not invite me?' For a horrible moment she wondered if she had misread the note from Lady Maria.

'Aunt Maria did not mention your name to me until just now,' he said in some constraint. And could have kicked himself when he saw her reaction.

Her dark eyes widened as her cheeks flushed crimson 'I…I beg your pardon, my lord. I assumed you were aware…' She floundered to a halt.

Oh, God! She thinks you don't want her here! There was nothing he could say to reassure her even if they didn't have an audience. Because in some ways it was true. Had he known in time he would have confided in his aunt and begged her not to invite Sophie. He could only repeat inadequately, 'A pleasant surprise. Come and talk to my aunt and be presented to Lady Stanford.'

Sophie greeted Lady Maria with real pleasure. The old lady tapped her on the cheek with her fan. 'Pretty colour. That gown suits you and at least there's enough of it to keep *you* warm. I fancy you know most of the others here. Ah! Aurelia, this is Miss Sophie Marsden. Sophie, this is Lady Stanford.'

Lady Stanford was very cool. She had heard an edited version from Lady Lucinda of the riding accident and considered it very likely that the scheming chit had engineered her own fall. She had said as much to Lucinda. Now, as she looked Miss Marsden over, she could see precisely why her daughter had considered the girl ill bred. That nose! Freckled! And the gown! It was positively archaic! No one with the least pretension to fashion would wear such an outmoded creation. And the way she held herself as though she were quite as good as her betters. Daring to come in with the Darlestons as though she were a member of their party!

Determined to show this little nobody the gulf that lay between the aristocracy and an encroaching little mushroom, she extended two languid fingers, uttered a brief, 'How do you do?' and turned away without waiting for an answer.

Lady Maria chuckled silently to herself. This was better than a play! David was quite obviously upset. Just far enough off balance to forget his manners and do something foolish for a change!

Lady Lucinda came up to Sophie and said with spurious interest, 'And how is your back, Miss Marsden? I do trust that Helford's services won't be required tonight.' She smiled sweetly at the look of embarrassment on Sophie's face. 'No doubt you find Helford's horse far better mannered than your, er…cob.' She could almost be said to have smirked.

This was too much! Sophie pulled herself together and replied with the utmost charm, 'He is very well mannered. And since you mention the incident, I do hope you had sufficient time... er...*left* to pull your own mount out of the way.' Her eyes rose challengingly to Lady Lucinda's.

Lady Lucinda stared at her in sudden doubt, but at that moment Miss Fanny Mclville was escorted into the room by her governess. Sophie could see at once that she was up to something. The green eyes were just too modestly downcast and she was looking just too innocent. She greeted her uncle and great aunt with pleasure before glancing around the guests.

Her eyes widened and a huge smile of delight transformed her face. 'Aunt Sophie! I didn't know you were coming. How is your back?'

'Much better, thank you,' said Sophie with a twinkle. 'Kit sent his greetings, by the way.' Now, what was there in that to make the child look so smug?

Fanny had turned to Lady Lucinda and was saying in her clear, bell-like tones, 'Oh, Lady Lucinda, I believe this is yours!' She was holding out a hat pin. 'I saw you drop it the other day and kept forgetting to return it.'

'Good God, child!' exclaimed Lady Lucinda impatiently. 'Give it to one of the maids!' Then, as Fanny continued to hold out the hat pin, she said uncertainly, 'You cannot be certain it is mine.'

'Oh, yes,' Fanny assured her, smiling seraphically as her victim whitened. 'I saw you drop it.'

Sophie stared at the smiling child in sudden understanding. So Kit was right! Heavens! No wonder Megs had bucked, having that thing stuck into her. What a pair of monkeys, though, to declare war on Lady Lucinda in this way! In front of everyone! For Sophie had not the slightest doubt that it was a declaration of war. Nothing could be clearer. Fanny Melville had flung down the gauntlet at Lucinda Anstey's satin-slippered feet with a re-sounding clang.

Lucinda took the hat pin and put it in her reticule with a forced little laugh. 'I suppose I must thank you, Fanny.'

'Oh, no,' said Fanny. 'Thanks are not necessary. Good evening.' She cast an affectionate smile at Sophie and said, 'Please tell Kit that he was quite right about the maids and that it will be done just as he wished.'

Sophie agreed to pass on the message with a perfectly straight face.

Lucinda was looking most uncomfortable and Sophie said, as Fanny went to greet Captain Hampton, 'Really, I don't know when I have met a child as bright as Fanny. She is charming, don't you think?'

Still flustered from the realisation that at least two people knew of what she had done and possibly three if, as seemed likely, Miss Marsden's horrid nephew had found out, Lucinda was betrayed into an unwise rejoinder.

'She would be all the better for the discipline of a good school rather than tearing about the countryside in unsuitable company!'

A deep voice behind them said, 'I would hardly consider Kit unsuitable. You do Miss Marsden a considerable injustice in saying so, Lucinda.'

Lucinda turned in consternation. Helford was looking down at her with a dangerous glitter in his brilliant eyes. 'Oh, I meant merely that a girl should be with a member of her own sex. Nothing more.'

'I see. Ah, here is Bainbridge to announce dinner. Miss Marsden, Tom Hampton will take you in. Mine is the pleasure of escorting Lady Darleston. I understand they brought you over. I need hardly say that had Aunt Maria had the sense to tell me she had invited you I would have sent the carriage. As it is, I am glad you did not drive yourself over.' He kept his tone light and cheerful, ignoring the leaden misery in his heart.

The light in his eyes warmed Sophie insensibly and she smiled up at him in relief. 'Naturally when I told Lady Darleston that it was impossible for me to attend if I *did* have to drive in the gig, she agreed that it would not do at all.'

He looked down at her, conscious of the usual desire to take her in his arms. Abruptly he said, 'Here comes Hampton. I shall talk to you later about Kit's affairs.' He turned away to seek his dinner partner, thinking that, despite the undoubted charm of Peter's wife, this was like to be the worst evening of his entire life!

Chapter Eleven

While Sophie was delighted to have Captain Hampton as her dinner companion, finding Sir Philip on her other side was a considerable penance, since he took the first opportunity to lean over and assure her that he would not mind their little misunderstanding.

'No doubt you were misled by the circumstance of Helford's attentions,' he said in an undertone, unaware that he was distressing her deeply. 'But you were not to know how a fellow of his rank views things. Stanford's chit, eh? A very fine young woman and will make him an excellent wife.'

Sophie swallowed a spoonful of the delicious turtle soup which suddenly tasted as though it had been seasoned exclusively with hyssop and wormwood. Would he never give up? She thought despairingly that it would take more than her word to convince him that she would never marry him! Or anyone else for that matter. It would be impossible now to surrender herself to any other man. Helford had seen to that.

She attempted to turn the conversation into more acceptable channels, aware that Lady Maria was not so much taken up by the outrageous flattery of Lord Darleston that she could not hear every word Sir Philip was saying.

Lord Darleston, thought Sophie, was simply delightful. He was every inch a gentleman, but she could see precisely why Lady Maria called him a rake. He would be irresistible to most women if he were not so obviously devoted to Penelope. She had met him for the first time that evening and his easy kindness and good manners had charmed her completely. Penelope was the luckiest of women, she thought.

With Lady Maria he was at his best, teasing the old lady by dredging up some long-forgotten scandal about her family and assuring her that the secret was safe with him.

The old lady snorted. 'Humph! All I can say is it's a good thing that baggage Penelope keeps you in line. You and your flummery!' She turned her attention to Sir Philip. 'And how are you keeping, Garfield?' Better draw his fire from Sophie. Chit was starting to look as though she were about to give him a set-down.

Relieved, Sophie returned her attention to her dinner, accepting a helping of duckling and green peas. She found Tom Hampton's kindly smile a positive Godsend and returned it with interest.

The unshadowed sweetness of her smile at Tom seared through Helford at the end of the table. His heart contracted as though a fist had tightened around it. No. Surely not. It would be appalling to see her married to Tom. *Better than Garfield!* He was surprised to find that the thought of Tom Hampton pursuing Sophie was almost as offensive as Garfield. Savagely he reminded himself that it could be none of his business if Sophie chose after all to marry. And Tom would at least be a kind and affectionate husband.

Not entirely oblivious to the fact that his host was toying with the idea of calling him out, Tom Hampton set himself to entertain and please Miss Marsden. Their conversation on the topic of boring punishments inflicted upon them in their youth was laced with laughter. Sophie's account of how she had made Kit add up her accounts after his last truancy impressed Hampton enormously.

'What a capital idea, Miss Marsden! I'll warrant he took the hint!'

'Well, yes,' acknowledged Sophie, chuckling. 'But I am bound to own that he did it a great deal better than I do. Even Thea, his governess, said so.'

'Should have taken a riding crop to the lad,' growled Sir Philip. Namby-pamby idea! Adding up accounts, indeed! 'Boy needs a man to show him what's what. I'll soon take care of that!' This remark was dropped resoundingly into one of those dreadful pools of silence which seem to attract embarrassing speeches.

Sophie flushed scarlet, every eye at the table was upon her and there was nothing she could say to rebut the impression made by Sir Philip without being appallingly rude to him.

David was not so nice in his notions. He could see the Vicar pricking up his ears, about to enquire if his services were to be needed. He had to head the man off at all costs before Sir Philip put Sophie into the position of having to refuse him at the dinner table. Despite the convention which dictated that conversation should be confined to the persons seated immediately to left and right, he fixed Sir Philip with an icy green stare.

'I thought it had been agreed, Sir Philip, that you were not to be granted that, or any other authority?' His voice held only mild inquiry, but it made Lady Maria shoot a startled glance at him over the forkful of game pie she was raising to her mouth. She almost laughed aloud. Lord! If ever she'd seen the boy so angry! Just as she'd thought—he'd completely forgotten his manners!

David returned to his conversation with Lady Darleston, supremely conscious of having made bad infinitely worse. He didn't dare look at Sophie. If he did he was entirely likely to find himself making a declaration over the dinner table. Damn Aunt Maria's scheming! She'd probably planned the whole thing!

It was a moot point as to whether Sophie was more horrified by Sir Philip's crass assumption of authority or the chilly way in which Helford had depressed his pretensions. It might not be convenable to converse across the table, but that wasn't stopping both Lady Lucinda and her mama from looking down their long noses at her.

While Sir Philip assumed an unwonted interest in his dinner, Captain Hampton was speaking to her very softly. 'Now that really was bacon-brained!' She looked up at him and found an expression of understanding sympathy on his kindly face. 'David,' he went on, 'has not the slightest notion of tact. It will be a wonder if any woman of rank can be prevailed upon to accept him.' This last was uttered so quietly that she could not doubt it reached her ears only.

Swallowing hard, she said with difficulty, 'I cannot understand why you should say such a thing to me, sir, but—'

His eyes twinkled as he interrupted her. 'Because I am as tactless as David, my dear. Do not allow this little contretemps to upset you, Miss Marsden. The only persons likely to be at all upset do not matter in the least. You may take my word for that.'

Both those unimportant persons had stiffened in

wrath at Helford's very proprietorial expression of interest in Miss Marsden. Lady Stanford was furious. How dare he have the effrontery to include his mistress at a dinner party where her daughter, his intended bride, was present! Let alone making the situation clear to everyone! No doubt that little hussy Kate Asterfield was laughing up her non-existent sleeve and planning to let everyone in town know just as soon as she could!

Lady Lucinda was no less disgusted than her mother, but her fury was somewhat tempered by the reflection that if Helford was planning to set Miss Marsden up as his mistress, or had already done so, it would keep him from sharing *her* bed more than was seemly. She looked up to find Helford's eyes on her and could not repress a shudder as she recalled the liberties he had taken with her person.

This reaction was not lost on David, who was of the opinion that he had completely lost his senses. How on earth was he to share a bed with this girl if he married her? With a shock he realised that he was casting serious doubt on their union for the first time, and that the thought of marriage to Sophie was suddenly far less terrifying.

Once admitted openly, the idea that he might not marry Lucinda Anstey refused to be banished. It developed itself into a fully fledged conviction as he continued with his game pie. But he was practically honour bound to offer for her now! How the hell could he get out of it? There had to be a way. A marriage of convenience was one thing, but he was damned if he'd spend the rest of his life tied to a female who made it clear she would welcome a crawling slug to her bed only slightly less enthusiastically!

And as for his reaction to Garfield's idiocy! What on earth had he been about to call attention to the situation in that way? He had meant only to erase the distressed look on Sophie's face and block the Vicar, but he had made matters immeasurably worse. For the rest of the meal he confined himself strictly to addressing his remarks to Lady Darleston and Lady Stanford, all the while trying to persuade himself that he was grateful for Tom Hampton's protective presence beside Sophie.

In truth, the fact that Sophie was so obviously comfortable with Tom galled him unbearably. He watched her surreptitiously as the first course was removed and the second course set out. She appeared to have recovered from her discomfiture and was talking happily to Tom while Lady Maria held Garfield's attention.

Gallant as ever, he thought. Far too proud to let any hint of her embarrassment show.

He smiled automatically at Lady Stanford as she informed him that his chef's way with a saddle of venison was quite something out of the way. She was far too canny to let Helford see her outrage. The last thing she wanted was for him to assume that an offer would not be acceptable. It was of the first importance now to marry Lucinda to Helford. If she returned to town unbetrothed, Lady Stanford would be the laughing stock of all her acquaintance.

So she continued to compliment Helford on his chef. 'I vow, I cannot imagine how you persuaded such a treasure to come into the country!' she said archly.

David said with a polite smile, 'I pay him very generously, Lady Stanford. There are few services that enough money cannot secure. Even a French-trained chef.'

'Quite so! A lowering reflection, is it not?' agreed Lady Stanford. Unguardedly she allowed her eyes to rest on Miss Marsden and a scornful smile curved her lips as she conjectured what price the little slut had put on *her* services.

Following her gaze, David's black brows snapped together as he realised what she was thinking. Sheer fury that anyone could think he would take advantage of an unprotected girl like Sophie rendered him utterly speechless. And the insult to Sophie was beyond anything! An insult he had laid her open to!

At this unfortunate moment Sophie happened to glance towards the end of the table to find Lady Stanford's sneering eyes on her and Helford glaring at her as though she had somehow offended him mortally. Her fork rattled uncontrollably as she set it down. Unable to help herself, she stared back at him, confusion and hurt evident in her dark eyes which could not tear themselves from his scowling face. *What have I done?* Trembling slightly, she dropped her eyes and schooled herself to an expression of cheerful interest as she turned back to Tom Hampton.

David saw the pain on her face, saw her turn back to Tom and flinched as he realised that he had unwittingly hurt her and that she had unhesitatingly sought comfort of his best friend. Dear God, would he never stop wounding her? It struck him with all the force of an exploding shell that she was just as vulnerable to being hurt as he was.

How the hell was he supposed to survive this? Never before had he been conscious of a desire to soothe away all hurt, protect a woman from the slightest breeze, ease all her burdens and make sure that she never looked at another man again. And he could do nothing but hurt her, forcing her to turn to one of his oldest friends for reassurance.

Love seemed to confuse everything. He couldn't think straight, he wanted her so badly. And even that had a different quality to it. In the past it had always been *his* desire, *his* pleasure that had been the main focus of his affairs. That was why he had always ensured that he bedded with women of experience, skilled in entertaining a man. To please them in return was simply part of the payment. Nothing more.

Sophie would have been different, he thought despairingly. It would have been...like...like... *making love for the first time*. For the first time he wanted to *give*, not just take his own pleasure in a woman's body. More, he wanted to give *himself*, not merely pleasure.

'Lord Helford?'

Penelope Darleston's warm voice drew him back.

He looked at her in confusion. 'I beg your pardon! My wits were wandering. What were you saying?'

'Merely that your aunt is signalling to me that it is time for the ladies to retire to the drawing room,' she said drily.

He looked down to Lady Maria, who had a particularly wicked smirk on her lined old countenance.

Turning back to Penelope, he said very softly, 'Tell Miss Marsden that I need to speak to her privately and will have her escorted home. Will you do that for me?' He could not allow her to think he had held her so cheap. He had to apologise to her. And he could not do it in front of an entire roomful of people!

Penelope looked at him with suddenly narrowed eyes and said slowly, 'Since you ask it of *me*, my lord, I can only assume that you will take all due care for her reputation.'

David blinked. Never had he heard such an implacable challenge in a woman's voice. Before he could answer Penelope had responded to Lady

Maria's signal and was standing up to leave the room for the servants to remove the covers and set out the port and brandy decanters. The gentlemen rose to their feet and waited politely until the door shut behind the ladies.

As they sat down again David resolved that they were not going to sit over their wine for very long. For a start the Vicar's presence made the usual round of ribald stories quite ineligible and even were this not the case he himself had no stomach for them.

He could not have borne to hear tales of loose living and even looser women bandied around while his mind was reeling under the appalling knowledge that he had left Sophie vulnerable to the worst of insults. The only benefit his love had brought Sophie Marsden was that it had prevented him from seducing her. It was not her quality or her unprotected situation that had stopped him. It was quite simply because he had fallen shatteringly in love with her, even if he had been such a fool as not to recognise the fact consciously soon enough—and to distrust it even when he did. Some deeper, surer instinct had held him back from an act which would destroy her. He would explain that to her and then he would let her go.

In the drawing room Sophie was conducting herself gallantly under fire. Lady Lucinda and her mama were probing with condescending insolence into the meaning of Sir Philip's insinuation.

'Are we to offer you our congratulations, Miss Marsden?' purred Lady Lucinda insultingly.

'Sir Philip has often been concerned enough to offer his advice on my handling of Kit,' Sophie replied with outward calm. 'I can hardly see that as a matter for congratulation.' Inwardly she seethed at the implied insult in offering her congratulations. It suggested that a woman had schemed successfully to snare a man. One wished a woman happy and congratulated a man!

'Oh, how disappointing! I quite thought he meant something else!' said Lady Stanford with vast insincerity. 'But I do think Sir Philip would be the very man for you. No doubt he would be able to mount you most satisfactorily. Far more so than Helford.' She smirked triumphantly.

Sophie went absolutely white with fury and opened her mouth to deliver a blistering reply, but Lady Lucinda chipped in first.

'Yes, indeed! I dare say *marriage* had never crossed your mind.'

'No, it hasn't,' said Sophie with deadly emphasis. 'I'm afraid the examples I have seen of women on the catch for a husband, the stratagems they use and the offensive insolence of their behaviour, have quite decided me to leave thoughts of marriage to others.'

'Well spoken, Miss Marsden,' came a light voice at her elbow. 'You remind us all of the pitfalls of vulgarity that await those who seek the married state too eagerly.'

Sophie turned in consternation to find Kate Asterfield twinkling at her in amusement. 'I did not mean—' she began but was cut off.

'Of course you did not,' Kate reassured her. 'Your meaning was plain to the meanest intelligence. Now come and explain to myself and Penny Darleston just exactly how to bring up boys. She is in despair over Darleston's heir, who has painted his sister's face bright blue! And I am expecting an interesting event in the winter and will take all the sensible advice I can get.'

So saying, she drew Sophie's hand through her arm and bore her off, leaving Lady Stanford and Lucinda seething at her effrontery.

'Well!' said the latter in tones of revulsion.

'Quite so, my love!' agreed Lady Stanford. 'How disgusting. To make such an announcement! And in that gown! But it is all of a piece. She was always a trifle fast and a dreadful flirt. One wonders that the Asterfields countenanced the match.'

Perfectly content that her character was being ripped to shreds behind her back, Kate said cheerfully, 'Now you are in the best of company, my dear! Helford's tactlessness will be in a fair way to being forgot with that for them to gossip over.'

'Are...are you really...?' Sophie was too shy to go on.

'I am indeed!' said Kate with a grin. 'But I haven't told Ned yet. I'll do that tonight. Penny has been warning me what a fuss Peter fell into when she was increasing. No doubt Ned will do the same!' She and Penelope kept Sophie beside them as they quizzed her on methods of dealing with naughty toddlers and even naughtier schoolboys until the gentlemen joined them.

Helford's eyes sought Sophie as soon as he crossed the threshold. Ah! There she was! He was relieved to see her with Kate and Penelope, apparently quite at her ease with them. He longed to go to her immediately, but he could see that the Vicar's wife was in urgent need of assistance.

Lady Stanford and Lucinda were discoursing to the long-suffering Mrs Henshaw on the best way to deal with a country parish and keep its members on the path of virtue. Mrs Henshaw had never before realised just what an atrocious piece of work she and Lucius were making of their job. She smiled with delight at his lordship as he joined their group, making it quite plain, as he bowed over her hand, that she was the object of his interest.

'Tell me, ma'am,' —and his voice radiated an unlikely innocence— 'that sermon your husband preached last Sunday on the power of faith—do you ever have the feeling that your prayers have unequivocally been answered?'

Emerald eyes quizzed her wickedly and she suppressed an undignified chuckle with difficulty. 'Sometimes, my lord. And I always find that my deliverance comes in the most unexpected guise.'

Lady Stanford rushed into speech. 'I was just explaining to Mrs Henshaw the importance of making sure the members of the choir are beyond reproach. One cannot be too careful and one must not condone sin.'

'No, indeed,' agreed Mrs Henshaw. She took the opportunity to change the subject. 'And speaking of music, I am sure Lady Lucinda is a most talented performer. Perhaps if it would not be too much...' It was uncommonly like toadeating, she thought ruefully, but...if it would shut Lady Stanford up...

Lady Maria, who had been having a quiet word to Penelope, heard this and said, 'Excellent notion. Go on, girl. A little music will be just the thing.'

Lucinda was not at all averse to displaying her talent. She had studied under the finest masters and knew her performance on the pianoforte to be superior. And it would remind Helford of her eligibility. No doubt Miss Marsden was but an indifferent musician. After all, the instrument in her parlour was a mere harpsichord, old fashioned and dowdy in the extreme.

With a fine show of demure reluctance she went to the Broadwood instrument and sat down. Having placed some of her own music there much earlier in the day, she found a piece quickly and began to play.

Her performance, thought David, was indeed superior. Touch and execution were faultless, but increasingly he felt that there was something lacking, some vital spark that would bring the music and the instrument to life. At the end he joined the clapping and nodded in polite agreement when Lady Stanford murmured to him that she considered Lucinda's taste to be irreproachable.

Lady Lucinda stood up and smiled graciously, accepting the applause as her due. She would have been quite happy to favour the assembled party further but Lady Maria had other ideas.

'Very well indeed. I think we'll have some more.' And then, just as Lucinda was about to sit down again, 'Lady Darleston, you play quite prettily.'

Sophie noticed with delight that Penelope did not bother to demur or protest archly that she was sure no one wanted to hear her poor fumblings. Instead she smiled at Lady Maria and went straight to the piano. Her fingers drifted over the instrument for a moment in rippling arpeggios as she explored its tone and feel.

Then she stopped, turned to her audience and said simply, 'Beethoven. *The Appassionata.*' Without any further ado and without music she plunged unhesitatingly into the first movement of the sonata.

Sophie had never heard music played like this. The instrument sang and wept under those slender fingers which held such an unexpected power to move the passions and senses. She found that she was actually trembling as Penelope unleashed the full strength of the music's fire and vigour.

As for David, he had realised the moment Penelope began to play what had been missing from Lucinda's performance. Passion of any sort. Certainly there had been no passion for music. To Lucinda the music was merely a means to display her cleverness and skill. To Penelope it was a means of entering another world where passion and emotion were paramount and she transported her audience with her.

At the end there was a moment's stunned silence, during which David sneaked a look at his old friend Peter Darleston. That gentleman was regarding his wife, still seated at the piano and seemingly oblivious to the wild clapping, with a burning intensity. He was seated on the edge of his chair and David somehow doubted that Penelope Darleston would get very much sleep that night. My Lord the Earl of Darleston was positively ablaze.

David swallowed hard. He knew exactly how Peter felt. Sophie was seated a few yards from him, her creamy complexion warm and flushed with her emotion, a sheen of tears in her expressive eyes as she stared at Penelope Darleston who had shown them all what music was for.

Lady Maria was looking at Penelope with an odd tilt of her head, David noticed suddenly.

Penelope returned that look as she said, 'I think a song is called for now.' She gazed straight at Sophie and said, 'Come, Miss Marsden. Kate, you must know, has a croak like a raven's. You sing for us.'

For one dreadful moment Sophie thought she would die as all eyes in the room rested on her, but Penelope's gaze held her. Those smoky grey eyes were full of encouragement and laughter as Sophie rose to her feet and went to stand by the instrument without the faintest notion of what she was to sing.

Wordlessly Penelope told her. Softly, without bothering to glance down at the keyboard, she slipped into the old tune Sophie had been singing the day they met. The haunting melody drifted through the room as she improvised an introduction.

Sophie stiffened. She couldn't sing that! Not with Helford in the room. It was impossible. Then her eyes met Tom Hampton's, full of confidence and with that kindly smile on his face. Imperceptibly he nodded at her. In a flash she realised that in this way she could say what was in her heart without shame. She had not chosen the song. If Helford understood, then he could make what use of the knowledge he chose. If he did not understand, then no harm was done.

On the final questioning chord Sophie drew a deep breath and began to sing. Penelope at the keyboard thought she had never before heard any voice echo with such poignant sorrow. There was a simplicity about the song and the performance which tore mercilessly at the heartstrings.

David listened transfixed, his heart pounding. She would give her love an apple without a core, a house without a door and a palace which he might open without any key. The riddle she had set hung between them in the quivering air as a simple interlude led into the second verse.

Her head was the apple without any core, her mind the house without any door and her heart…oh, God! Her voice soared in the final pleading phrases…her heart was the palace where he might dwell and for which he did not require a key because it was his. His mouth suddenly dry, he realised what she was offering. Herself, body, mind and soul. And something in the plangent voice told him that she had not the slightest expectation that her gift would be accepted. True to her nature, she had taken the risk of telling him what she felt in the certainty that her sentiments were not returned. Leaving herself wide open to the full hurt of his rejection. She'd done the very thing he had most feared to do.

As the song closed he stared at her in disbelief. Such a slender, vulnerable figure in her amber silk, the wide dark eyes unfocused as she waited for Penelope to strike the final chord. In that moment he knew only one thing. Sophie Marsden was his!

He couldn't possibly offer for Lucinda! If it caused a scandal, that was just too bad! He might have been able to sacrifice himself on the altar of duty, but he was damned if he'd immolate Sophie!

Sophie was conscious of a burning regard as she curtsied to the applause. Shyly she looked up at Helford and turned a fiery crimson as she met his searing gaze. He seemed to devour her with his eyes, daring anyone to gainsay him. He alone was not clapping, but what she saw in his face made her swallow hard. She had openly declared her love for him and he was telling her that he had understood. What he would choose to do with the knowledge she did not know. She had offered herself unconditionally whatever the cost.

The Vicar, sitting next to Lady Maria, thought he must have misheard the old lady. Surely she couldn't really have said, 'About bloody time!' No, it must be his hearing. Unless, of course, her ladyship was becoming a trifle peculiar.

The tea tray was brought in half an hour later. The talk in the meantime had all been of music.

Kate was positively bubbling over Sophie's singing. 'It was wonderful! Where *did* you learn that song?'

She was delighted at Sophie's explanation. 'How lovely. I must ask my maids at home if they know any like that.' She twinkled at Penelope. 'I may have a voice like a raven. Indeed, I do not deny it. But I still know a good song when I hear one.'

Lady Lucinda turned to her mama and said audibly, 'A maidservant's song! I suppose the tune is well enough in its way, but the words! I dare say its origins account for the very vulgar sentiments expressed.'

'Quite so, my dear!' agreed Lady Stanford fervently. 'And I believe it to be a sad mistake to shower too much praise for what may be achieved by any person of moderate taste and talent. And I am not quite sure that I approve of Beethoven. After all, he was a supporter of that monster, Bonaparte.'

'Vulgar?' asked a lazy, husky voice just behind them. 'Do you reckon love as a vulgar emotion, Lady Lucinda?'

Lady Lucinda turned to meet the faintly sardonic brown eyes of Lord Darleston. She drew herself up proudly. 'I think persons of our rank should be above being moved by the sway of strong emotions, yes. There is something most unseemly in such things, be it temper, excessive grief or…love.'

Darleston nodded. 'I see. Well, well, well. I never knew I was such a vulgar fellow. Poor Penny, she won't want to know me now. Unless—' in tones of discovery '—unless, of course, she feels vulgar too. Perhaps, since she chose Beethoven, there is yet some hope for her poor, vulgar husband.' With a friendly smile he strolled away from the two speechless and furious ladies.

Lord Mark Reynolds, upon hearing this masterly

set-down, nearly choked on the cup of tea just handed to him by Lady Maria. 'Good God, Darleston, what on earth are you about?' he spluttered. 'Are you aware that Helford is about to offer for that chit?'

The black brows rose slightly. 'Do you care to have a little wager on that, Mark?'

'A wager?' Lord Mark was astounded that Darleston should suggest such a thing. 'You ought to know I don't bet on certainties like that! Be robbing you, dear boy.'

'I'll lay you a monkey Helford doesn't marry Lucinda Anstey,' said Darleston calmly.

Lord Mark goggled at him.

'You see, Mark,' he continued, 'Helford is not quite that much of a fool.' He smiled at Lord Mark's stunned countenance and went over to sit down beside Lady Maria.

She handed him a cup of tea which he accepted with thanks. 'I trust you are satisfied with the evening's results.' His countenance was gently mocking.

Shooting an irritated glance at him, Lady Maria asked bluntly, 'How much did Penelope tell you?'

Darleston grinned. 'Not much beyond the fact that you had set her on to stop the match. She certainly didn't give any clue as to what she intended, apart from asking if David liked music. Put it down to my knowledge of David and my powers of observation.'

She chuckled wheezily. 'You always were as sharp as you could stare. Lord! How could David be such a zany as to contemplate...' She paused. 'Well, I suppose that was my fault. I handled him badly. Should never have mentioned the word *duty*. But I think we've done the trick, with a certain amount of help from the lady herself, I might add. It now remains to be seen whether he has enough brains to offer for the right girl.'

Darleston's roar of laughter attracted the attention of his wife who was speaking quietly to Sophie. 'Heavens! Lady Maria must have said something utterly outrageous.' She turned back to Sophie and said, 'He asked me to tell you he would have you escorted home in one of his carriages.'

At this point they were interrupted by Sir Philip, who came up and said, 'I have ordered my carriage, Miss Sophie. We will be leaving very shortly.'

Sophie looked at him innocently. 'Oh, did you bring the Vicar and Mrs Henshaw? I hadn't realised. Goodnight, Sir Philip.'

A look of annoyance crossed his face. 'I will escort you home, Miss Sophie. I wish to...to discuss certain matters with you.'

Penelope watched with fascination as a hint of steel entered into Sophie Marsden's face.

It was echoed in her voice as she replied, 'I find your manner of discussing the matter repugnant, Sir Philip, and have no wish to endure it again. My opinion on this topic remains the same as ever. I have no need of your advice, no need for your carriage and no need or desire for your discussions. Goodnight, sir.' And, as he looked as though he would have argued further, 'Sir, I have spoken elliptically out of respect for your feelings, despite the fact that you have shown none for mine! Unless you wish me to speak more plainly, leave this subject!'

Red with bottled fury, he turned on his heel and stalked away to bid farewell to his host and hostess.

'Goodness!' said Penelope, visibly impressed. 'Do you always refuse offers so categorically?'

A little conscious, Sophie said, 'Oh, dear. I suppose it was rather obvious.'

'Moderately,' agreed Penelope. 'Never mind. He did ask for it.' She had every expectation that Miss Marsden would not respond to Lord Helford's inevitable offer in the same way.

Chapter Twelve

The house party had made its way up to bed without realising that their host had disappeared. He had handed them their candles on the landing and bidden them all goodnight with every appearance of having all night at his disposal. Lady Lucinda had lingered slightly, thinking that he might like to take the opportunity to make her an offer since Lady Maria had interrupted them so tactlessly before dinner. She thought that even if he wished to kiss her again, she was prepared now, and could endure it without too much difficulty.

Her affront when Helford smiled at her charmingly and thanked her for her pretty playing as he handed her the candle was considerable. He did not move as she went off down the corridor to her chamber, but as soon as he heard the door close behind her he was off the opposite way along the corridor at a run. Down some narrow back stairs, usually frequented by

servants, three at time. Down another corridor to a
side entrance and out into the night.

Sophie was waiting in the Great Hall for Helford.
All the others had gone and he had disappeared
muttering something about bidding his house party
a goodnight. She waited with increasing nervous-
ness, wondering if Penelope had made a dreadful
mistake, until a familiar face appeared at the door.

'Evenin', Miss Sophie. Got yer carriage outside.'
Jasper smiled at her in a friendly fashion.

'Oh.' Sophie looked around wildly. There was
only a sleepy-looking footman who appeared to be
waiting for her departure to lock up.

'Should I…should I not bid his lordship
farewell?' She was conscious of a feeling of sickening disappointment. Helford had not returned. If
he had wished to speak to her, he must have changed
his mind. He was probably avoiding her. She could
not tell his servants that she wished to see him. It
would look as though she were throwing herself at
his head.

Jasper was shaking his head. 'His lordship asked
me to tell ye to go straight home, miss.'

She blushed in mortification. Damn Helford! If
he couldn't keep to what he himself had arranged,
then he could go to the devil! Throwing her cloak
around her, she said, 'Very well, then. Thank you,
Jasper. I am ready.'

Proudly she went down the broad flight of steps

to the waiting carriage. Jasper handed her in. After the brightly lit hall and the flood of light pouring from the open door, her eyes took a moment to adjust to the darkness inside the carriage. She heard Jasper spring to the box and call, 'Let 'em go!'

The pair of horses moved off and she suddenly realised that there was someone else in the carriage, sitting in the darkest corner. For a moment she thought she must be mistaken, but the figure moved and she found herself caught in a hold as tender as it was unbreakable. A seductive mouth was on hers, warm and caressing. A gentle hand was under her chin, stroking her throat, her cheek, adding its mite to the persuasive lips which held her in thrall.

At about this moment Lady Lucinda, having rung for her maid, was removing her pearls at the dressing table when a movement in the glass caught her eye. She spun around, but could see no one. Just the flickering candles in the sconces, she thought. Shrugging her shoulders, she removed her bracelets and began to unpin her hair. She could not remember ever having been so disgusted by an evening's entertainment in her life. How dare that insufferable man Darleston give them such an insolent set-down! And Helford! Making it plain for anyone to see that that little trollop was his current inamorata! While as for the girl herself! It was obvious enough what Helford saw in her!

Again that movement caught her attention. She turned again, but could see nothing. As soon as her maid came she would have her light a lamp, this candlelight was quite inadequate. The girl should have come up earlier and lit the lamps. And where was her maid? How long must she wait for the lazy wench?

And then she saw it. Sitting up on the middle of her bed with a piece of apple between its paws was a rat. And not just any rat. A big rat. In fact, a *very* big rat. It did not seem to be particularly concerned about Lady Lucinda's presence. But then, given its size, it really had no need for concern. It just sat there, nibbling on its apple, bright eyes gleaming in the candlelight, looking totally incongruous on the silken counterpane.

That was before Lady Lucinda screamed. At the very first scream the rat whisked around and disappeared into the shadows of the bed hangings. Lady Lucinda kept on screaming, becoming more hysterical by the second.

Within half a minute Lady Stanford came racing in, brandishing the poker from her bedchamber, clearly convinced her daughter was being raped. She found her standing on an elegant bergère chair as far away from the bed as she could get, clutching a smaller gilt chair in an attitude of defence. A second later her maid burst into the room from the corridor, closely followed by the entire house party,

Lady Maria, the butler and two footmen who appeared to have left behind their usual expressions of bovine stolidity.

A babble of noise broke out as everyone tried to ascertain from the shaking lady exactly what had induced her to seek the dubious sanctuary of a French chair. Eventually Tom Hampton's calm voice got through to her, after he had silenced everyone else by the simple expedient of telling them plainly to shut up.

'Come now, Lucinda, tell us what has alarmed you.'

She raised one shaking hand and pointed at the bed. *'A...a rat! On...on my bed!'*

'A *rat*?' exclaimed Lady Maria in disbelief. 'We do *not* have rats at Helford Place!'

'Ugh!' Kate Asterfield was for once entirely in sympathy with Lady Lucinda. 'How utterly revolting!'

'A rat, eh?' said Asterfield, not at all convinced by Lady Maria's belief in the ratless state of the house.

The butler, Bainbridge, however, drew himself up and said in tones of deep disapproval, 'Her ladyship must have seen a large mouse. I do not deny that there may have been a mouse in the room, but it cannot have been a—'

This categorical denial was rudely interrupted by a startled exclamation from one of the footmen. 'Gor...bloody 'ell! It's enormous!'

Never in all his life had Bainbridge been so

shamed by one of his underlings. Turning to anni-
hilate the offender, he found James staring and
pointing at the canopied top of the bed hangings.
The forceful rebuke died on Bainbridge's lips as he
beheld the largest rat he had ever seen perched on
the apex of the canopy.

'Gawd!' gasped the other footman. 'What a
whopper! That ain't no mouse, beggin' your pardon,
I'm sure, Mr Bainbridge, an' yours, milady. That's
a *rat*, that is!'

Screams of horror erupted from all the women,
who scrambled as far away from the bed as
possible. Except, of course, for the redoubtable
Lady Maria, who stalked over to the bed and peered
up at the rat with an outraged expression on her
countenance.

Satisfied that it was not, after all, a mouse, she
pronounced, 'There seems little doubt. It is a rat.
Remove it *at once*!' She swung around to glare at
the hapless footmen and Bainbridge.

'Remove it?' James seemed to have totally forgotten his place. 'Remove it? Just like that? Not
bloody likely… milady.' This last did not in the
least suggest that his respect for Lady Maria would
lead him to tackle a rat of these proportions. His
colleague and boon companion Samuel nodded
vehemently in support of this revolutionary
attitude. Even Bainbridge looked flabbergasted at
the suggestion.

'I say!' said Lord Mark, 'I've got a capital idea! Helford's head groom Highbury has a champion terrier. He was tellin' me the other day. It kills rats on sight. What say I nip down to the stables and fetch him up with the dog? Be capital sport!' He rubbed his hands together in glee. And, as all the ladies stared at him in outrage, he added lamely, 'Get rid of the rat, you know. Capital terrier it is…just the…er…job.'

Trying not to laugh at a scene which was rapidly deteriorating into a farce, Hampton looked at his hostess for guidance. 'Ah…Lady Maria…what do you say?' It seemed like a good idea to him, although he would not have cared to wager any sum on the motives behind Lord Mark's enthusiasm. He could not, however, adopt the idea over Lady Maria's head. And where the devil was Helford? he wondered. Damn it all! It was his job to deal with things like this. His chamber wasn't so far away that he wouldn't have heard all the racket Lucinda had kicked up, let alone the rest of them.

Lady Maria snorted and said shortly, 'If that seems best to you, Hampton. I have no experience of rats, I am happy to say! Lucinda! Another room will be made ready for you while the gentlemen amuse themselves!' She shot an ironic glance at Lord Mark, who blushed deeply. 'You will not wish to sleep in this chamber again. Come, Mrs Asterfield.' Accompanied by Kate, she stalked out, her rigid back proclaiming her complete disapproval.

'I'll fetch the terrier, shall I?' suggested Lord Mark with unconvincing diffidence. At Hampton's nod he went out quietly, but a moment later he could be heard fairly running down the corridor. A faint cry of, 'Yoicks! Tally ho! Gone awaaaaay!' drifted back to them. Only the knowledge that Lady Stanford, apoplectic with fury, was observing him enabled Tom Hampton to keep a straight face.

'Oh, I say!' said Asterfield in tones of deprecation. 'That's a little off! Mean to say, he don't need to be that pleased!'

Lord Mark returned fifteen minutes later with Highbury and an excited terrier whose tattered ears bore mute testament to his many battles with the foe. Lucinda and her mama were, with the assistance of their maids, removing all her belongings to Lady Stanford's room for the night where the sofa bed was to be made up.

'Evenin', milady,' said Highbury, not at all averse to being called upon to perform duties outside his province. 'Now, where's this 'ere rat 'is lordship's tellin' me about?'

James pointed silently to the bed hangings and there was the rat, scuttling back and forth. The terrier did not need to ask, his nose alerted him to the presence of his greatest enemy and he pranced forward, barking loudly.

Highbury swore softly. 'Righto. Clear the room. We'll soon 'ave 'im down and then Nelson can do 'is stuff.'

Asterfield spoke up. 'Hope we didn't drag you out of bed, Highbury. Jolly sporting of you to bring the dog along.'

'Oh, I weren't in bed, Mr Asterfield, sir,' Highbury assured him cheerfully. 'I never goes to bed without all the 'orses is in safe. An' Jasper an' Bob ain't brought 'is lordship in yet.' Patently unaware of having uttered anything at all out of the way, he turned his attention back to the rat.

Oh, my God, thought Hampton. It only needed that!

Lady Stanford and Lucinda had frozen on their way out. Lady Stanford turned back and enquired icily, 'And where, may I ask, is his lordship?' Her tones suggested that no excuse for his absence would be sufficient to redeem him in her view.

'Hmm?' Highbury's thoughts snapped back to his betters. 'Where's 'is lordship? Gone in the carriage to see Miss Marsden 'ome safe. Now… Captain Hampton, sir, if you'd just fetch me that chair, I can stand on the bed an' give 'im a bit of a poke, like…'

A stunned silence greeted this revelation. Lady Stanford's jaw hung open in disbelief. Not all her spouse's infidelities over the years had prepared her for anything this outrageous. Shameless! Utterly shameless!

A stifled snort of laughter from Ned Asterfield settled the issue. Her head held high, Lady Lucinda said, 'Come, Mama. It is clearly not at all the sort of establishment with which we wish to be connected. In any way whatsoever!' She stalked from the chamber in what could only be described as suppressed fury. Lady Stanford followed in full agreement. Had Lucinda shown the least disposition to accept his lordship's suit after this comprehensive insult, she would have disowned her!

Twenty minutes later Hampton strode back to his bedchamber, having persuaded Asterfield and Lord Mark that to finish up an evening's sport by returning to the library to try and drink each other under the table would be in the worst of bad taste. They only agreed when it was pointed out that they didn't even have the rat's mangled corpse to gloat over as it had hurtled around the room to evade the terrier and had found an open window. The rat had disappeared along the ornate stonework which afforded ample holds for a rat, if not for a terrier, who had had to be forcibly restrained from attempting to follow his craven enemy.

As he settled into bed, he resolved that in the morning he was going to give David Melville the finest trimming of his unregenerate life for putting

Sophie Marsden in such an appalling position. He ground his teeth in rage. If Helford hadn't already offered for her he, Captain Thomas Hampton, was personally going to stand over him while he did it!

On reflection, though, he had to admit David had certainly solved his problem about having to offer for Lucinda. Someone with David's best interests at heart was plainly looking out for him, he thought with a chuckle. Where on earth had the rat come from? On the heels of this question came another: just what had Fanny had in that box she'd brought home from Willowbank House the other day?

'*Helford!*' Sophie gasped, stunned, unable to think. His kisses were possessive, demanding. Her mouth was released briefly as he whispered against her hair. 'Call me David, please, Sophie…oh, God! Sophie! My little sweetheart…' She could feel his ragged breath on her ear, creating the most dizzying sensations, and then he took her mouth again. She felt his tongue flicker against her lips, seeking entrance.

She opened her mouth with a moan of pleasure, feeling his tongue plunge in and take complete possession, boldly plundering and exploring as his hands gripped her waist, pulling her closer to his hard muscular body. She yielded totally, pressing herself against him, returning his kisses, her arms clinging to him desperately as he removed her cloak.

David felt as though he were on fire. He could think of nothing but the innocent response of the girl in his arms, the sweetness of her trembling body and mouth. Desire raged in him fuelled by her passionate embrace. One hand slid up her bare arm to her sleeve and slid it off her shoulder, easing her bodice and chemise down until the breast was exposed. He touched it lightly, wondering at the texture of velvety flesh. He felt, rather than heard, her instinctive murmur of protest. He smothered it with his lips and tongue, ravishing the vulnerable, moist mouth in a way which brooked no argument.

Her senses entirely overwhelmed by his sensual onslaught, Sophie offered no further resistance, but gave herself up to the utterly wonderful way he was making love to her. His teasing fingers were fondling and stroking her breast in a manner which made her gasp in pleasure.

Circling and tantalising at first, he at last brushed his thumb very lightly over the nipple. He groaned deep in his throat as he felt it hard and erect. He could feel the tremors running through her body and lifted his mouth from hers. Then with another groan he lowered it to her breast and ran his tongue over it lightly before sucking and biting with gentle savagery at the rosy peak.

Sophie was conscious of a feeling of intense heat burning through her whole body; it seemed to be concentrated in her breasts and in an increasing tension in her belly and even lower. David was now beside her, encouraging her to lie back along the seat. She knew she ought to resist, but lacked the willpower to do so. It felt so wonderful, so right to be lying in this intimate embrace with him practically on top of her and his mouth literally devouring her breast.

She felt one hand slide down the silk of her skirt, caressing the line of her thigh through the fabric, then he was lifting her skirt, pulling it up to expose her bare leg to his hand. It glided up past her knee and on to her thigh. Shock blazed through her, partially recalling her to sanity. The last remaining corner of her brain screamed feebly that she had to stop him. Right now! At once! Before things went too far. But that mesmerising hand crept further to tease and caress her soft thighs, which fell apart in obedience to his seductive probing.

His mind reeling, David's mouth lifted from her breast. Never in his life had he felt so totally out of control, so totally possessed by his own desire. The carriage lamp outside cast a faint glow and he could see her face very dimly. Tenderly his free hand stroked a wayward curl back from her brow, then drifted over her cheek to linger by the corner of her mouth. Oh, God! Her mouth, so soft, so yielding, like her body! With a shuddering groan he took her mouth again, his tongue echoing the rhythm and action of his searching fingers.

Dazed, melting in surrender, yet that small, sane part of Sophie's mind still shrieked its warning. This must stop! Her fainting reason panicked. Soon it would be too late! If, indeed, it were not so already. Desperately she tried to summon the will-power to tear herself free. But she wanted him, longed to give herself. She sobbed in passion, words of love germinating in her heart, where they had lain dormant, ready to flower on her lips in response to his loving.

Releasing her mouth momentarily, David whispered in a deep voice, cracking with emotion, 'Sophie, dearest Sophie. I want you so much!' His lips drifted over her temples, her cheek, to the wildly beating pulse at the base of her throat.

She froze. He wanted her...was that all? Suddenly Sophie's mind cleared and she realised where this was going to end. That she had to stop him. Before...before he could not be stopped... before she begged him to take her.

His mouth was on hers again, seducing her to his will, his fingers teasing and probing until he found the tangle of soft curls at the base of her belly. Tenderly he cupped the mound and one long, expert finger slid down to caress the quivering dampness between her thighs. Shock lanced through her at the sensation. Aching, empty, her body throbbed to the gentle rhythm, to the overwhelming temptation to yield. But a vision of Kit flashed before her dazed mind. What was the use of remaining single to protect his inheritance if she ruined herself in this way? Desperately she pushed against the solid wall of his chest, crying out in protest as she wrenched her lips away.

'My lord, no! Please!'

She felt him pull away from her, heard his groan of frustration as he released her. Frantically she pulled and pushed her skirts down over her trembling thighs, dragged the bodice of her gown back over her aching breasts. Her hands shook uncontrollably as she realised what she had so nearly permitted. What it could have meant to Kit.

Her whole body sang with the burning, raging need his caresses had unleashed. She prayed that he would not press his advantage, try to overcome her resistance. She knew if he did that her defences would crumble swiftly, that she would not be able to stop him, would not even want to stop him.

To her horror she felt him reach for her, his hands gentle but compelling, drawing her into the warmth and strength of his embrace. Terrified of her own melting response, she clung to reason as to a life line and flung herself to the other side of the carriage.

'No!' It was a cry of despair.

And finally the blind terror in her voice got through to David. It shook him to the core. *Oh, my God! What the hell have I done? She's terrified!*

Shame surged through him that he could have lost control so totally as to actually scare her. *She trusted you!* Breathing hard, he forced himself to sit back against the squabs, forced his limbs to relax. Tried, with even less success, to force his mind to think about something other than the girl sitting shaking in the darkness not three feet from him. And conscious all the while of the frantic urge to wrap her in his arms again. To comfort her, to reassure her. He dared not.

The pain of his arousal was appalling, but it was as nothing to the pain of guilt in his heart. She had told him…No! Begged him to stop. And he hadn't wanted to. He knew even now that if he pressed her she would not have any real defence against his lovemaking, that she would surrender to his demands, give herself without reservation.

He couldn't do it. She deserved better than that.

They sat in shaken silence, letting the rumble of the carriage wheels soothe their ragged breathing, each as insanely aware of the other as if they were still in each other's arms.

Sophie was beyond speech and even if she hadn't been she had no idea of what she could possibly say. So she sat, grateful for the friendly veil of darkness that masked the tears slipping down her burning cheeks. So close had she been to declaring her love for him, that she could still feel the words bursting to escape, clamouring in her heart for release.

David, his mind still reeling from the sheer intensity of his physical and emotional response, drew a deep breath, and said as evenly as he could, 'Sophie…you must not misunderstand me. I did not mean to insult you…I never intended…' His apology trailed off. What hadn't he intended? To make love to her? Nearly seduce her?

To his horror he heard her response. Light and bitter.

'You need not fear, my lord. I have not misinterpreted your actions.' The briefest of pauses. 'I am well aware of your intentions…' He thought her voice shook slightly, but an instant later it was as cool as ever. 'I confess I had no idea you meant to go beyond flirtation. Forgive me if I decline to join your game.'

At this extremely inopportune moment the carriage began to slow down.

David cursed fluently. And then realised he was wasting time.

'Sophie, listen,' he said urgently. 'You must know I love you. I…I know I shouldn't have even touched you tonight. God knows I find it hard enough to keep my hands off you at the best of times, but you can't think I merely want a quick tumble with you!'

At this inopportune moment, the carriage drew to a halt. And before the horses' hooves had fully stilled, Sophie had the door open and had leapt out into the road.

She did not dare wait to find out just how long a

tumble his lordship envisaged. The likelihood of her acquiescing in his ideas was too great to be risked. 'G…good night,' she whispered, staring up at him with wide, dark eyes.

'Sophie! Wait!' His voice was frantic. 'My house party is going tomorrow. I will come the next day to see you, to…to arrange everything…'

She bit her lip and turned away before she could respond to the urgency of his tone. She fled to the open gate and up the path without a backward look. Fumbling with the latch, she opened the door and slipped inside. The house was quiet and she could hear the rumble of hooves as the carriage was turned. Holding her breath she listened…there it was, the sound of the carriage leaving. With unsteady hands she shot the bolts home and went up to her chamber quickly.

Still shaking, she sank on to the bed, her thoughts in turmoil. *Arrange what?* He had not said what he was offering. She did not dare hope that he offered marriage. He was as good as betrothed to Lady Lucinda. At the most he wanted her to be his mistress. At the worst he wanted a brief affair. She dismissed that. *He said he wanted you. Surely if all he wanted was to have you, he had every opportunity. He must have known how little effort it would have taken to persuade you.*

She flushed in shame, knowing that, had he chosen to press her, one touch, one word of love, would have done it, would have had her in his arms, begging him to take her. Bitterly she realised that he had only spoken of love when it was plain that she would resist him.

She shuddered. He knew she loved him after that song. Would he realise how easy it would be to breach her defences even now? What would her answer be when he returned? She knew what it *should* be, but she could not bear him to think her a tease. Or, worse, that she was trying to lure him into marriage by refusing him. And she did not want to refuse him. Had it just been herself she would have surrendered and taken the risk. Taken what he offered.

She could not afford to think of just herself. She had to protect Kit. And now that meant shielding him from her own disgraceful impulses. Fiercely she forced herself to envisage how his life would be ruined if she accepted a *carte blanche* from Helford and gave Strathallen a weapon with which to challenge her guardianship in court.

Slowly she undressed and readied herself for bed, laying aside the crumpled silk gown. As she washed herself at the jug she found that her thighs were sticky, that cleansing between them was enough to set her trembling at the sensations which coursed through her. She pulled on her nightgown and slipped into bed as she faced the undeniable fact that if Helford came to take her and claimed to love her the temptation to surrender would be overwhelming.

Furiously she gritted her teeth and fought for control over her unruly heart and body. She was *not* going to add her name and heart to the list of Helford's innumerable conquests.

David watched her go and collapsed on the seat with a groan of frustration. He sat with his head in his hands, trying to regain some measure of control over his body. Never in his life had he felt so utterly insane with desire. The pain in his loins was beyond bearing. He tried hard not to think of Sophie's warm, yielding body, and wondered if she would ever forgive him for what he had done. The only saving grace, he told himself grimly, was that he wanted to marry her.

It was at this point that he realised he'd been so damn flustered that he had not made his intentions absolutely plain even at the last when he'd told her he loved her. He had not actually asked her to marry him. Swearing, he sat back against the seat as he realised that she had every reason to think he wanted an affair!

Chapter Thirteen

The following morning David was somewhat startled to hear from his valet that a rat of large and ferocious aspect had been discovered in Lady Lucinda's bedchamber.

'A rat?' he asked in amazement as he flung back the bedclothes. 'We don't *have* rats here! Not in the house. I suppose there are bound to be a few around the stables. It must have been a big mouse.' He drew on a resplendent grey silk dressing gown.

Meredith shook his head mournfully. 'No, my lord. It was a rat. Mr Bainbridge will bear out James and Samuel. They all say it was the biggest rat they'd ever seen. Even Lady Maria agreed it was a rat.' He handed Helford his shaving water.

David nearly dropped the jug. 'Lady Maria saw it? Why on earth did she see it?'

'Every one in earshot saw it, my lord, as far as I can make out,' he explained. 'Very upset the young lady was, which I'm sure she's not to be blamed. She wouldn't stay in the room, I'm told, but had a bed made up on the day bed in Lady Stanford's chamber.'

'What happened to the rat?' asked David in failing tones. If everyone had appeared in Lucinda's bed-chamber to discover what the disturbance was, then his own absence must have been glaringly apparent.

With a singularly abysmal effort to maintain a straight face Meredith said, 'I am…er…given to understand that Lord Mark, who is, as your lordship knows, much addicted to sports, he…er…suggested that Highbury and his terrier might be fetched up from the stables.'

'What?' David stared at Meredith in patent dis-belief in the shaving mirror as he lathered his face.

'Yes, my lord,' affirmed Meredith. 'Mr Bainbridge and James and Samuel refused to budge when Lady Maria told them to remove the rat. Very outspoken on the subject James was, I am informed.' The corner of his normally well-trained mouth twitched convul-sively.

'It must have been a bloody big rat to make them disobey my aunt!' said David with a shout of laughter. 'Come on, Meredith, what happened? Did Highbury bring Nelson up? Lord, what a kickup!'

'As to that, I was not an eyewitness, my lord,' said Meredith, in tones of infinite regret. 'But Captain Hampton is in the library, I believe. He asked me to tell you that he would appreciate a word with you before breakfast.'

David snorted. 'Did he, now? And tell me, was Captain Hampton present at this bloodbath?' He carefully negotiated his chin.

'I believe so, my lord.'

'God help me, then,' said his lordship in restricted tones as he shaved around his mouth. Tom, of all those present, was bound to have a very fair idea of where his host had been. He comforted himself with the thought that Tom was far too discreet, not to mention too good a friend, to have given him away.

Half an hour later his lordship, immaculate in breeches, top boots and a coat of dark green superfine, strolled into his library to find Tom Hampton sitting at his own *bureau plat*, by the open French window, writing a letter.

He slewed around when his host walked in and said grimly, 'Good morning, David. I hope you are up to a few shocks.'

David cocked his head and said, 'Well, I know about the rat. Something, however, tells me the mere fact that a rat invaded Lucinda's bedchamber would not be sufficient to make you look like bull beef. Out with it. What am I supposed to have done?'

Hampton's mouth did not so much as quiver at this. 'I will rather ask you, David, what are your intentions towards Sophie Marsden?'

'And if I give the wrong answer?' asked David, the lightness of his voice at odds with the watchful gleam in his green eyes and the alertness of his stance.

Hampton stood up slowly. He was not quite as tall as Helford, but just as strongly built. And he looked positively dangerous. 'I tell you, David, if you mean to take that child and make her your mistress, I'll call you out.' Despite the softness of his voice, no one in possession of his senses could have doubted that he was in deadly earnest.

David relaxed. 'Well, I certainly mean to take her,' he began and flung up his hand hurriedly as Hampton started towards him. 'Oh, take a damper, Tom! I want her as my wife, not my mistress.'

'Thank God for that!' said Hampton, sitting down again. 'I couldn't believe that you were really going to seduce her, but when it came out that you had taken her home…'

David stiffened. 'Who the hell let that out? I didn't realise anyone knew!'

'Highbury,' said Hampton. 'I dare say he was distracted by the rat! Mind you, we were all wondering where you were. You missed a scene of high drama, let me tell you. And you may yet be thankful for Highbury's lack of discretion! Sit down, David! You're making me nervous, looming over me like that.'

'I thought you were going to call me out,' protested David, sitting down on the edge of the *bureau.*

'Only if you were planning to seduce Miss Marsden,' Hampton replied.

David thought it might be as well not to tell Tom how close he had come to doing just that the previous night. 'For God's sake, tell me about this blasted rat, Tom! I can't believe it, we don't *have* rats!'

Hampton complied, explaining in laughing detail what had happened. He looked a bit more serious at the end. 'When Highbury said you'd taken Miss Marsden home, well! You should have seen the look on Lucinda's face! Not to mention Lady Stanford's. You're in trouble there, my boy. Made it quite plain that you would not be accepted. Er…just how deeply were you entangled with Lucinda?'

'Deep enough,' acknowledged David with a grimace. 'It's going to cause a lot of talk, but I'm damned if I'll marry her just to avoid unpleasantness. And if she's indicated so publicly that an offer won't be welcome, it doesn't matter. I approached Stanford before leaving town to ask his permission to pay my addresses, but I hadn't actually asked her to marry me. You and Kate put paid to that in the last week, didn't you?'

'Mmm,' said Hampton with a twinkle. 'Don't leave Lady Maria out of the reckoning. She was quite as determined to prevent the match. May one ask why on earth you even considered Lucinda? I don't say anything against the girl, but I wouldn't have thought she was quite your style.'

'She's not,' said David promptly. 'Put it down to sheer stubbornness. I intended a marriage of convenience because I thought myself incapable of falling in love after Felicity. Thought it didn't really matter who I chose as long as she was a girl of breeding, beauty and virtue. You must own Lucinda is all that.' He shrugged. 'It never felt quite right. I knew I wasn't in love, but that didn't worry me at first. Nor that Lucinda doesn't know the meaning of the word. But I kept seeing Peter and Penelope. I suppose it gradually dawned on me that a marriage doesn't have to be convenient to be happy. And that just because a man makes one mistake he doesn't have to keep on making it. And then I met Sophie!'

'I see,' said Hampton. 'And that was it. She bowled you out!'

David looked at him. 'You could say that. One day I'll tell you how I met her. But now, if you will excuse me, I need to write a note to reassure her that I really do intend marriage. Unless, of course, you feel that you could make a better fist of it. I suppose I should be thanking you and the others on bended knee for your kind offices.'

'No, no!' said Hampton with a grin as he stood up. 'I'll leave you to it in the sure and certain knowledge that Lady Maria approves your choice this time.'

'Oh, go to the devil,' recommended David, sitting down at the *bureau*. He watched Captain Hampton depart with a light step and wondered just how quickly his friend would be able to tell his co-conspiritors of the success that had attended upon their efforts. With a shudder he contemplated just what might have occurred without their intervention. He would have offered for Lucinda and been accepted.

He groaned as he realised just how close he'd come to an appalling scandal. He had no doubt that he would not have married Lucinda. Would probably have jilted her for Sophie, which would have made the position for both women intolerable. Thanks to his aunt and his friends and…yes, and that impossible rat, he'd been spared all that!

The chiming of the clock on the marble chimney-piece warned him that he was running out of time and that if he wished to write to Sophie before breakfast, he'd better stop dithering.

His lordship found paper, mended his pen and wrote hastily for a moment. It would have to be a brief letter if he were not to be hopelessly late for breakfast. To his exasperation his seal was missing.

'Hell and damnation!' he muttered. 'Where is the confounded thing?' He thought hard and remembered that he had put it in his pocket the day before to take down to the estate room. 'What I need,' he said to the standish, 'is a seal ring. I shall suggest it to Aunt Maria as a wedding present.' He folded the letter over and wrote *Miss Sophie Marsden* on the outside. Then he left the room to find his seal.

As soon as the door clicked shut a tall slim figure gowned in pale blue muslin stalked into the room through the open window. Fury and chagrin blazed from cerulean eyes; even Lady Lucinda's black ringlets seemed to radiate anger. How *dare* he! It was bad enough to think that he had been pursuing the Marsden wench right under her nose with a view to making the slut his mistress. But to find that he actually wished to marry the little trollop in preference to herself was insupportable!

Never mind that she would not now accept him if he got down on his knees and begged. Lady Lucinda Anstey had never been so insulted and humiliated in her entire life. She'd make the pair of them pay for this if it took her the rest of her life!

She clenched her fist in rage and brought it down on the vacated *bureau*, making the quill pen and standish jump slightly. The unsealed letter to Sophie caught her eye. Her hand went out to it and drew back. There was no point in destroying it. He would only write another.

But her hand went back to the letter as if drawn irresistibly. She hesitated, never in her life had she read someone else's letter but the temptation to see what sickly, vulgar rubbish Helford had penned to the presumptuous whore was too great. Quickly she unfolded the letter and conned it.

My dearest Love,

I thought that I had better write and reassure you as to my intentions after my behaviour last night. We arrived at Willowbank House far too soon. Believe me, Sophie, I mean to have you with all honour. I am rather rushed now but please accept this in earnest of my intentions.

All my love, David.

She snorted in disgust. How pathetic! Had she not actually heard Helford tell Hampton point blank that he intended marriage she would doubt it from that letter. She was about to refold the letter again when a sudden idea presented itself for her inspection.

Carefully she re-read the letter. It was as she thought, he did not actually mention marriage. Not that she doubted his intention. But would Madam Marsden see it like that? If, as the letter implied, he had taken liberties with the wench, then she might well be expecting a very different sort of offer.

Lucinda thought fast. Helford could be back at any moment. He must not find her here! Swiftly she opened her reticule and drew forth two ten-pound notes. Swiftly she folded the letter around them, and placed it back on the desk. At the worst, if Helford found the money, he could prove nothing, might even think he had got the notes muddled with the letter. At best, it might even ruin the marriage if Miss Marsden thought he had considered making her his mistress.

With a coldly triumphant smile Lady Lucinda left the room, giving all her consideration to how she could ensure that Miss Marsden should be as sullied as possible by the fact that Lord Helford had taken her home and not kept the line with her!

Entering the room a bare two minutes later, Helford sat down his desk and pulled the letter towards him.

Just as he was about to open it the door opened and a small voice said, 'Uncle David?'

He looked up in some surprise. 'Hullo, Fanny. Something wrong?'

Inserting her self into the room, Fanny nodded. 'It's…well…it's about that rat.'

Smothering a smile, he said comfortingly, 'You don't have to worry, sweetheart. Highbury's Nelson saw it off. It won't come back.'

'It's not that,' muttered Fanny. 'All the maids are quite hysterical and Aunt Maria is talking about having the whole house gone over and…and…I thought I'd better tell you…'

'Tell me?' he prompted as she hesitated.

'That it was me.'

A feeling akin to awe stole through David as he eyed his shamefaced niece. 'You put the rat in Lucinda's room?' He couldn't quite believe it.

'Yes, sir.'

Choking back a wild desire to laugh, he asked simply, 'Why?'

She hesitated and then said, 'Because I didn't want her to marry you. And I thought…'

'That if she believed the place to be infested with rats she wouldn't,' he finished drily. 'You were quite right, but why tell me now?'

Fanny blushed even more deeply. 'Because I heard Captain Hampton just now telling Aunt Maria and Mrs Asterfield that you'd decided to marry Aunt Sophie instead…and…and…well, we…I wouldn't want *her* to say no because of the rat! And, he…he kept on looking at me and saying that Lady Lucinda wouldn't have you because of the rat…and…and I thought I'd better tell you before he did!'

'I see,' said David, wondering if he was allowed to laugh or should, in the name of discipline, preserve a disapproving front. But for the life of him, he couldn't find it in him even to pretend to be cross. 'Well, since you've saved me from a fate worse than death, to wit, an appalling scandal, I'll let you off this time.' He shook slightly. 'Just don't unburden your soul to Aunt Maria!' Seeing her look of puzzlement, he explained. 'Don't tell her what you've just told me. I think that it had better be our secret.'

He held out his hand to her and with a smile of relief she ran across to him. He hugged her and said lightly, 'Just don't import any more rats, pet. Where on earth did you catch one anyway?'

She looked very conscious and said, 'I think I'd better not say...really, Uncle David. I promise I haven't been anywhere I'm not allowed, but I can't say...'

Memories of his own misspent boyhood suggested only one reason that she would refuse to answer; an ally to incriminate—which meant—no, he wasn't going to ask! There were some things a wise guardian just didn't want to know. Officially, anyway.

'Very well,' he said. 'Now, you'd best be off. I have to get to breakfast and be extra polite to everyone! Out!' Then, as she reached the door, he asked casually, 'By the way, Fanny, how big was it?'

She turned and shuddered. 'Oh, it was enormous! I nearly screamed when it came out of the box on her bed and I saw it. I didn't think rats got that big!'

'Hmm,' managed David in the face of this innocent revelation. 'Greater love hath no niece...my thanks, Fanny. Off you go now, and remember—don't tell Aunt Maria!' That joy, he vowed, was going to be his, and his only.

Only after the door shut behind his niece did he give in to his laughter. Kit and Fanny! And he'd have the pair of them under his guardianship! What on earth was he letting himself in for?

Belatedly remembering his letter, he cast a horrified glance at the clock on the chimney-piece, sealed the missive hurriedly and rang the bell. When James appeared, he merely gave it to him and said, 'Have one of the grooms deliver that to Willowbank House immediately.'

'Very good, my lord.' James took the letter and prepared to depart.

'Oh, James, about last night…'

James turned with what could only be termed reluctance. 'Yes, my lord?'

'It must have been an extremely large rat.'

The corner of his lordship's mouth was twitching uncontrollably and a wide answering grin split James's normally stolid face. 'It was that right enough! Cor! I never seen the like! Even Mr Bainbridge was shocked!' He flushed. 'I hope her ladyship didn't take it too badly amiss, me speakin' out of turn like as how I did. Don't know what came over me.'

'Never mind, James,' said his lordship with an even broader grin as he wondered how Fanny had steeled herself to the task. 'Should her ladyship chance to mention the incident, I will undertake to convince her that had she given me that command, my response would have been even less respectful. I understand Highbury's terrier put the beast to flight?'

'Aye, he did that all right,' said James, with a chuckle. 'Shame it got away. Not but what it would of made a nasty mess which the maids wouldn't of liked. All for the best, like as not, my lord.'

'I dare say!' said his lordship in heartfelt agreement. He was sorry that Lord Mark and Ned Asterfield had been disappointed in the evening's sport, but a rat fight in the State Apartments would have been in very poor taste. Besides, he owed the rat a debt of gratitude!

An hour later Sophie broke the seal of Helford's letter in the privacy of her bedchamber. Her fingers shook as she slid the knife under wax. As she opened the letter something inside fluttered to the ground. She frowned. It was a bank note, no, two bank notes. Her stomach lurched sickeningly as she bent to pick them up.

Shaking with horror she read the letter...*accept this in earnest of my intentions*... She dropped letter and money as though they had burned her. She could not blame him after the way she had behaved last night, but somehow she had allowed herself to hope that he had meant...she could scarcely think the word...marriage. It was plain he did not! *I mean to have you in all honour*... What did that mean? That he would engage to keep their liaison secret?

It was not, however, his intent to take her as his mistress that really hurt. Were it not for Kit, she would have gone to him regardless. It was the money. And she'd allowed herself to think he might mean marriage! Doubtless he'd decided that having her in bed would be far more comfortable than a draughty carriage!

What does he think I am? Her mind shied away from the obvious answer. He had sent the money as a down payment on her services. No more, no less.

He calls you his dearest love! He told you he loved you!

Not as you understand it, obviously. Grow up, Sophie Marsden, and stop dreaming. He regards you as a cheap little strumpet. Just imagine what he would have sent if he hadn't decided that it would be more comfortable for him in bed!

'I hate him!' she said furiously. 'I hate him!' But she didn't. That was the problem. She loved him and she had thought he at least cared for her. Even if he hadn't been able to marry her…she had thought…now she knew that she had been close to destroying herself for a man who thought of her as a…a…business transaction…a filly to be bought, and doubtless sold when she tired him or if her action did not please. All that had saved her was Kit.

She sat for a long time, staring at nothing, dry eyed although her throat ached with unshed tears. It would be impossible to stay here after this. She could not allow Kit to ride with him any more or have Fanny here even if Helford would have permitted it. She did not think he was unprincipled enough to use the children to disguise an affair. No, she would leave as soon as possible. She would be able to think of some reason to satisfy Thea and Kit.

At last, though, a solitary tear trickled soundlessly down her cheek. It was followed by another and another until her face was wet and her shoulders shook with the force of the sobs that racked her slender frame. Never, not even when Emma died, had she known such complete despair. Emma's death, she had known, would in time be accepted, and in truth she never felt that Emma was far away. She was always conscious of her as a silent but friendly presence.

This was not something that could be transmuted into a joyful memory as Emma had become. This bitterness would haunt her for the rest of her life. Never would she be able to seek or accept love again. She felt soiled. Helford might not have actually taken her maidenhead, but she knew that any man would consider the distinction to be academic. She felt it so herself. She was damaged goods now.

When she finally emerged from her chamber her face was white and her eyes red-rimmed. Her cold expression forbade anyone to ask what was troubling her and she went about her household tasks with unwonted efficiency and vigour. When Lord Helford came tomorrow, he would be sent about his business and requested not to call again.

Discovering the next morning that the milk had gone sour, Sophie took a can and walked down the lane to Gillies's farm. It was usually a pleasant walk and she was always sure of a welcome at the farmhouse. Mrs Gillies was never so busy that she didn't have time for a comfortable chat.

On this occasion, however, Sophie was met at the door to the dairy by one of the maids, who said cheekily, 'Missus don't hold wi' your sort! She says ye can go elsewhere fer yer milk after this. She'll fill it this onct but not anymore.' The girl grabbed the pail and departed before Sophie could utter a word. When she came back she said, 'There y'are. Now ye're t' go. Missus don' want none on us ter be dirtied wi' your sort.'

Her cheeks flaming, Sophie took the can and left, crossing the farmyard with her head held high. Two farm hands on seeing her, made it clear that they considered her fair game, standing in her path, calling out obscene remarks as she approached.

She ignored them and walked on defiantly. Something in her eyes made them give ground, but one of them grabbed her bottom as she went past, squeezing it hard and saying, 'Sure an' 'is lordship was on to summat sweet an' juicy 'ere!' As she kept going he yelled, 'I can give yer what 'is lordship give yer! Stuck-up slut!'

By the time she reached home she was raging. The driver of a passing farm wagon had offered her a lift in return for a kiss. It was obvious that the entire countryside had been informed of Helford's intentions. So much for his promise to have her in all honour! She opened the front door and heard Thea's voice in the parlour. 'No doubt this is Sophie now, my lord.'

Damn him! He must have sent his horse around to the stable. Just as if he owned the place! Which he did, of course. No doubt he thought he owned her too. He was about to discover his mistake.

As Thea came out of the parlour Sophie said, 'A moment, Thea. There is something I must return to his lordship. I will be down directly.' She ran upstairs to her bedchamber and took the letter from a drawer. It was refolded with the note inside and resealed. Holding it, she went back downstairs with her head held high.

Upon her entering the parlour Helford stood up and smiled at her tenderly. Then the smile faded. His little love was looking anything but loving. Thea Andrews was excusing herself and he politely bade her farewell. Then he turned to Sophie warily.

She was holding out his letter, her eyes cold and her pale face like a mask. 'I would prefer you to take this back. I am afraid that I cannot entertain your obliging proposals, my lord, and I would infinitely prefer it if you ceased your visits to this house.' Her voice was laden with contempt.

'What!' He couldn't believe his ears. She was actually refusing him! 'You...you can't be refusing... Sophie, why?'

'I do not return your sentiments, my lord!' She had expected that question. Her answer was true enough, she considered. She didn't return his sentiments. She was in love with him and he thought of her as a convenient bit of game, just as he had once implied.

Helford's temper began to rise. What the hell did the chit mean? She'd returned a fair bit in that blasted carriage all right and tight! Fair enough if she had thought him to be suggesting a less respectable union before she received his letter, but now! What more did she want?

'Damn it all! You certainly gave a good imitation of it the night before last! I wasn't the only one making the running!'

She had no answer to that but blushed a deep crimson. 'Please leave, my lord. There is nothing more to be said.'

'Isn't there?' Helford's voice was savage. 'I'll say one thing more, Miss Marsden! You have behaved like the veriest trollop! If I *had* taken you in that carriage, it would have been no more than you deserve! Obviously I should have availed myself of the opportunity! Good afternoon!'

He snatched the letter from her and stormed out, leaving a white-faced girl behind him. She stood rigidly until she heard the thunder of his horse's hooves on the road, then she sank into a chair and sobbed her heart out. Thea Andrews, returning to the room, stood dumbfounded on the threshold and then ran to kneel beside her, slipping an arm around her shoulders, murmuring softly and stroking the brown curls. Gentle, soothing words flowed from her but Sophie continued to weep until Thea thought she must break apart.

Thank goodness Kit was out of the way, she thought. Finally she managed to urge Sophie to her feet and up to bed. After tucking her in and drawing the curtains she went back down to the kitchen to consult with Anna on this puzzling departure from the norm.

Anna had been to the village and had got a fair idea of what was being said.

She passed it on to Thea at once, saying, 'If'n we don't do summat fast, Miss Sophie's ruined. His lordship oughter be ashamed of hisself! But what to do is beyond me, Miss Thea.'

'It can't be true!' said Thea, shocked. 'I mean, I have suspected that she is not so indifferent to him as she would like us to think, but she wouldn't—'

'Lor', miss! You don't need to tell me that. I've knowed Miss Sophie since she was a baby. It's what others'll believe that's the problem. An' there's no gettin' around it, if 'is lordship did bring 'er 'ome then 'e oughtn't 'ave done!'

Thea racked her brains. 'Lady Darleston!' she said at last. 'I'll write to her at once and have Grigson take the note over. She'll know what to do!'

Anna nodded her approval. 'Aye, that might help. Not a blind bit of notice would they take of us what've known Miss Sophie fer years, but they'll take the word of a Countess what's known 'er five minnits!'

Chapter Fourteen

After pushing through a hedge into the fields and urging his horse into a gallop for some four miles, Lord Helford was no closer either to regaining control of his temper or understanding why Miss Marsden had refused his offer. Surely she didn't think he would object to her settling her money on Kit! Not that the boy was likely to need it if Strathallen could be brought up to scratch.

At last he turned for home, his mood bleak. His temper had finally ebbed, giving way to a numb despair. As much as he tried to convince himself that Sophie Marsden was a teasing little trollop, his heart stubbornly refused to take the slightest notice. If anything had been needed to assure him that what he felt for her was love, it was the fact that he could not shrug her off. Bitterly he remembered the morning he had gone to beg Felicity to marry him. He had felt only rage and hurt pride, he now realised. Not this aching, leaden despair.

Briefly he considered offering for Lucinda Anstey after all, only to dismiss the notion with a shudder. Even if she accepted him, which he seriously doubted after the cool way she had spoken to him in farewell the previous afternoon, the knowledge that all his friends were dead set against the match was enough to give him pause. Had he loved her, that would not have signified, but it would hardly be a convenient marriage if his friends and aunt actually disliked his bride. Besides, he could not bear the idea of making love, or rather consummating a union, with Lucinda. Not after the innocent abandon of Sophie's passionate response.

Which brought him back to Sophie. Why the devil had she refused him? He found it hard to believe that she did not return his love. He hoped he was not the arrogant coxcomb she had once called him, but he had been sure that she loved him. There was something odd about this and he didn't know how to deal with it. All he knew was that if Sophie didn't marry him, the name of Melville would die with him. He could not imagine ever wishing to marry someone else.

Upon reaching the stables he dismounted and threw his reins to Jasper without even a grunt of greeting and stalked up to the house, prey to the blackest despair he had ever known. Far worse even than when Felicity had chosen to marry James and the title rather than himself. He'd thought he'd hit rockbottom then, but somewhere deep down he had known that it was inevitable. That had Felicity truly cared for him, she would not have hesitated for a moment.

Somehow it hurt far more that Sophie had rejected him. She was not choosing something else. Merely rejecting him. He thought he could have borne it better had he thought that she was in love with someone else. *Dear God! Was she? But who? Not Garfield. That was unthinkable. But Tom?*

He groaned. That was not at all unthinkable! Tom would make her, indeed any woman, a splendid husband. Comfortably circumstanced, kind...and he'd made it quite plain that he liked and admired Sophie. Even if he had not encouraged her, he had supported her through that ghastly dinner party. David realised that the thought of Sophie being in love with anyone save himself did not help in the least. It merely made him want to plant Tom a facer and drag Sophie to the altar by the hair!

Jasper had watched his master's bleak-faced departure with interest. He had a great deal to say to his master when opportunity presented itself, but he judged that now was not the moment. The master would be settling down for a long session this evening. Jasper decided to slip up to the kitchen later on to visit his good friend, Jeffreys the chef. Time enough to ask his lordship what the hell he was playing at with little Miss Sophie once he'd had time to down a decanter or so of brandy.

* * *

By the time Lord Helford was halfway down the decanter, his leaden misery had settled firmly and showed no sign of responding to the time-honoured remedy known as drowning one's sorrows. The noble vintage he was quaffing so recklessly might as well have been drained off from the kennels for all the satisfaction it afforded his numbed heart. His determination never to darken Miss Marsden's doorstep again had been replaced by an equally irrational desire to leap back into the saddle and ride straight back to Willowbank House, sweep her into his arms and force her to consent to marriage. It would not do, of course, she'd tell him to go to the devil in as many words.

By the time Bainbridge came to the library to announce dinner he was extremely well to live and merely favoured the butler with a morose grunt.

'Should I, er…take the brandy decanter into the dining salon or would your lordship prefer to dine here?' enquired Bainbridge tactfully. 'Lady Maria is dining off a tray in her room, being rather tired.'

'Neither,' was the reply. 'I am not hungry. Apologise to Jeffreys for the trouble he has been put to.' It would be too much to say that his lordship's deep voice was slurred precisely, but it was evident that he was expending a great deal of effort to avoid that indignity.

Bainbridge tottered away, quailing inwardly at

the likely reaction of Jeffreys at this cavalier rejection of his labours. What, apart from the jug, of course, had bitten the master? He bore all the signs of a man badly crossed in love, but that was impossible! It was common knowledge that his lordship had been on the point of offering for Lady Lucinda Anstey, and it would be news to Bainbridge if love had entered into his master's dealings with her.

Steeling himself for the inevitable explosion, Bainbridge entered the kitchen and relayed the fell tidings in as placatory tones as he could muster. On the whole Jeffreys took it quite well. Apart from jumping up and down forcibly expressing the desire that, if England had a revolution, his ungrateful master should be the first to mount the block, he only threw the rolling pin he happened to be holding and one silver chafing dish which had the misfortune to be close at hand. His underlings all ducked for cover and the scullery maid, who had put her nose in from the scullery to see what was amiss, retreated at once to her pots and pans.

Of all the occupants of the kitchen, the only one unmoved by Jeffrey's wrath was Jasper, who was seated at the table devouring bread and cheese.

He pricked up his ears and said, 'In a tweak, is 'e?'

Bainbridge eyed him with marked disfavour. His lordship's tiger had no business whatsoever in the kitchen, but if Jeffreys chose to allow it, he had nothing to say in the matter.

'His lordship,' he intoned frigidly, 'is not at all himself.'

'Jugbitten, eh?' Jasper correctly interpreted this genteel euphemism. He grinned cheekily at Bainbridge. 'I'll deal with 'im. Where might 'e be?'

Not for all his disapproval of his lordship's vulgar, makebait tiger, could Bainbridge deliver a fellow man up to such a fate as he reckoned would be in store for anyone disturbing the master.

'Don't you do it, Jasper!' he said earnestly. 'Be more than your job's worth. If I didn't know better I'd say he'd been crossed in love!'

'Would you, now?' said Jasper slowly. 'Then thankin' yer fer the warnin' all the same, but I'd best see 'im afore 'e shoots the cat, as the saying is! Jeffreys, you keep things warm a bit. There's no sayin' but what 'e mightn't fancy a bite after I'm done with 'im. Now, where is 'e, Mr Bainbridge?'

'In…in the Library,' said Bainbridge, thinking that no doubt his lordship, having an affection for Jasper, would re-employ him in the morning if he turned him off tonight.

Upon entering the Library, one look was enough to inform Jasper that his master was in as bleak a mood as ever he'd known. He hadn't even noticed the door opening but was gazing into the empty fireplace with an expression of bitterness, twirling his empty brandy glass. The usually immaculate cravat had been loosened and his black hair tousled.

Jasper shut the door quietly, watching as his master reached for the brandy decanter on the floor beside his wing chair.

'Beggin' your pardon, sir, but I'd say ye'd had enough.'

David turned sharply, focusing his gaze with difficulty on the figure by the door. 'Jasper? What the hell are you doing here?'

'Need a word with yer lordship afore you gets any further,' said Jasper bluntly. He walked over to the fireplace and looked down at his master with friendly concern.

'Damn you, Jasper!' exploded David. 'You go too far!'

'Aye,' said Jasper equably. 'An' I'll go a bit farther. 'Tis about Miss Sophie—'

David erupted from his chair. 'Jasper, if you mention that name again, you'll be seeking a new master!'

Seemingly unperturbed, Jasper nodded. 'That's as may be, my lord, but was you wishful to have all the folks around Little Helford talkin' about how Miss Sophie was your bit o' muslin?'

'*What?*' David was dumbfounded. 'But she's not! I mean…I didn't…why the hell am I explaining myself to you?'

'I didn't think ye knew,' said Jasper. 'But that's what they're all asayin'. That she's no better than what she oughter be an' that she's a disgrace to the…'

'My God!' He felt sick. 'Does she know what's being said?' Could this be why Sophie had refused him? Had she been misled by scurrilous gossip? Had she thought he intended to recant his offer of marriage? Take her as his mistress? That he would callously ruin her?

'As to that my lord, I did hear as 'ow she got a pretty nasty greetin' at Farmer Gillies's farm this mornin'. Full of it the village was when I was down at the smithy afore.' Jasper watched his master sympathetically. Not a doubt but what it was a facer for him.

Ashen, David swallowed hard. It was all his fault! If only he hadn't decided to take Sophie home! Somehow the story must have got around. Damn Highbury! He shuddered to think what she must have thought. That he was laughing at her naïvety. That he had let it be known she was his mistress. No wonder she had refused him if she thought he was offering her a *carte blanche*! But what about his letter? He had offered her marriage, hadn't he? Surely, even if people were talking, she must have been reassured by that. But then why had she returned it to him as though it were the embodiment of an insult?

At this juncture the door opened and Bainbridge announced, 'Captain Hampton, my lord,' in tones which suggested he envisaged an immediate entry to the workhouse.

The groan which broke from his lordship betokened that the unexpected sight of one of his closest friends was in no way welcome.

Captain Hampton, taking in the scene with an experienced eye, said, 'Bainbridge, have dinner served at once in the small salon before we have to put his lordship to bed in a bucket, there's a good chap.'

The door closed behind the outraged butler.

'What the hell are you doing here?' asked David. 'You were going home.'

'Broken wheel about thirty miles from here. Thought I might as well come back. So I hired a horse. But do enlighten me. What now have you been about that Jasper feels called upon to give you one of his jobations?' enquired Hampton as he lowered himself into the vacated wing chair.

'Ruining Sophie Marsden!' said David in accents of utter despair. 'Tell him the worst, Jasper, and then you may as well leave me to my fate.'

'You did *what*?' Hampton stared at him. 'You said you were going to offer for her!'

'I thought I had, too!' said David. 'Tell him, Jasper!'

Jasper obeyed, noting that the Captain, usually so cheery, looked as though he was like to give the master a fair bit more than a jobation.

'But didn't you write to her, David?' Hampton was puzzled. 'Maybe the letter was not delivered.'

'Of course I wrote to her!' said David. 'And, yes,

the damned letter was delivered. She almost threw it at me when I saw her!' He paced the floor in frustration. 'She must have thought that I...that I...had... Oh, God! Tom, what she must have thought? She told me she did not return my sentiments! And well she might if she thought I meant...to...to...take her as my mistress!'

'It all hinges on that letter,' said Hampton thoughtfully. 'I don't suppose you can recall precisely what you wrote?'

David shook his head. 'No. I was in such a damned hurry. I had to go and find my seal and just as I got back Fanny came in and told me she'd put the rat in Lucinda's room...'

'It was her, was it?' Hampton choked on a laugh. 'How very enterprising of her. Where the devil did she get it? And why?'

David grinned. 'Yes. She thought you'd smoked her. I'm prepared to wager she got it from Kit. As for why—she told me that she wanted to make Lucinda think the place was infested with rats to stop her marrying me. Anyway, what with trying not to laugh in front of the child, and thinking I'd better get to breakfast on time and smooth Lucinda down a trifle, I was a little rushed. Turned out she was breakfasting upstairs, though.'

'What?' Hampton was surprised. 'But I passed her in the hall on my way to the library that morning.'

Helford shrugged. 'Must have changed her mind.

I dare say she was furious with me. If Highbury let out that I had taken Sophie home…and with the rat thrown in…'

Jasper piped up. 'Not me place, o' course, to say, but…' He hesitated.

David looked at him in resignation. 'Since when has that consideration ever stopped you, Jasper? Out with it.'

'Well, I was agoin' ter say that mebbe 'twas her ladyship what started all the talk 'bout Miss Sophie,' said his henchman reluctantly. "Twas her maid talkin' the loudest in the servants' hall. Could be she was takin' out a bit o' spite.'

'You're sure you can't recall that letter, David?' asked Hampton.

'Quite…no, hold on! I think I've got it with me!' exclaimed David. 'I shoved it in my pocket and stormed out. It's probably upstairs.'

'Well, for God's sake go and get it!' recommended Hampton. 'And bring it to the small dining salon, I'm famished.'

With a broad grin, Jasper opined that it would be as well if so be they were wishful to keep Jeffreys in good skin.

Ten minutes later the two gentleman were seated at one end of the dining table, a vast expanse of mahogany even with all the leaves taken out. The letter lay unopened beside Helford while the first course was set out.

'We'll serve ourselves, Bainbridge,' said David impatiently.

Scarcely had the door shut before he picked up the letter and broke the wax. As he opened it the twenty pounds fluttered to the table top.

He stared at it as though he had never seen a pair of ten-pound notes in his life. 'What the hell is that doing there?'

Hampton blinked. 'You didn't…no…of course not.'

David was reading the letter with a gathering frown. When he had finished he put it down and said in constricted tones, 'I should have let you write it after all, Tom. I don't actually say anything about marriage…here, you read it.'

He passed it over. What a bloody fool he was! For want of a bit of care, he had ruined Sophie and made her life hell. He wouldn't blame her if she refused to have anything more to do with him, even after he explained.

Hampton read the hurried note and handed it back. 'Not exactly explicit, is it? You damned idiot! But what really has me gapped is the money. How did that get there?'

David shook his head. 'I couldn't hazard a guess. I certainly didn't put it there! She…she must have thought I was…buying her…services.' He buried his face in his hands with a ragged groan.

Hampton was thinking hard. 'You know, David, if Lucinda started the gossip, then I think we need

look no further for the origin of this twenty pounds.'
He nodded at Helford's dropped jaw and darkening
brow. 'Think about it. You didn't put it there. And
I spoke to Lucinda just before going to the library.
In fact, I told her that I was going to see you. The
window on to the terrace was open and…you didn't
re-read it, did you, when you came back? Didn't
you say you left the room to find your seal? And
then Fanny came in?'

'The little bitch!' David exploded. 'I'll…I'll…'

'Do nothing,' finished Hampton. 'You can't prove
it and you've already done quite enough to stir up the
tabbies. The only thing you can do is marry Sophie
Marsden as fast as possible and get her up to London
with Lady Maria and Penelope Darleston to silence
the gossip. The pair of them can launch her in the
Little Season.' He looked at David sympathetically.
'You know, old chap, I think when you explain
yourself and apologise for being such a bloody fool,
she might just forgive you. There's really no occasion
for quite such despair. After all, the girl's tail over top
in love with you, for some God-unknown reason!'

'How the hell would you know anything about it?'
asked David irritably. 'Or did she tell you that when
you were making up to her at dinner the other night?'

'Oh, take a damper!' recommended Hampton
good-naturedly. 'I should imagine everyone in the
room knew what was going on when Penelope
Darleston got the girl to sing that song. Damn it all,

if she'd been singing it for me, I'd have fallen in love with her myself!'

By the end of dinner David had talked himself into a more hopeful frame of mind. Tom was in the right of it. He'd see Sophie tomorrow and sort things out. Have the banns called immediately. And if Sophie tried to kick him out again, he knew perfectly well how to get her attention and stop her talking for long enough to convince her that his intentions were entirely honourable.

In the event Lord Helford did not arise from his slumbers at all early on the following morning, and when he did he came to the immediate conclusion that the sun was far too bright and the sky far too blue. That was before Meredith drew back the curtains of his bedchamber to reveal a cloudy, weeping day outside. At which point he winced audibly and visibly as he buried his aching head under his pillow.

'Should I return later, my lord?' asked Meredith solicitously.

'What time is it?' asked David carefully.

'Nearly noon, my lord.'

Nearly noon? Oh, God! He'd have to get up. He couldn't leave Sophie in this damned coil any longer.

'Coffee,' he said shortly as he eased himself out of bed. 'Black and strong.'

And blinked as it was handed to him in a delicate basaltware coffee cup.

'Captain Hampton's orders, my lord,' explained Meredith, laying all blame squarely where it belonged.

David throttled an overwhelming urge to laugh. It was bound to make his headache even worse than it was already. Instead he accepted the coffee and sipped at it gratefully. Gradually he began to feel less scratchy and was able to contemplate getting dressed in a more optimistic spirit. He still didn't feel quite so sanguine about facing Sophie.

He would have to explain that damned twenty pounds for one thing, and despite being morally certain Lucinda had been responsible, he had no proof and hesitated to make an accusation he could not substantiate. Besides which, he just had a sinking feeling that everything was not going to be quite as simple as Tom had suggested.

For God's sake, David! Just tell her you're head over heels in love with her, beg her to marry you, in as many words, and kiss her senseless! How difficult is that?

Which was all very well, thought David. The last time he'd tried to do that, he'd got the order confused and kissed her first. And just look at the bumblebroth that had landed him in!

Having made a brief stop at the Vicarage on his way through the village that was guaranteed to stir up even more gossip, he rode up to Willowbank

House alone in the middle of the afternoon to discover a chaise and four standing in the road outside. Frowning, he wondered who could possibly be visiting Sophie in a chaise. The crest on the door was unfamiliar, but when he looked more closely he realised that what he had taken for a leopard was actually a Scottish wildcat.

Shock lanced through him as he realised who must own it.

'Is this Lord Strathallen's chaise?' His question was addressed to the lad holding the wheelers.

'Yessir.' The boy touched his cap politely. 'Come special all the way from Scotland he has, sir. Hold your mare, sir? Jim ain't doin' much.'

David nodded. 'Thank you.'

Another boy came forward and took the mare's bridle.

Steeling himself, David walked up the path, breathing the misty, heady scent of the lavender that lined it brushing against his sleeves. He always smelt it when he came here, he realised suddenly. And Sophie always smelled of it.

Smiling slightly, he went through the open door into the hall and wondered where she might be.

A harsh voice from the parlour, raised in anger, gave him the clue.

'D'ye think I've not heard all the gossip, ye little southron whore? Full of it the village was! Twasn't hard to pick up that his lordship's taken you as his latest lightskirt! Aye, and I only wish Jock had had as much sense with your sister! Why he had to marry her I'll never know! But since he did, I'm damned if I'll have my heir raised by you! Ye'll hand the lad over and there's an end of it! D'ye hear me, ye little doxy?'

David froze in horror. The countryside must indeed be humming if a chance traveller had heard the gossip. Despairing guilt racked him. No wonder Sophie had refused him if this were the sort of thing to which she was being subjected!

Sophie's answer came furiously. 'You have not the least right, my lord! You have known of Kit's existence for years! Emma named me his guardian and I have the deed to prove it! You are entirely welcome to visit him and I will be happy to bring him to visit you so that he may learn to know his family and become familiar with your people, but...'

A bark of scornful laughter interrupted her. 'Aye, so ye may have a deed! And how long do ye think that will stand in court if I bring a claim and can prove ye're not fit morally to have charge of the lad? Precious little good Helford will be then!'

This had gone far enough! Rage exploded through David that anyone might threaten his love in any way whatsoever, let alone with a weapon he had forged.

He stalked into the parlour without even bothering to knock.

Sophie, facing the door, was on her feet, her face white and stricken. 'You…you can't…it's not true…you *couldn't* be so cruel…*Helford*!'

She broke off as she saw him, shock and despair evident in her wide eyes and trembling mouth. Unbelievable pain pierced through David as he realised that in his arrival she saw the vindication of Strathallen's claim.

The old man had turned to face him. Nearly as tall as David, he was a striking figure in his kilt. Fierce blue eyes glared forth challengingly over a beak of a nose in a face lined with years. A thick head of white hair was the only other discernible evidence of his advanced age. He held himself as straight as a man half his age and exuded a vigour that many a younger man might have envied.

When he spoke his voice held nothing but scorn and triumph.

'Ye're mighty prompt, Helford! Come for a word with this little doxy, have ye? Or have ye been here all along?'

'You may thank God for your advanced years, Strathallen!' rapped out David, white-lipped with fury. 'Only they protect you now, and if you insult my betrothed wife any further, I can assure that they will not continue to protect you!' His voice was icy. 'I have no idea what gossip you have been listening to, but I made Miss Marsden an offer of marriage yesterday morning and I am here to inform her that the banns will be published next Sunday. I suggest that if you have any further requests to make of her, that they be made through me. I would point out to you that once Miss Marsden marries me, I will automatically assume all legal responsibility for Kit. And perhaps if you have any doubt of the nature of our relationship you might better apply to my aunt, Lady Maria Kentham, or to the Earl and Countess of Darleston, rather than the taproom of whatever hostelry you are dignifying with your custom!'

Thus my Lord Helford at his most arrogant and overbearing.

It was probably fortunate that Strathallen was too taken up with goggling at David to observe the shocked disbelief on Sophie's face. Her jaw had dropped open and she was clutching at a chair back for support as the room whirled around her in a very dizzying manner.

Marriage? Had he said marriage? That he was here to inform her that the banns would be called on Sunday? She had to be dreaming…it just wasn't possible!

Strathallen was speaking. 'Do I understand you, my lord? You are betrothed to…to this…'

'To Miss Marsden!' grated David. 'And you will speak to her and of her with respect, Strathallen! Starting now! You owe Miss Marsden an apology, I believe.'

A harsh laugh broke from Strathallen. "'Tis no matter to me if ye're fool enough to marry the little slut just because the whole county is awash wi' the tale…'

'*Take that back!* Or…or I'll *kill* you!' Kit had stormed into the room. Small fists were clenched and hazel eyes were bright with childish rage. The black eye he was sporting suggested that he had already been defending his aunt's honour. 'Aunt Sophie isn't a…a…what you said. Take it back, I say!' He advanced threateningly on Strathallen, evidently intent on ramming his insults down his throat.

'That will do, Kit,' interposed David, laying a firm hand on his shoulder. 'Lord Strathallen is under a misapprehension. You may trust me to protect your aunt.'

'She's *my* aunt!' said Kit fiercely. 'And I won't let anyone insult her!' Suddenly he rounded on Helford. 'Not even you! Do you know what they are saying?' His distress was plain in the overbright eyes, the wobble in his voice. For a moment it looked as though he would fly bodily at Helford, but all of a sudden he seemed to regain control of himself.

Fixing David with a steely glare, he said, with commendable steadiness, 'My lord, I…I demand to know what your…your intentions are towards Aunt Sophie!'

Sophie froze. She saw David's jaw tighten.

'Kit, no!' she said frantically.

David held up one hand. Meeting Kit's fierce gaze, he said quietly, 'A moment, Sophie. He has every right to ask that question.'

Drawing a deep breath, he continued. 'Yes, Kit, I am aware of what has been said. It was all a misunderstanding which has made both me and your Aunt Sophie very unhappy. People did not realise that my intention is to marry your aunt. But I assure you that I intend, have always intended, to marry her.'

Tension ebbed visibly from the small body. 'You're going to marry Aunt Sophie? Well, that's all right and tight then!'

'If she'll have me,' said David diplomatically.

'Why ever wouldn't she?' asked Kit in surprise. 'Fanny thought you were going to marry Lady Lucinda.'

David strove to keep a straight face. 'Lady Lucinda is not at all fond of rats, Kit.' He raised one brow in mute query.

'Oh.' Kit grinned. 'Well, serves her right. I mean, after she stuck that beastly hat pin into Megs! Does this mean that we will live with you and Fanny at Helford Place? I mean, it's bigger than this house. And Lady Maria wouldn't like it if you came here, would she?'

David's jaw dropped slightly as he realised the full extent of his erstwhile intended's perfidy, but he managed to say, 'No. But she has already informed me that if I mean to fill the place with scrubby schoolboys she will remove to the Dower House. Now, might I suggest that you take yourself off about your business and leave us to ours?'

Kit seemed to remember Strathallen's presence. 'Oh, very well, but if *he* starts slanging Aunt Sophie again, will you tip him a leveller?'

David's face was grave as he said, 'Something of the sort. But it's not good form to hit a man twice your own age. Not at my age anyway.'

This was given frowning consideration. 'I suppose not.' He swung around to Strathallen again. 'Then if you insult Aunt Sophie again, you'll be the most rotten skirter, since Helford won't hit you. I don't care who you are!'

'Kit,' said Sophie. 'Out! I am sure Lord Strathallen has understood your position.'

'Just long as he does!' said Kit trenchantly. He left the room with a final fierce glare in his grand-father's direction.

A stunned expression on his face, Strathallen turned to Sophie. '*That* was my grandson? Jock's lad? That young varmint who juist aboot called me oot and challenged a mon he knows to be a peer?' His accent became decidedly more marked.

Sophie swallowed hard. 'My lord, recollect, Kit had no idea of your identity and he is well ac-quainted with Helford…please do not—'

She was rudely interrupted. 'Losh, girl, I'm not repining! If any mon had spoken to my mother as I spoke to you, I'd be after rammin' the words back down his gullet wi' me ridin' whip! The sperrit of the lad! An' he's been kept frae me all this time!'

'No doubt if you had acknowledged the letter Jock's widow sent you eight years ago you might have known the boy! And he would have known who you are!' snapped David. 'You must have known the boy was your heir long before Hampton and I wrote to you!'

'Aye. I knew,' admitted Strathallen. 'But no one else knew of his existence. Ye may be sure I did not boast of the whelp of a—' He caught David's eye and stopped. 'Weel, I was wrong. Any lad who could do what that lad juist did has no cause to complain of his dam or his raisin'! Lord, he looked as though he'd be at me throat!'

'As he would have been at mine,' said David drily. 'That is, if he didn't persuade my niece to put a rat in my bedchamber.' He went on, 'Seriously, my lord, there has been no attempt to keep Kit from you. You were informed of his birth in the letter Emma Carlisle sent you when she wrote of Jock's death. A letter which I understand it cost her great pain to write.'

Sophie's eyes flew to his face. She remembered telling him of that, how he had comforted her grief. That had been the first time he'd held her, his powerful body a refuge from pain, his arms a barrier to ward off all trouble. And now...what was he trying to do now? Simply protect her with his name since, contrary to expectation, the story of his intent had got about? Did he actually think she would accept such an offer? Or was he merely intending to smooth things over with Strathallen before breaking the engagement?

Strathallen's voice, low and ashamed, broke in on her thoughts. 'I barely read the letter before I burned it. Sure, it hurt so much... And ever after I wished I'd not done so, or that I'd copied the extracts she included...' The old eyes were suddenly misted over, their fierce blue softened.

'The original letters are here,' Sophie told him gently. 'If...if you would like to read them...copy them...I am sure Kit will bring them when he comes to see you. He is so proud of Jock. I am sure he will wish to show them to you.'

The old man sighed. 'I've been a damned fool, then. Alastair tried to tell me for years and I refused to listen. I never intended to deny the lad his inheritance. 'Twas just so damn hard to climb down...an' when I heard what folks were sayin'...weel, I juist saw red. I'll be takin' meself back to the Helford Arms. Your servant, Miss Marsden, an' I beg your pardon for...for everything. Bring the lad to me when it suits you to do so. I'll not be raisin' a claim against ye.'

He left quietly, leaving Sophie and David facing each other.

She supposed that she would have to sort the mess out. Now would be best. There was Kit's future to arrange. As long as he didn't renew his offer. Over the past day she had forced her battered heart and pride to accept the hand dealt by fate.

Despite what Penelope Darleston had said when she visited yesterday evening, Sophie did not believe he had ever intended marriage. Why should he when she had made it quite obvious that with a little effort he could have her without? Had he chosen to press her the other night, she might well have given herself. No doubt with Penelope's support and that of her husband the scandal would blow over, but the fact remained that she had nearly ruined herself.

She would not destroy herself for the gratification of his desire no matter how much she wanted to do so. He could go to the devil and leave her in peace. If such a thing were possible for her now.

Bleakly she told herself, as she met his eyes, that it would come to that in the end anyway. He would tire of her and leave, his only legacy a load of bitter memories. She did not delude herself. The memories would not ease the pain of parting. Rather the nature of the relationship would sour the memories. And there was Kit to consider. She could not ruin his life for the transient joy of Helford's arms.

She was the first to break the silence. 'I have to thank you, my lord, for your intervention. It was most timely.' Her voice was cold and light, a brittle armour for a breaking heart. Gallantly she continued. 'You may be sure that I will not hold you to your foolish declaration. Lady Darleston has been kind enough to engage herself to scotch the unfortunate consequences of the other night.'

The strange glint in his eyes disconcerted her. 'Is that what you think, Sophie? That this is merely a ploy to mislead Strathallen?' He smiled oddly. 'I am desolated to contradict you, my dear, but I can assure you that nothing less than our marriage will satisfy him. You will marry me or see Kit whisked off to Scotland before the cat can lick her ear.'

She stared up at him in horror. 'You...you mean I have to marry you to keep Kit?' She had thought it was painful enough to be offered a *carte blanche* by the man to whom she had given her heart. That was as nothing in comparison to the pain of being forced to accept an offer of marriage from him, an offer he had made only under duress.

For a wild moment she considered hurling the offer back in his teeth. But the vision of Kit arose before her, as it had done the other night. She couldn't, simply couldn't, betray his trust now, just to salvage her own pride. If she didn't accept Helford's offer, then Strathallen would have no trouble at all in convincing a court that she was unfit to be Kit's guardian. For Kit's sake she had to accept. Furiously she suppressed the surging joy in her own heart, the joy which cried out in exultation that now she would belong to Helford, no matter on what terms.

From between clenched teeth she said, 'Then I have no choice but to accept your very obliging offer, my lord. You will forgive me if I am less than enthusiastic about accepting your very reluctant hand in marriage!'

'Sophie, you cannot possibly think that I am only offering for you out of obligation...' In absolute horror, David realised that his final, instinctive attempt to mask the terrifying reality of his own need had backfired very badly. Her next words confirmed it.

'What else should I think?' she blazed at him. With a massive effort she drew a deep breath and forced her voice to calmness. 'You had no thought of *marriage* the other night, my lord. You can hardly expect me to be flattered at an offer made out of necessity. And made, no doubt, at the prompting of your friends.'

The cool steadiness of her voice was gratifying, but she hoped keeping it that way was going to get easier rather than harder. A flutter in her breast and a rising lump in her throat were not helping in the slightest.

'David.' He corrected her with a challenging look. 'I asked you to call me that the other night if you recall.' A hot flame flickered in his eyes. 'Of course you might not. You were somewhat distracted at the time, I believe.'

'No!' What had been intended as a firm and categorical denial came out as a frightened squeak as his words brought the memory flooding back to her body as well as to her mind. Horrified, she felt her knees turn to jelly and that same melting sensation take control as her body remembered the power this man had wielded over it.

Desperately she forced her brain to keep functioning. She had to keep him at bay—had to remind herself that this marriage would be one of obligation—on both sides.

He came closer, green eyes glinting, reminding her irresistibly of a prowling cat, one of the larger ones.

'No!' This time there was a note of panic in her voice. Furious with herself, she forced a lighter note. 'And marriage is a high price to pay for your pleasure, is it not, my lord? Yesterday morning it was only worth a down payment of twenty pounds to you!'

She was unprepared for his reaction. Embarrassment she would have understood. Or outrage at her most improper suggestion. But not this sudden and genuine roar of laughter. His whole face was alive with it, green eyes sparkling as he continued to chuckle.

'Oh, Sophie! What next will you say?'

Her hold on her temper, which had been precarious to say the least, finally slipped completely.

Scarcely knowing what she was doing, she grabbed for the nearest available missile and hurled it at him. Years of bowling for Kit had given her an enviable aim and she heard with immense satisfaction the thump as the heavy family bible struck him above the eye.

He staggered backwards, clutching his head. 'For God's sake, Sophie! Calm down, you little termagant, and give me a chance to explain myself! I didn't put that money in the letter!'

She stared at him in disbelief. If he hadn't put it there, then who had?

He sat down on the sofa and tenderly felt the spot where the bible had struck him. 'You've got a better aim than most females, I'll grant you that. I should have dodged!'

His voice held tender amusement and his eyes laughed up at her. She saw that he was going to have quite a bruise and felt a twinge of remorse. Ruthlessly she stamped on it. But his smile was turning her bones to water as she clung desperately to her resolution, reminding herself that he didn't really love her. That he must never know how much she loved him.

He was speaking again. 'Tom and I think that Lucinda overheard when I told him I intended to marry you. That she slipped the money into the note when I left the library to find my seal. Tom thinks she was on the terrace.' He sighed. 'I'm sorry,

Sophie. That letter was the most useless bit of cor-respondence I've ever penned. My only excuse is that I've never actually written a proposal of marriage before, or even a genuine love letter. And I was a bit pressed for time. Can you forgive me?'

It was becoming harder and harder to breathe, let alone speak. The lump in her throat combined with a burning prickle in her eyes to make speech nigh on impossible.

At last she spoke in a voice that seemed to break. 'My lord, surely there need be no pretence between us. You offer marriage because you have acciden-tally compromised me and in so doing have given Strathallen a weapon to use against me. I have accepted your offer because if I do not, I must lose Kit. What more remains to be said?'

She saw his fist clench.

'Just this, Sophie.' He dragged in a deep breath. Their misunderstanding had gone far enough. 'I'm offering marriage because I damned well have to!' This was said with considerable violence. And then, as the bitter agony of despair flooded her soft eyes, he added, 'But not for any of the reasons you might be forgiven for thinking.'

He stood up and crossed the remaining space between them and set his hands on her shoulders, looking straight into her overbright eyes. Her whole body stiffened at the touch of his hands, his nearness, his overwhelming masculine strength.

There was a hint of laughter in his voice as he said, 'Leaving aside the minor circumstance that there are four people in line to call me out if I don't marry you as fast as possible, namely the Earl and Countess of Darleston, Tom Hampton and my Aunt Maria, to which you might as well add Anna and Thea Andrews as well as Kit and Fanny—I have to marry you because if I don't, I'm going to be infernally unhappy!' A sudden responsive tremor ran through her and he went on. 'And I did think marriage was necessary the other day, you little idiot! I know that letter of mine was less than explicit and I grant the money must have been a facer, but didn't it occur to you that if I didn't want marriage I would have just taken my pleasure with you in the carriage? Do you think I don't know how easily you could have been persuaded the other night? For God's sake, Sophie, I'm in love with you! Take my word for it—that's the only reason you're still a virgin.'

There was a moment's silence while Sophie took in this impassioned declaration. She wanted to believe it, her heart begged for its release, but still she hesitated. The shadows of doubt still weighed in on her. That he desired her was obvious, and she knew that he was fond of her, but marriage? Was that really what he wanted? And if so, why on earth had he been courting Lucinda Anstey?

Lord Helford, however, did not hesitate. Seeing

her mouth open and feeling that enough had been said and that further explanations or arguments could wait, he swept her into his arms and stopped her mouth in the only effective way he knew. His lips claimed hers irrevocably in a searing kiss and she was held in a grip which threatened to break several ribs. Despite her lingering doubts, she yielded completely, her mouth opening under his assault with all the sweetness he remembered.

With a wrenching groan he deepened the kiss, whirling her into the vortex of a dizzying passion. Irresistibly he backed her to the sofa until her calves hit it. And then with a satisfied grunt he scooped her up to dump her unceremoniously upon it, where he joined her at once without ever breaking the kiss.

His hands were everywhere, caressing and stroking. The light muslin gown was no protection against his wicked expertise. He revelled in the softness, the sweetness of her breasts, kneading and teasing until with a deeply plundering kiss his long, experienced fingers found a taut nipple and massaged it tenderly. Encouraged by her moan of pleasure, he abandoned himself to the task of convincing her that their marriage was inevitable, a glorious necessity.

Her mouth clung to his, a miracle of loving surrender. Her whole body under his was warm and pliant. But when he finally raised his head to gaze down at her, her eyes, when they fluttered open, told him that he had only been partially successful. She had yielded…she loved him…but the shadowed eyes told him that still she doubted—could not quite believe that he loved her.

'Sophie…' he whispered, despairingly.

She trembled in his arms. 'I…I have agreed, my lord. Please, I do not require protestations of devotion… When are we to be married?'

His heart contracted in pain as he sat up, releasing her. So calm, so hurt. How the hell could he reassure her? Passion was patently useless. It might bind her to him, thereby increasing her sense of hurt, but would she ever believe that it meant anything to him? Unthinkingly he said bluntly, 'The banns will be called for the first time on Sunday. It's all arranged.'

'Arranged!' Sophie stared at him in dismay. Had he been so sure of her? So sure that she would be so desperate to retrieve her reputation that she would leap at his proposal? Did he care so little for her that he had actually arranged the wedding without so much as asking her who should be invited? Fury surged up again to mingle with the mind-numbing pain. She was not going to be organised and…and managed like one of his mistresses!

Seething with hurt outrage, she scrambled to her feet.

'If I am going to marry you, my lord,' we had better get something clear.' she said in shaking tones. 'Firstly, even if I do manage the word *obey* without choking on it, I haven't said it yet, and I do not appreciate being ridden over roughshod! I have no intention of being treated as one of your *convenients.*' She blushed fierily as she said this, and added, 'Not even a convenient wife.'

He stared up at her. And then he groaned. 'Oh, hell! I'm sorry, Sophie. I didn't mean to be so damned officious! Tom's right, it's a shocking habit and I'm counting on you to cure me of it. For God's sake, don't think I take you for granted, or that I mean to be arrogant. It's just that I want you so much that I tend to get carried away! And when I found out what was being said…I saw the Vicar on the way over because I wanted to straighten everything out as quickly as possible…'

Sophie flinched. She was right, then. For a moment, when she had seen the hurt in his face, she had hoped… But he was, after all, marrying her only to protect her name. Every nerve in her body tightened.

'No!' His voice, harsh and shaking, dragged her eyes to his. He surged to his feet and grasped her hands, drawing her to him inexorably. The green depths held a fear and a pain that shocked her, the planes of his face set and tense. 'For goodness' sake, you have to listen to me, Sophie. I do want to protect you. I can't deny that. But it's because I love you. Not because I nearly ruined you.

Sweetheart, it's not my honour, but my heart that's begging you to marry me. Please, Sophie.'

'You…you really want me?' She still couldn't quite believe it. Didn't dare to believe it.

Her heart trembled at the intensity in his voice as he said, 'Three weeks, Sophie. The banns will be called on Sunday. Give me that time to convince you, my love. I know I've been a fool, that I've hurt you and confused you. Will you trust me, just this one last time?'

Words would not form, and even if they had, would not have made it past the choking lump in her throat. She could only nod helplessly as he raised her hand to his lips.

Chapter Fifteen

The following morning Penelope Darleston descended upon Willowbank House like a whirlwind and removed Sophie to Darleston Court, effortlessly squashing David's plan to remove his bride to Helford Place. She said cheerfully that her chaperonage was the best way of stopping any malicious tongues dead in their tracks and forestalling any more difficulties. Just what she meant by difficulties was left unsaid.

And somehow her matter-of-fact attitude did wonders for Sophie's uncertain spirits. She seemed to take it for granted that Helford was tail over top in love and that his near betrothal to Lucinda had been a minor aberration.

'Peter did exactly the same, you know,' she confided in the carriage. 'The only difference was that he actually chose me, for all the wrong reasons, but then had the sense to fall in love. Helford has merely muddied the waters a bit more. The main thing is that he has come to his senses at last.'

* * *

David swiftly realised that, despite Lady Darleston's amused attitude towards his very obvious frustration, she had actually assisted him indirectly. As had Lady Maria by inviting Kit and Thea Andrews to move into Helford Place immediately. She had also invited Lord Strathallen to remove from the Helford Arms, in order that he might become acquainted with his heir.

Not unnaturally, Kit was eager to see his aunt nearly every day and, since this involved Helford and Strathallen escorting both Kit and Fanny over on their ponies, David's visits to his betrothed were thoroughly and unexceptionably chaperoned. A situation which his supposed friend and ally, Peter Darleston, laughed at openly.

Nevertheless, despite the fact that he could barely steal a kiss without interruption, David had to admit that the three weeks' enforced propriety gave him the opportunity to fully convince Sophie of his love for her once and for all. He found that taking the children riding was the best way of at least being able to talk to Sophie without interruption.

With their innocently efficient chaperons cantering ahead with Strathallen on one of their earliest rides, he was able to explain all his confusion to Sophie without being distracted by the passion simmering beneath the surface, flaring into life.

As they rode he was able to tell her what a fool he'd been.

'I never intended to offer you a *carte blanche*, sweetheart,' he assured her. 'At first I didn't realise why I kept wanting to see you, why I worried about you.' He groaned. 'I should have realised when Garfield tried to persuade you to marry him, but I was so damn confused. I was practically betrothed to Lucinda and I'd convinced myself that she...or rather the sort of marriage she offered...was what I wanted.'

'A marriage of convenience?' she asked quietly. 'You never cared for her?'

'That was not part of the bargain,' he answered. 'Lucinda made it quite plain that ours was to be a...a union of dynasties, not individuals. And I was so damned cynical about love and women that I thought I wanted it as well. Until I met you and you turned all my stupid notions inside out!'

'Me?' Sophie was stunned. 'What did I do?'

He laughed harshly. 'What did you do? You risked your life to save that wretched urchin. You refused to marry for money or security, instead you protected Kit's interests just as gallantly as you saved Jem. And the day I saw you with the Simpkins baby, realised how much you longed for your own children, and tried to warn you to protect yourself from hurt, you forced me to see that I'd spent twelve years running scared, rather than living.'

He saw joy leap into her eyes and understood at

once. 'It's not just desire I feel for you, my love,' he avowed very softly. 'I won't deny it's there, but that didn't prompt me to marriage. If I had simply desired you, I'd have been able to control my longing to see you. I would never have asked you to be my mistress under any circumstances.' He laughed oddly. 'I also wanted to protect you, even from myself. A fact which was brought home to me when Garfield tried to force his attentions on you. I'd never felt like that in my entire life. Oh, I dare say I'd have defended any woman in that situation, but I wouldn't have felt so...so personally involved...as though something belonging to me had been violated.'

Trembling, her hand stretched out to him. He grasped it at once and held it reassuringly. 'Trust me, Sophie. If I hadn't loved you, my betrothal to Lucinda would have been announced before we sat down to dinner that ghastly night. At that point I was still dithering. I knew I loved you and it scared the hell out of me. What your song did was force me to realise that I couldn't run away from what was between us. That all my supposed conviction that I wanted a marriage of convenience was no more than a smokescreen for my own fear of being hurt again. I meant to offer for you in the carriage, but like a fool I kissed you first and lost control. I was so stunned by what I felt for you that I couldn't even express it.'

He felt her fingers cling. Her voice, soft and shaking. 'Then you have relieved my mind, my heart, of its only fear: that you were marrying me for a combination of obligation and desire. That you were fond enough of me to sacrifice what you really wanted.'

Tears hung on her lashes as he said harshly, 'No, Sophie. I've made the right choice. I've chosen love.' To his inexpressible joy he saw the shadows lift from her eyes and knew that she was his. That she had finally and irrevocably accepted the truth of his love. As he had.

With that concern off his mind, by the wedding morning the only consideration weighing on David was how soon he could decently remove his bride from the wedding feast and take her back to Willowbank House. To the enormous bed that he had arranged to have installed in Sophie's bedchamber.

As weddings go, it was small, with only close friends and family. To wit, Lady Maria, the children, the Darlestons, Tom Hampton, Strathallen, the Asterfields and, to David's startled delight, George Carstares and Miss Sarah Ffolliot. Kate had sent a letter announcing that they were coming. And would Helford please ensure that there were no more rats? George and Sarah simply appeared at Darleston Court, the day after the notice appeared in the *Morning Post*.

"Fraid we just assumed, old chap,' had said George, wringing the groom's hand in obvious delight. 'We're not getting married for another month so we left Sarah's mother with the preparations and came!'

So David Charles Melville, Viscount Helford, took to wife Miss Sophia Ann Marsden, a woman who embodied none of the virtues he had so coldly deemed necessary in a wife. And he spoke his vows in the full and certain knowledge that he had finally got it right. The blast of approval at his back from family and friends assured him that they knew it too.

By eight o'clock that evening he was settling his dazed and sweetly exhausted bride safely in his arms. Her naked, pliant body was intimately entangled with his, her head resting on his shoulder. He viewed with intense satisfaction the fact that Sophie was, at long last, his. Totally and irrevocably.

Completely ignoring Anna's offer of refreshment when they arrived back, he had picked his bride up and carried her upstairs to her bedchamber. He had not even dared to kiss her in the carriage on the way over. He was going to have her in bed, but he was not going to wait a moment longer!

Sophie lay stunned in his embrace. Not even his near seduction in the carriage after the dinner party had prepared her for the joy and ecstasy that had flooded her when he at last took possession of her trembling, arching body. He had been so tender with her, despite the blazing desire that was consuming him.

When he had set her on her feet after carrying her up to her bedchamber, he had taken her mouth in the most gentle of kisses, framing her face in his hands. It was only after several minutes that she realised that one of his hands had somehow found its way to her lacings and that her gown was in some mysterious way sliding down over her breasts, her waist and pooling in a silken whisper around her feet.

He had drawn her back into his arms as he released the bow of her chemise and cupped one breast in a large possessive hand, rubbing his thumb back and forth over the nipple, calling forth a whimper of pleasure as her senses spiralled in a dizzying vortex of passion. This time at last, there would be no drawing back, no more frustration. This time he would take what was his and she pressed herself to him urgently, eager to give him everything he wanted.

She had felt him feather burning, searing kisses along the neck line of her chemise, teasing her until she wriggled to be free of the wretched thing and with a deep, seductive chuckle he had obligingly removed it as well as her petticoat. Then he had swung her into his arms again, placing her gently on the bed, which she had dimly realised was rather larger than she recalled.

His eyes had never left her as he stripped. Blazing with incandescent desire they had roamed her quivering body as she had watched him divest himself of his clothes. Only when he unbuttoned his breeches had her virgin shyness asserted itself, her eyes fluttering shut almost unwillingly.

Then he was beside her on the bed, his arms enfolding her to lie in his embrace, a large, compelling hand on one satiny hip moulding her to him as he moved his throbbing loins against her in a slow, yet inexorable rhythm.

Despite his screaming need, David had held himself in check as he made love to her. Never rushing her, he lavished untold attention on every exquisite detail, bringing into play all his expertise. He savoured to the full her unhesitating and glorious surrender to his demands, to his caressing hands and his increasingly possessive mouth.

When at last his hands and mouth had brought her to the point of insanity she had heard a sobbing voice she could barely recognise as hers begging him to take her. It seemed that was all he had been waiting for. His weight had shifted immediately, pinning her to the bed, vulnerable in the aching emptiness that cried out within her. His hand had pressed her thighs apart in unspoken command, a groan of deep satisfaction tearing from him as he settled himself between them…for a moment he had continued to caress her, his arousal pressing against her…and then with a tender murmur…oh, God…he had taken her in one gentle, but masterful movement of his loins…he had lain motionless for a moment, soothing her involuntary cry of pain, waiting for her to relax before he allowed himself to move…and when he had! She had thought she would die of the agony of delight his powerful body evoked as gradually he allowed her to feel the full force of his passion.

His loving had brought her to the limits of ecstasy and further, to a place where thought was suspended and only passion and breathless, searing sensation existed…a world of feeling where she had soared in unfettered joy. And now as she lay nestled in his arms, her body relaxed in sweet exhaustion, his tender, adoring whispers assured her beyond all doubt that she was loved.

She was his. Completely and irrevocably. David held her and gloried in the thought as she drifted towards sleep, her silken limbs and body entwined with his. Never had he felt like this in all his life. This sense of completion, of total possession, of being possessed in return. That he had not merely taken, but had actually given. He remembered that he had once thought that in lying with Sophie he would be truly making love for the first time. It was all that and more.

His arms tightened about her and she sighed peacefully. 'Dearest.' His voice was husky, the merest whisper, but she turned slightly in his arms, her silky softness caressing him, and pressed a kiss on his shoulder. Smiling, his lips gently brushed her hair.

Finally, after all his years of wandering, he had come home. And love was, after all, the most convenient choice he could possibly have made.

* * * * *